INTER OFFICE MEMO

To: Mackenzie Donahue
From: Chief Daniels
Subject: Holly Reynolds

Donahue—Enclosed find details on your new assignment and a dossier and photos of the subject. We want you to get close to Ms. Reynolds and see what she knows about her brother's activities. Don't get distracted by her big brown eyes or the sweetness of her smile. Don't think about the softness of her skin or the way she feels in your arms. And, whatever you do, don't fall in love with her!

MEN at WORK

✈ —MILLIONAIRE'S CLUB 🍎 —BOARDROOM BOYS ☀ —MAGNIFICENT MEN

🔧 —TALL, DARK & SMART 📁 —DOCTOR, DOCTOR 🔫 —MEN OF THE WEST

⚙ —MEN OF STEEL ⬟ —MEN IN UNIFORM

MEN at WORK

DALLAS SCHULZE

MACKENZIE'S LADY

MEN
IN
UNIFORM

Harlequin Books

TORONTO • NEW YORK • LONDON
AMSTERDAM • PARIS • SYDNEY • HAMBURG
STOCKHOLM • ATHENS • TOKYO • MILAN
MADRID • WARSAW • BUDAPEST • AUCKLAND

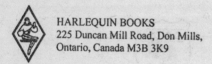

HARLEQUIN BOOKS
225 Duncan Mill Road, Don Mills,
Ontario, Canada M3B 3K9

ISBN 0-373-81014-8

MACKENZIE'S LADY

This edition published by arrangement with Harlequin Books S.A.

® and TM are trademarks of the publisher. Trademarks indicated with ® are registered in the United States Patent and Trademark Office, the Canadian Trade Marks Office and in other countries.

Printed in U.S.A.

Dear Reader,

I am so pleased that *Mackenzie's Lady* is being rereleased. This was my first book for Harlequin and, rather like a mother with her first child, it holds a special place in my heart. Looking back through it, I found myself smiling as I renewed my acquaintance with Mac and Holly.

Mac wasn't the first tall, dark and handsome hero I wrote—nor was he the last!—but he remains a personal favorite. And Holly is a sweet, funny heroine—just the right woman for him.

I hope you'll enjoy them as much as I did.

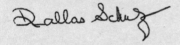

Chapter One

She didn't belong. It was obvious from the moment she walked in the door. That had been almost half an hour ago and this was the fourth time that Mac had found himself watching her.

He pulled his eyes away from the small corner table where the woman was sitting and scanned the room. Long fingers curled around the squat glass in front of him. The liquid that half filled it was a virulent shade of yellow. The one ice cube gracing it seemed to be fighting to stay afloat as if some monster awaited in the murky depths of the glass.

He lifted the glass but the liquid barely touched his lips, though his throat moved as if he were swallowing a hearty gulp. A keen observer might have noticed the faint twist of hand that tilted a thin stream of liquid onto the warped wooden floor before the glass returned to the table, the level of alcohol considerably lowered.

"If Baldwin doesn't show soon, we're going to have a lake under this table. We must have dumped a gallon of this stuff on the floor already."

Mac's eyes slid to the man seated across from him and one dark brow lifted in amusement.

"There's too much dirt on the floor for a lake, but we might manage a small swamp."

"Complete with crocodiles probably."

"Oh, the crocodiles are here already, along with assorted snakes and rodents." A subtle nod of his head indicated the other patrons.

His companion grinned, revealing a black hole where his front teeth should have been. "You're not casting aspersions on the clientele of this luxurious establishment, are you?"

"I'd rather cast a small hand grenade and get rid of all of them. The world would be a healthier place without them."

"Not quite all of them, I bet." Mac's brows rose questioningly at his friend's sly comment. Ken jerked his head toward the woman Mac had been watching. "I've noticed the way you've been giving her the eye. I bet you'd want to rescue her before dropping your world-cleansing grenade."

"Since she's sitting behind you, how did you know who I was looking at?"

Ken's lean features settled into a superior look that clashed with his unshaven jaw and grubby clothing. "Elementary, Watson. A trained mind can detect these things. It's obvious that you have much to learn." He stopped as Mac's face set in lines of exaggerated boredom. "I can see you're not buying this. Okay, I'll confess. There's a mirror behind the bar and, when your attention kept drifting, it wasn't hard to figure out where it was drifting to."

Mac let his gaze settle on the woman again, aware that Ken was watching her in the mirror. "Not bad." His mouth quirked upward in acknowledgment of Ken's comment, but his gaze didn't waver from the woman.

What was she doing here? She was as out of place as a daisy among thistles. Short dark curls framed a face that was at once womanly and pixieish. Her features were refined but she fell short of classic beauty. Her mouth was too wide and her chin too pointed, but the whole came together in a roguishly appealing package.

He had seen her walk in, her pale yellow sundress standing out against the dingy gray of the cantina's walls. He pegged her as a tourist who had gotten off the beaten track and ventured a little too far into the side streets of Tijuana. She would turn around and leave as soon as she saw what kind of a place she had stumbled into.

She *had* hesitated a few feet inside the door, and he had seen her swallow hard as she took in the filthy room and its equally filthy inhabitants. Her gaze skimmed over the table where he and Ken sat, and the flicker of contempt in her eyes hadn't changed. Well, at least their disguises looked bad enough to fool an American tourist, he thought with amusement.

His amusement had faded somewhat when, instead of turning around and walking back out into the relative safety of the street, she had continued into the room, the click of her delicate heels loud in the sudden quiet of the bar as every man's eyes turned to watch her progress. Admiration mixed with irritation as she seated herself as calmly as if she were in a quiet café in the heart of the Midwest. Either she was too stupid to know what she had gotten herself into or she had more guts than was healthy.

Now, watching her, he decided it was the latter rather than the former. She knew she was in a potentially nasty situation and for whatever reason, she was choosing to stick it out. Her eyes were as restless as his own, searching the bar frequently and glancing at the door every time it opened. She had ordered nothing but a soft drink, which she sipped through a straw.

"She'd never give you a second glance the way you look now."

Mac dragged his eyes back to Ken, meeting the mocking commiseration in his friend's eyes. "What's wrong with the way I look? Do you know how long it took to find a suit like this in my size?"

Ken's eyes slid over the blinding white of Mac's suit jacket. The exaggerated points of the lapels were edged with gold sequins, and the matching pants carried a similar stripe down the outside of the pant leg. A black silk shirt stretched across the width of Mac's chest, the front opened almost to the navel, revealing a mat of dark hair and a multitude of heavy gold chains. A gold ring pierced one ear, lending a rakish air to his strong features. A puckered line of scar tissue ran down the left side of his face from the corner of his eye almost to the bottom of his earlobe, drawing the eye so that the rest of the features seemed blurred. Gold rings studded with jewels adorned every finger of his big hands.

Only the indolent ease of his long body and the sleepy droop to his eyes would have been familiar to anyone who knew him.

Ken finished his inspection and grinned. "You sure do make a great pimp. I don't know many men who could carry off that suit and all that jewelry as well as you do."

"Thank you, I think. Actually I think it's the boots that really make the outfit." He extended his foot out from beneath the table so that Ken could admire his footwear. The other man choked slightly before agreeing that it was definitely the boots that completed the look. "I've always wanted a pair of black patent boots with gold condors on the toes. I suppose I'm going to have to give them back when we're done." Mac sounded so wistful that Ken almost believed him.

"I think those are eagles."

Mac's brows drew together in a frown and he gave the boots considerable attention. "No, I'm sure those are condors. Look how skinny the neck is."

"It's an eagle. The only reason his neck is skinny is that the brush slipped when they were doing the paint-by-numbers design."

Mac's brows rose. "Do you mean I'm wearing one-of-a-kind boots, hand-painted in Hong Kong? Maybe they'd do a custom design."

Ken choked and coughed as he swallowed a laugh. "Careful. You're going to make me fall out of character. A man in your powerful position would hardly be seen laughing with a common junkie."

Mac shrugged, his eyes scanning the bar again. "I don't think Baldwin is going to show. Either he chickened out on making the sale or this was just a trial run to see if we'd show."

"You want to split?"

Mac hesitated, his eyes touching on the woman in the corner, and Ken grinned, revealing the gaping hole in his teeth again. "We can hang around a little longer. Edwards isn't expecting to hear from us for a while yet."

"Something's got to give soon. Nobody is stupid enough to push his luck forever. Unless she's dumber than she looks, she'll leave before trouble starts."

"I think she's too late already."

At Ken's murmured words, Mac jerked his eyes back to the

corner. In the time the woman had been there, two men had approached her. Each time, Mac had tensed, wondering if he was going to be forced to intervene and risk everything he had worked for in order to rescue the stranger. On both occasions, the men had spoken to the woman and she had sent them away with a brief shake of her head. Even in the dimly lit bar, he had been able to see the flush that rose in her cheeks, or perhaps he only assumed that it went with her mortified expression.

Ken's comment that it might be too late referred to the man who now swaggered up to the woman's table. He was a big man, not only tall, but bulky. A huge gut hung over the waist of his faded denims, but the corded muscles in his arms were ample evidence that it would be foolish to dismiss him as harmless.

Mac drew his feet out from under the table. Everyone in the bar was watching the confrontation in the corner, so he was able to openly observe the apparent negotiations without being conspicuous. His gaze barely flickered in answer to Ken's exaggerated sigh.

"I suppose we're going to have to interfere. You know, you really should have picked another line of work. Slaying dragons would have suited you just fine." The woman shook her head violently and there was no mistaking the dark flood of color that rose in her face.

"Look. She's grabbing her purse. Maybe he'll let her leave."

Mac shook his head, pulling himself into a more upright position. "Something tells me that he isn't going to be that obliging. Stop complaining. You couldn't walk away from this any more than I could. Baldwin isn't coming. If we're careful and lucky, we can still get out of this without blowing our cover."

"Complaining! Who's complaining? I'm really looking forward to getting my head beat in by these overgrown gang members. There's nothing I enjoy more than a thoroughly impossible fight. I love the feeling that I can't possibly win. Besides, my last hospital stay wasn't nearly long enough. If I'm lucky, maybe I'll be able to get a permanent room set aside for me after they scrape me off the floor of this bar. Oh, damn! He's definitely *not* going to be a gentleman about it."

Mac got to his feet in one easy movement, throwing a reckless grin over his shoulder at his friend. "Look at it this way. We've poured enough booze on this floor to sterilize it. You might as well reap the benefits of being scraped off the only sterile floor in Tijuana."

Ken rose to his feet slowly. "I knew I should have listened to my mother when she told me to become a doctor," he muttered. "If I'd listened to her, I could be vacationing in Mazatlán instead of barhopping in Tijuana."

Despite his mumbled complaints, he was following Mac across the small room. Damned if he was going to let the other man have all the fun.

IT HAD BEEN a big mistake. Holly had decided that almost as soon as she had walked into the bar. Sheer stubbornness had made her stay. This was where Jason had told Maryann he would meet her. As Maryann's representative, she would wait for him there. But half an hour later, she decided that not even for her best friend was she going to spend another minute in the place.

She had already turned down two advances when the third man approached. The first two men had been particularly unprepossessing, but they had accepted her refusal with reasonably good grace. Something about this man told her he was not going to be so obliging. He swaggered across the room, his small eyes shifting from side to side to confirm that all his cronies were watching him approach the foreign woman.

She picked up her purse hurriedly, but he reached her table before she could rise. He spoke English but he didn't need verbal reinforcements. His gestures were unmistakable. Color surged into her face until she thought she might catch fire from the heat of it. At twenty-eight, Holly thought she'd heard it all, but this was something new to her.

"No, thank you." The polite words echoed ridiculously in her mind as she shook her head quickly, getting to her feet and wishing that she were an imposing five-foot-eight instead of a less-than-threatening five-three. She edged her way around the table, hoping that the cold distaste in her face would conceal the frightened pounding of her heart. When he reached out and put his filthy hand on her bare arm, she felt her stomach knot. She dragged her eyes from the grimy nails that dug shallow indentations into her pale skin to the cold gleam in his narrowed eyes.

His eyes met hers for a long, frightening moment before he turned his head and spit on the floor next to them. Holly's stomach heaved and she swallowed hard, tightening her grip on her purse and wishing that she had thought to put a lead weight in it before she came to Tijuana. She didn't bother to look around for help; she would find none in this place.

She met her captor's gaze head on, refusing to flinch away from the menace in his eyes. "Let go of my arm." The faint tremor in her voice lessened the impact of the demand, and he grinned, revealing a mouth full of broken, rotting teeth.

He drew her rigid frame closer, bending down until his fetid breath wafted across her face. She fought the urge to gag and tried to jerk her arm away, but his hold was unbreakable.

Before she could decide on her next move, a new player entered the game. A long hand, glittering with gold rings, reached between Holly and her tormentor, grasping the man's wrist.

"I think the lady asked you to let her go."

Holly's gaze jerked to the newcomer. The flicker of hope that had entered her frightened eyes died. He was an American, but from the looks of him, he was not the type likely to be chosen for a chamber of commerce advertisement. She didn't even want to speculate what he had done to pay for the quantity of jewelry he wore, or how he had acquired the puckered scar that ran down the left side of his face.

He stood next to them casually, his eyelids drooping down over eyes that were a dark, indescribable blue. He looked as if he just might drop off to sleep at any moment.

Her tormentor spat out a short phrase in Spanish and it didn't take an interpreter to know that he was not being complimentary. The other man smiled gently.

"It's possible but I don't think so. Anyway, I didn't plan on discussing my family with you. The lady asked you to let go of her arm." The long, graceful fingers tightened, the smile never leaving his face.

To Holly's surprise, the first man released his hold on her arm. She rubbed at the faint red marks left behind, tightening her already white-knuckled grip on her purse. All she wanted was to get out of the bar before some new disaster arose, but she was hemmed in, caught between the two men and the table at her back.

They faced each other, their respective attitudes a study in contrast. The first man's eyes blazed angrily, his thick body tense. The American was totally relaxed. His arms hung languidly at his sides, and Holly had the distinct impression that he was stifling the urge to yawn. But then, that impression might be deceptive. His eyes never left the other man when he spoke to her.

"Maybe you should leave now, and if you take my advice, you'll avoid this area of Tijuana next time you visit."

She bristled a little at this unasked-for advice but he was too right to argue with. Her thank-you was strangled as she began to edge her way between the two of them, trying very hard to avoid contact with either of the men. She was caught squarely between them when the first man grabbed for her arm. She stiffened but didn't have time for more than that.

The bejeweled man behind her moved faster than she would have thought possible, his hand coming out and catching the grimy fingers before they touched her.

"You don't learn very fast, do you?" The voice was still soft and gentle, but Holly could feel the tension in the arm that skimmed her shoulder. "Why don't you get out of here before all hell breaks loose?" The last words were directed at her.

She dragged her fascinated gaze away from the sight of his long fingers wrapped around the other man's wrist. She took two steps and then stopped. The sound of a pin dropping would have echoed in the unnatural stillness of the bar. All eyes were glued to the sudden confrontation in their midst. Boredom had filled the day for most of the men there. Any diversion would be welcome, but the building tension between the fancy Americano and Paco Ramirez—this diversion offered more possibilities than most.

Holly had no way of knowing exactly what was going on in the minds of the bar's other patrons, but it was obvious that no one was going to try to stop the imminent fight. Common sense told her not to worry about it, to take the stranger's advice and get out of the bar. She didn't like the looks of him any more than of the other man. He could undoubtedly take care of himself. Her conscience rebelled, however.

She turned back reluctantly, her eyes skimming over his scarred face. He had released the man's arm but, other than that, their positions were unchanged.

"What about you?"

His gaze did not flicker away from his opponent. "I'm touched that you care, but I'll be fine. Now get out of here."

Holly Reynolds had never taken orders well. Her family and any of her friends could have told him that. Unfortunately, none of these people were around to give him this piece of information, though it might have saved him some grief.

If he had asked her to leave, she might have taken him up on it and ignored her conscience. But he ordered her to leave and she immediately decided that nothing would get her out of that bar until she was sure that he was unhurt. After all, she reasoned, he had come to her rescue. What kind of a person would she be if she left him all alone?

"I'm not going anywhere until I'm sure you'll be all right." The mulish tone would have warned anyone who knew her.

"For God's sake, lady, have you got a death wish?"

She set her teeth. "I'm not going without you. I couldn't live with myself if I did."

"Oh, great! I don't believe this. You're going to get us both killed." He might have expanded further on the subject but he didn't get a chance. He saw the blow coming, despite trying to watch both the crazy woman he was attempting to help and the man he faced. His left arm came up to block the blow while his right hand shot out to shove the woman farther back, following the motion with an awkwardly angled blow to the other man's stomach.

A ragged shout of excitement went up from the men in the bar. Only the cantina's owner was in disagreement with the opinion that a good fight was just what was needed to liven up the day.

For the next few minutes Mac had his hands full just trying to prevent his thick-set opponent from beating his head in. He and Ken were outnumbered, and Ken's prediction of being scraped off the floor might have come true if most of their would-be opponents hadn't gotten sidetracked into personal battles of their own.

Mac's memories of the fight were stored in brief images: Ken's wild war whoop as he waded into the fray until he and Mac stood back to back, the look of stunned surprise on Paco's square face when Mac's fist connected with his chin, snapping his head back. Without the need for words, he and Ken worked their way slowly toward the door. Mac searched the wild crowd for the woman who had been the cause of all this, and his eyes caught what would remain his favorite image. She stood on a chair near the door, wielding a heavy beer bottle with delicate—if indiscriminate—precision. More than one of the men went home with a headache that night.

"Are you ready?" Ken's voice was breathless with exertion as he dodged another fist and backed a little closer to the door. Mac disposed of his current opponent with a quick uppercut.

"Now!"

The two of them broke for the entry. Mac's longer strides brought him to the door two steps ahead of his friend. The high wail of sirens in the distance added an extra urgency to his steps.

Holly felt as if she were being swept up by a hurricane. She was standing on a chair, trying to visually sort the twisting mass of humanity into something recognizable. It seemed as if her eyes had just located the tall frame of her rescuer near the center of the room when he came surging toward her. She had a brief glimpse of his face and then one arm caught her around the knees, dumping her over his shoulder and knocking her breathless as he continued out the door.

Stars danced in front of her eyes and her ears rang as her lungs struggled to function. It wasn't easy, with the pressure of his wide shoulder knocking the air back out of her with every loping stride he took. She didn't have enough wind to protest his cavalier treatment or to demand that he put her down. She couldn't even be too worried about where he was taking her. All she wanted was a chance to draw a breath in comfort. The ringing in her ears gradually merged with a high, incessant sound that she vaguely identified as a siren. Before she had a chance to react to this new information, the sound was cut off as her captor made a quick right and came to a halt next to a high adobe wall.

He bent down and dropped her gently to her feet, and Holly backed away from him as quickly as her shaking legs would allow. The man looked even more disreputable in daylight than he had in the dingy bar. The scar that slashed his lean cheek competed for attention with a rough scrape high on the other cheekbone and an oozing cut on his lower lip. The pristine whiteness of his garish suit was marked by streaks of dirt.

The smile he gave her might have been intended to reassure, but the thick black mustache and horrible scar combined to give him a ferocious look that made her already overworked heart go into double overtime. Only the brilliant blue of his eyes kept her from trying to dart past him. The eyes held her attention, whether she willed it or not. She took another step back and came up hard against the wall. Her wide eyes stayed focused on his face. She tried to maintain an air of calm control while her thoughts whirled madly around.

Holly swallowed hard and began to edge her way to the side. He blocked her path out of the narrow alley, but maybe she could dart around him. She refused to consider that it would be impossible to outrun those incredibly long legs if he chose to recapture her.

"Sorry for the rough transportation. Are you all right?" His voice was a slow drawl. Not a Southern drawl but just a lazy intonation that softened and lengthened his words.

She nodded and managed a tentative smile. "I'm fine," she told him huskily. Maybe he was going to let her go without a fight. "Thank you for coming to my rescue in there." That was the way to do it, remind him of his good deed. Maybe he'd decide he didn't want to spoil his record.

She edged a little farther along the wall and sighed with relief when he moved a step or two in the opposite direction. There was plenty of room for her to get around him now and he didn't show any signs of wanting to harm her. Everything was going to be just fine, and she and Maryann would have a good laugh about this once Holly was safely back in Los Angeles.

"We're all clear. If anybody saw us come this way, they're not telling the local police."

Holly screamed and spun around, almost losing her footing on the loose stones that surfaced the alley. The new voice coming from directly behind her was totally unexpected. The man who had spoken raised his sandy eyebrows, surprised by her reaction. "I didn't mean to startle you, lady. I figured you must have heard me."

She shook her head, realizing even as she did so that she *had* heard him but had been concentrating so hard on the first man that she hadn't really registered the sound of his approach.

The newcomer grinned at her, and despite the empty space where his front teeth should have been, there was something so boyish in the expression that Holly relaxed slightly.

"Boy, you sure know how to cause trouble, lady. I thought I was going to end up with six broken ribs when Mac decided to play knight in shining armor."

Holly's eyes flickered to the other man, trying to imagine him as a knight in armor. The newcomer grinned again, seeing the doubt in her dark eyes. "Believe it or not, lady, he can't resist a damsel in distress. You wouldn't believe the number of times I've had to fight for my life just because I happened to be with him when he decided someone needed to be rescued."

The alleged knight gave his smaller companion a tolerant smile. "You're exaggerating, Ken. It must be that streak of Irish in you that can't resist embellishing every story you tell."

Holly relaxed even more. The bantering between the two of them reminded her so much of her brother, it was impossible for her to hang on to her fear. Besides, now that she'd had a chance to catch her breath, she realized that her fear had been more of the situation than of the individuals. Despite their daunting appearance, neither of these men seemed threatening to her.

The man called Ken gave his large companion another grin before turning back to Holly. "Are you okay, lady? Mac carried you out of there like a sack of potatoes. Any lasting damage?"

"Only to my dignity," she answered truthfully. "And I wish you'd stop calling me lady. It makes me feel like a cocker spaniel."

"Sure," he said obligingly. "If I knew your name, I'd call you something else."

She hesitated only briefly, her common sense wrestling with her instincts. "Holly Reynolds."

"Holly." Ken murmured her name and then shook his head. "I think I prefer Lady. It suits you better."

"I'll be sure to tell my parents that you don't approve of their choice," she told him dryly.

She ran her hands over the full skirt of her sundress, grimacing faintly as she noticed the streaks of dirt on the soft cotton.

"So, what's a nice girl like you doing in a place like this?" She couldn't help but smile at Ken's cheerful delivery of the hackneyed line, but Mac spoke before she could answer him.

"You'll have to excuse him, Ms Reynolds. I'm afraid Ken is under the mistaken impression that everyone wants to tell him their business."

Her eyes flickered over him and then away. There was something about him that disturbed her.

"Of course she wants to tell us what she's doing here, don't you, Holly?"

Holly was grateful to turn her attention back to Ken. She understood him. He reminded her of her brother James. She could cope with that feeling more easily than the confusing emotions the other man inspired.

"Well, actually, it's not all that interesting. My roommate was dating a guy a couple of months ago, and when they broke up, he ended up with a watch that belonged to Maryann's grandfather. He had supposedly taken it to a repair shop run by a buddy of his. Personally, I think Jason sold it and pocketed the money. Anyway, Maryann has been trying to get the watch back ever since.

"Jason called last week and told her that he had moved back East but he was going to be in Tijuana this weekend and if she wanted the watch, she could pick it up down here. My brother was going to come with Maryann but he got called out of the state. And then Maryann got the flu, so I volunteered to come instead. I bet Jason set this whole thing up as some kind of sick joke. It would be just like that weasel to send her to a place like that bar and then have a good laugh when he imagined her trying to cope. Maryann could never have handled that whole situation.''

Ken and Mac exchanged amused looks, but neither of them pointed out that Holly hadn't been coping too well before Mac's intervention.

''Damn, I must have dropped my purse in the bar.''

''I'm afraid you're going to have to write off the loss,'' Mac told her.

''I suppose so. It had my favorite lipstick in it and they don't make that shade anymore.'' She seemed to contemplate this loss for a moment before shrugging. ''Oh, well, it could have been my head that got lost. Luckily I didn't have much money in my purse and I left my credit cards and driver's license in the car, so I'll be able to get home with no problem.''

''Where's home?'' Mac asked the question so casually that Holly answered without hesitation. Her attention was on a newly discovered broken strap on her sandal.

''Los Angeles,'' she murmured absently as she tried to tuck the strap under the edge of her foot to hold it in place. She missed the sharp look Ken threw his friend and then the knowing grin that followed it. He whistled softly to himself. Mac gave him a warning scowl that was completely ignored. Ken continued to whistle ''Some Enchanted Evening.'' The tune seemed out of place in a deserted alley in one of the less enticing areas of Tijuana.

Holly set her foot back down, giving a pained sigh as the strap promptly popped back out again. ''I guess my shoes are going to be a write-off, too. If I ever lay my hands on Jason Nevin again, I think I'll hold him down and pluck every hair out of his beard, one by one.'' Ken chuckled at her vengeful tone and Mac's face creased in a lazy smile.

''It's probably safe to leave now. The police must have rounded up their quota of bar patrons.'' Mac's words gave Holly an oddly unsettled feeling. Of course, she was delighted by the thought of putting the whole embarrassing incident behind her. And she had to keep in mind that no matter how charming Ken seemed and no matter how disturbing Mac was, they were obviously not the kind of people that the average kindergarten teacher needed to list among her acquaintances.

Her eyes shifted awkwardly between the two men, her next move uncertain. Was she supposed to just walk away? Should she offer to pay them? But she didn't have any money and, somehow, she couldn't picture asking them for an address to mail a check to.

The silence in the narrow alley grew until she could almost hear herself breathe. In the distance she heard the sound of cars, traffic, people, civilization. All of those things seemed very far away. Nearby she could hear a dog barking. On the other side of the wall, a goat bleated mournfully and a little farther away children laughed.

She swallowed and gave the two men a strained smile. Funny, she didn't even know their last names. She would never see them again—and she certainly didn't want to see them again, she assured herself—but it was hard to just walk away.

The children laughed again and her smile grew a little more natural. The familiarity of the high childish sound helped her to regain her balance. "My students would never recognize their neat and tidy Miss Reynolds now. I look like something the cat dragged in."

"Barroom brawls are a little hard on the wardrobe," Mac agreed quietly. He nodded his head down the alley. "If you go out that way and turn right, you'll hit a major street in about a block. You should be able to find your car from there."

It was a dismissal. As clearly as the bell ringing at the end of a school day, he was telling her that it was time for her to go home now. It was time to put this frightening incident behind her and go back to the real world. And she did *not* feel hurt by his tone.

She nodded briskly, holding her chin high. "Thank you for coming to my rescue. I hope it hasn't caused you any problems." She started to hold out her hand, then realized how absurd the conventional gesture looked and quickly tucked it back behind her skirt. She smiled nervously and forced herself to turn away and walk down the alley.

She was almost to the corner of the wall when she couldn't

resist turning back for one last look at her strange benefactors. Ken raised his hand and gave her a cocky grin. Mac's hands remained in his pockets but the intensity of the look in his eyes remained with her long after she was safely in her car and driving back to L.A.

Chapter Two

Mac leaned indolently against the wall and let his eyes drift shut, closing out the quiet bustle of the big room in front of him. He must be getting old. There had been a time when just the smell of this room had been enough to make his pulse skip a beat. It had been a long time ago, when he had been new at the job, convinced that he was going to solve at least some of the world's problems.

He couldn't even dig up much curiosity about being called into the chief's office. He assumed it was a new assignment but he wasn't all that interested. His dark brows pulled together in a frown. Maybe it was time to get out. He'd seen cases where agents burned out on the job and he didn't want to become one of them. Maybe he needed to start seriously considering the future and what he wanted out of it.

"Hey, Mac, wake up. The chief is ready for you." He straightened away from the wall and smiled at his boss's secretary.

"I wasn't asleep, Livvie. How are the grandchildren?"

The woman's round face lit up in a smile that was reserved for a special few. "Growing like weeds, as always."

"Remind me to give you a package for them before I leave."

"You shouldn't be buying presents for them, Mac," she scolded lightly, but her dark eyes twinkled with pleasure. "You ought to be spoiling little ones of your own."

A shadow slid over his face, momentarily dimming the azure of his eyes before it was banished by a lazy smile. "I didn't buy them anything major, Livvie, just a couple of things I picked up the last time Ken and I were in Mexico.''

She opened the door to the chief's office. "Just as long as that's all you picked up in Mexico,'' she murmured wickedly.

Mac was still smiling as he shut the door behind him. Chief Daniels turned away from the window and limped heavily across the room to shake the agent's hand. His left knee was twisted at an awkward angle, the result of an exchange of bullets between government agents and drug runners. A cane lay propped against his desk but he refused to use it unless he absolutely had to.

Once the two men were seated, the older man's cool gray eyes studied Mac thoughtfully. Mac returned the gaze without discomfort. The chief liked to think out his words before speaking.

"What's your interest in the Reynolds case?'' The question was abrupt, without preliminaries.

"Reynolds case?'' Mac started to shake his head. "I don't know anything about a Reynolds case.''

"No? Then why have you been making inquiries that relate to it?''

"I didn't know I had been.''

He caught the file Daniels tossed him. "It's in the records that you've been asking for information regarding one Holly Ann Reynolds. Age: twenty-eight. Occupation: schoolteacher at the kindergarten level.''

Mac's fingers tightened around the folder. "I don't know anything about any case involving Holly Reynolds. The inquiry was made for personal reasons.'' The chief's sandy brows rose sardonically but Mac refused to say anything more. He knew as well as his boss that using the agency files for personal reasons was strictly forbidden.

Daniels let it pass without comment. "What do you know about Holly Reynolds?''

Mac shrugged. "Not much. Ken and I ran into her in Tijuana a month or so ago. She got into trouble in a cantina down there and we came to the rescue.''

"Oh, yes, the damsel in distress you mentioned in the report.'' He nodded, his fingers toying idly with a duplicate of the file Mac held. Suddenly his eyes came up to look at Mac intently. "Why were you trying to find her?"

The color in Mac's face deepened slightly but his gaze didn't waver. "I wanted to see her again."

"Humph." The snort expressed the chief's opinion of using the agency computer as a dating service, but once again, he let the subject drop. He leaned back in his chair.

"Holly Reynolds's father was a career diplomat. Retired a couple of years ago. Her older brother, James, followed him into the field. James is thirty-three and was just assigned to one of our embassies in Europe."

Mac listened carefully. Whatever the agency's interest in James Reynolds, he wanted to know every detail and exactly how it might affect Holly. He hadn't spent a month waiting for an answer to his strictly illegal inquiries only to lose interest now she was within reach.

"Do you know much about fine art?"

Mac shook his head, taking the apparent change of subject in stride. Daniels always had a reason.

"I don't know the difference between a Renoir and a finger painting," Daniels admitted without regret. "During World War II, a lot of the great works of art in Europe were either hidden by the people who owned them or were stolen. Some of the stuff reappeared after the war, of course, but there's still a lot of it missing. Caches are discovered from time to time.

"Shortly after James Reynolds was transferred to the embassy, paintings that hadn't been seen in over forty years began to turn up in private collections. Our agency wouldn't be involved if it wasn't for the fact that several of these works of art have been smuggled into this country."

Mac swallowed against sudden anger. If James Reynolds was involved in smuggling fine art, he was dealing with a very tough crowd. The mere fact that she was his sister could be enough to put Holly in danger. Remembering those wide brown eyes and stubborn little chin, Mac felt a stab of fear that was out of proportion, considering he knew little more than her name.

"I'm assigning you to keep an eye on her and, through her, on her brother."

Mac's head jerked up. Daniels met the blazing blue of his eyes calmly. "Is there some suspicion that Holly is involved?"

"None. Her record is absolutely clean. But she and her brother seem to be quite close. If we stay close to her, we may be able to pick up something on Reynolds."

"You want me to run surveillance on her?"

Daniels's mouth twisted to acknowledge Mac's deliberate obtuseness. "What the agency wants is for you to get close to Ms Reynolds. Get to know her and let us know if you find out anything about her brother."

The folder hit the desk with a soft splat and Mac moved across the room to the narrow window. Tension tightened the heavy muscles of his back. "What you're asking me to do is to spy on her."

The older man leaned back in his worn chair. "I'm not asking you to do anything you haven't done before. You don't have to torture her for information." He let the silence stretch. "Since you broke the rules to find out about her, you obviously had much the same plans yourself. All I'm asking is that you do a little work for the agency at the same time. What you do with your relationship with the woman is entirely your business."

"There's a big difference between getting to know her for purely personal reasons and suckering her into revealing information about her brother," Mac growled without turning.

"Look at it this way, Mac. If her brother *is* smuggling stolen art, it's better that he's caught before he drags his family into it. If he's innocent, then it's better that it be proved before his career is ruined. Either way, we have to know the truth."

Still Mac said nothing and the chief let the silence stand for several long moments before adding the clinching remark.

"Would you rather I assign someone else to her case?"

Mac spun away from the window and glared fiercely at the older man. Daniels met the raging frustration with calm implacability. The two men battled silently for a moment and then Mac strode angrily to the desk and snatched up the folder, his long fingers crumpling the edge.

"I'll take the damn case."

Daniels nodded. "I thought you would."

HOLLY RUBBED HER FINGERS surreptitiously along the top of her thigh. The hasty massage did little to ease the aching muscles. She glanced at the clock and gave a sigh. Another half hour and she could go home and sink into a tub of steaming hot water. Then she was going to kill Maryann.

She looked out over the quiet classroom and her wide mouth tilted in a smile. Twenty studious little faces were bent over twenty battered desks, with small fists clenched around thick crayons, intent upon creating self-portraits.

It was impossible for her to feel blasé about the world when all around her children were just discovering all its wonders. The only thing she'd rather be doing was raising her own children, but that was going to have to wait until she found a man with whom she wanted to share her life.

She doodled aimlessly on a sheet of paper. Her other hand rubbed unconsciously at her aching muscles. Usually she enjoyed her time in the classroom. She shifted and stifled a grimace of pain as her muscles protested. Yes, she was definitely going to have to kill Maryann.

On the other hand, she couldn't entirely blame her roommate for her current discomfort. Maryann had only suggested that Holly take up running; she hadn't dragged her out of the house and forced her to pant and puff her way around the block. Still, Maryann *had* caught her at a vulnerable moment. She knew that Holly had been restless lately.

Perhaps she wouldn't actually kill her, just maim her a bit. Maryann insisted that it had been less than a mile but Holly couldn't believe that. It was impossible to become a physical wreck after running less than a mile.

She glanced at the clock again. Twenty more minutes. The days had been getting longer for the past month, ever since that ridiculous trip to Tijuana. Damn! Why couldn't she just put that whole foolish incident out of her mind? It was over a month now and she still thought of it at odd moments. It even haunted her dreams.

Holly felt her cheeks grow warm. He had no business intruding on her sleep like that. And she had no business remembering him as vividly as she did. She was not going to think about it anymore.

She made the same promise to herself every day, and one of these days, it was going to come true.

It was over half an hour before she was able to turn the light off. Her small charges had gone home to cookies and milk, and the room had been tidied. She bent to pick up her tote bag and groaned softly as she straightened. Damn. What was wrong with being comfortably out of shape? Where was it written that everyone should have a rock-hard body and the ability to leap tall buildings in a single bound? She would settle for being able to get from one place to another at a brisk walk. The idea of dragging her sleepy body through the streets at dawn, all in the name of being fit, was ridiculous and painful.

It was raining—a damp, depressing drizzle. Holly stared across the parking lot at her car. Why hadn't she thought to bring an umbrella? Because if she had, it wouldn't have rained. With a resigned sigh, she left the shelter of the brick school building and picked her way through the puddles in the parking lot.

She was damp and chilled when she reached the car. Her cold fingers struggled for a moment with the key before the lock yielded and she was able to slide into the car. She murmured a soft plea as she turned the key in the ignition. The ten-year-old Fiat had been a graduation present from her parents and she dearly loved the car, but there was no denying that Baby could be very temperamental, especially when it was cold and wet. Holly had never gathered the necessary courage to actually tackle the intimidating mass of wires and mysterious parts that resided under the hood. Besides, no matter what people told her, she was convinced that the reason Baby balked was simply that she hated the rain.

Today was one of those days. Holly coaxed and pleaded to no avail. The engine turned over with a sullen whine but it refused to catch. She finally gave up and sat staring at the instrument panel in frustration. There was no sense in calling home. Maryann was working the evening shift at the hospital this week. Everyone else Holly could think of was either working or out of town. A glance outside the window told her that it was still raining and the heavy cloud cover was blocking out the sunlight.

She jerked her head around, startled, as someone tapped on her window. She blinked several times to clear her vision, convinced that she was hallucinating. The last time she had seen that man, he had been standing in the hot sun in an alley in Tijuana. He tapped on the window again, gesturing to her to roll it down. She obliged dazedly, still unable to believe her eyes.

He rested one hand on the top of the door, leaning down to meet her astonished eyes. A battered canvas hat was pulled down over his forehead, shielding his face from the worst of the rain. The rakish angle as it tipped down gave him the look of a movie adventurer. Holly was not surprised that she had no trouble envisioning his swinging across jungle chasms and fording snake-infested swamps.

"Hi. Remember me?" His voice was the same soft drawl and the eyes that had burned into hers in fantasy now stared at her in reality.

She swallowed and nodded her head. Yes, she remembered him. Even without the spangled suit, he was unmistakable. Maybe it was the running yesterday that had caused this. She had never heard of anyone hallucinating after attempting to exercise but there was a first time for everything.

His dark mustache tilted up and she caught the gleam of white teeth. "Having car trouble?"

"Yes." She had to clear her throat to get the word out. She resisted the urge to touch his strong jaw and thereby confirm his presence.

His smile deepened and Holly thought she could see a twinkle in his cerulean eyes. "Do you have any idea what's wrong with it?"

"It?"

"Your car," he reminded her softly. "Do you know what's wrong with your car?"

She shook her head, forcing her paralyzed brain to function again. "Baby doesn't like rain. She always refuses to start when it's wet."

He shivered as a cold breeze blew the rain in under the brim of his hat. "I can't say I blame Baby. Listen, I might be able to fix it, but quite frankly, the idea of peering under the hood in the dark and rain doesn't sound too appealing. My car is parked just across the street. I could give you a lift home if you'd like."

Holly hesitated. Common sense told her that this was insane. She knew almost nothing about him and what she did know definitely wouldn't serve to nominate him to the PTA board. Her dark eyes studied his face uncertainly. There was something different about that face, but she couldn't quite place what it was.

His smile deepened appealingly as he sensed her uncertainty. "I can't give you a written recommendation but my mother thinks I'm relatively harmless."

She made up her mind with customary abruptness. "I'd appreciate a ride." She grabbed her purse and tote bag from the passenger seat and swung her slim legs out as he opened the door for her.

"Don't you have a coat or an umbrella?" Holly shook her head and then almost jumped out of her skin when he draped his coat around her shoulders. It was a leather aviator jacket, well worn and smelling of a dark woodsy cologne that made her nose twitch. Before she could form a coherent protest, his arm circled her shoulders and he was hustling her across the parking lot.

His warm, vital presence was almost too much to absorb. She felt surrounded by him—the warm comfort of his jacket draping her body, the heavy weight of his arm around her shoulders, his tall frame sheltering her from the soft rain. He unlocked the door of a dark sedan and she sank gratefully into the cozy warmth.

She turned to look at him as his long legs slid beneath the steering wheel. He started the car but he didn't immediately put it into gear. Instead, he stretched his arm along the back of the seat, his fingers resting mere inches away from her cheek. He tugged his hat off, dropped it onto the seat between them and ran his fingers through his flattened hair.

Holly's eyes flickered over the blue cotton shirt and faded jeans, noting the scuffed boots that covered his feet before she glanced up into his face again. She wondered if this was haute couture in casual wear for off-duty pimps. If he had been appealing in the gaudy suit, he was devastating—too devastating—in the worn clothing he now wore. Her heart skipped a beat in response to the lazy charm of his smile.

"How did you know where I worked?" She flushed as soon

as the words were out. What if it was just an incredible coincidence that he happened to show up outside her school?

His smile deepened. "There aren't all that many women named Holly Reynolds who teach school in L.A."

"I didn't tell you I was a teacher."

"You mentioned your students. It wasn't hard to interpret that to mean that you were a teacher."

Her brows drew together and her forehead wrinkled as she considered this. Her toes curled inside her soft pumps, responding to the warm air from the heater. Her name and the fact that she might be a teacher didn't sound like much of a clue to her, not enough of a clue to track someone down in a city the size of L.A. Her frown deepened. Maybe it would be safer not to inquire about his methods.

Holly cleared her throat and gave him a tentative smile. "It seems as if you always turn up just in time to rescue me, Mr.... umm..." She let the sentence trail off. She didn't know his last name and she wasn't sure she wanted to use his first name. That implied an intimacy her common sense urged her to avoid.

"Donahue. My friends call me Mac, short for Mackenzie."

"I don't know that we're friends," she told him bluntly, wanting to make her feelings clear from the start.

"Maybe not yet, but I hope we will be."

Holly dropped her eyes away from that compelling gaze and studied the pale pink polish on her nails, comparing it to the warm gray of her wool skirt. She might be impulsive, but not even Maryann could accuse her of being completely devoid of sense. The man who sat next to her looked like an all-American boy right now, but all-American boys did not hang out in sleazy Tijuana bars wearing white spangled suits and getting into brawls. She could overlook the brawl. After all, he had been coming to her rescue, but there was still the question of what he had been doing there in the first place. She was not going to get involved with someone that she strongly suspected of being a pimp.

Holly cleared her throat again. "I don't think we will get to be friends. I mean, I appreciate your help and all that, but I don't think I'd cope too well with your line of work. I'm not making any judgments or anything," she added hastily, "because I think everybody has a right to do whatever makes him happy." She trailed off uncertainly, wondering how anyone could be happy selling someone else's body. She shook the thought away and continued, wishing that she hadn't rolled her car window down, wishing even more that she'd never gone to that stupid bar in the first place.

"The problem is, I'd be uncomfortable and I'd make you uncomfortable, so I think maybe I'll just walk home, but thank you very much for the offer of a lift." She rushed the end of the sentence out, feeling acutely uncomfortable in the face of his continued silence.

She gave a startled gasp as his hand came out to catch her shoulder when she tried to reach for the door handle. The eyes she turned to him were wide, with a hint of fear in their depths.

He gave her an appealing smile. "Look. I think you've got the wrong idea about what I do for a living."

"I don't want to know any details," she assured him hastily.

"You don't understand, Holly." Despite her wariness, hearing her name on his lips sent a shiver of awareness through her. "The way I was dressed down in Tijuana was part of my job."

"I understand," she told him. "Believe me, I understand. I'm not making any judgments but I..."

He interrupted her with a hint of exasperation lacing his deep tones. "I'm a cop, Holly."

"A cop?" she exclaimed, her mouth hanging slightly open until she shut it with a snap.

He nodded. "I was working on a case in Tijuana. I could hardly go into that area wearing a uniform."

"A cop?" Her voice rose to a squeak as she stared at him. She giggled. "A real live honest-to-goodness, you-have-the-right-to-remain-silent cop?" She began to laugh. "I don't believe this. Do you have any idea how guilty I felt every time I thought of you? I couldn't believe I was actually attracted to some sleazy—" She broke off, feeling a burning tide of red surge into her face.

Why didn't she just tell the man that he'd been the main attraction in several dreams that would have been banned in Sweden? When was she going to learn to think before she spoke?

His soft laugh held pleasure but no mockery. This time when

his hand slipped to rest lightly on her shoulder, Holly didn't stiffen. Her mouth curled up in reluctant amusement. It *was* funny, even if the joke was on her. Besides, the fact that he had gone to the trouble of finding her was evidence that the attraction was not only on her side.

"Sleazy?" he murmured teasingly. "I thought I looked rather stylish."

"You didn't look like the kind of a guy that a woman takes home to meet her mother. Are you really a cop?" She was unaware of how much her tone revealed. She wanted to believe he was telling her the truth, wanted an excuse to like him.

"Scout's honor. I'm really a cop."

Holly let herself relax completely, returning his smile with a wide dimpled grin, her brown eyes sparkling with relief.

"Now that I've established a respectable reputation, I was hoping you'd have dinner with me."

"Tonight?" Her voice rose on the question, revealing her surprise.

Mac gave her an apologetic smile. "I know it's short notice but I only tracked down where you worked today. I was hoping you'd be impressed by my diligence and go out with me."

Holly hesitated only a moment. It *was* short notice and she was tempted to tell him that she had other plans.

"I'm hardly dressed for going anywhere nice." Her words were an acceptance and he rewarded her with a devastatingly sexy smile.

"I'm not exactly dressed for L'Ermitage myself." His eyes skimmed appreciatively over the slim gray skirt and pale pink blouse. "I know a place where we can get the world's greatest hamburgers. Real hamburgers, not pieces of cardboard covered with Thousand Island dressing."

"It sounds fantastic." She settled back into the seat with a comfortable sigh as he put the car into gear and backed it out into the street. Maryann would say she was crazy, but Holly couldn't remember the last time she had felt so secure. She watched his hands on the wheel, admiring their broad strength. Something inside her insisted that she trust him.

They spoke very little during the short drive to the restaurant.

It was an easy silence, odd for two people who had known each other such a short time. But then Holly felt as if she had known him forever.

The restaurant was crowded. A harassed-looking waiter in a Hawaiian shirt and shorts showed them to a table and took their order. Holly looked around at the semi-South Pacific decor and smiled. Only in Southern California would one find a restaurant with giant plastic birds sitting on perches that hung suspended from the ceiling.

She glanced across the table at Mac, wondering if he shared her amusement. Her eyes met his and slowly the smile faded. The warmth in those electric blue depths made her heart falter for an instant. She swallowed, trying to fight the intense surge of desire that washed over her, leaving her skin tingling in its wake. She dragged her gaze away from his, skimming her eyes over his strong features. There was a deep tuck in one lean cheek. In a woman it would have been called a dimple, but she couldn't imagine applying so feminine a term to this very masculine man.

"Your scar's gone!" she blurted out, finally realizing why his face had looked different earlier. It had been nagging at the back of her mind ever since she'd seen him standing in the rain outside her car.

He shrugged. "Makeup. People don't notice your face much if there's something to draw the eye away from your features. If you'd been asked to describe me, what would you have remembered first?"

"Your eyes. They're beautiful," she answered without thinking. Those eyes had appeared in far too many of her dreams.

"Thank you." His voice was muffled, and peering at him in the dim lighting, Holly was almost positive that the color in his cheeks was darker than it had been. "You just ruined my lecture and one of the treasured theories on the art of camouflage," he told her reproachfully. "You were supposed to say the scar. A scar like that sticks in the mind and it makes the rest of the features fade out of sight. At least it's *supposed* to make them fade out of sight."

She shrugged. "Sorry. You shouldn't have eyes like that if you don't want to be remembered."

Any reply he might have made was lost as their waiter returned with two hamburgers and a giant basket of french fries. Conversation was postponed in favor of biting into the thick, juicy burgers. Once their initial hunger was eased, they began to talk.

Holly set down her hamburger and nodded toward one of the hanging birds. "My brother would love this place."

Mac stiffened but she was looking away and missed the intense look he gave her.

"Your brother?" he murmured.

She nodded. "James loves tacky places like this. It's ridiculous, really. He minored in art in college. You'd think he'd have better taste."

"Is he teaching art now?" he asked casually, wondering if she'd notice the tension in his voice. Damn! He hated this assignment!

"Uh-uh," she mumbled through a bite of meat. "He followed Dad into the diplomatic corps. He's working in Europe now. In fact, that's why he didn't come to Tijuana with me last month. He had to fly to Washington to get the details on his new job. I'm really going to miss him."

"You sound as if you're close." *That's right, torture yourself by finding out just how hurt she'll be if you help put her brother away.*

Unaware of her companion's dilemma, Holly nodded. "James and I have always been close. We think a lot alike, I guess."

"Well, I can't really say that I'm sorry he didn't go to Tijuana with you. You might not have needed my help if he had." His slow smile made her heart pick up an extra beat and her mouth trembled slightly as she nodded her agreement.

The conversation moved on casually. Holly told him some of the more adventurous aspects of dealing with a group of five- and six-year-olds, selecting all the funniest stories just for the pleasure of seeing him smile. It was odd, she thought as she nibbled on one last fry. She didn't know this man at all and yet she was so comfortable with him.

That feeling of safe familiarity lasted until he pulled the sedan into a parking place outside her apartment building. The car suddenly seemed remarkably small and the warmth that had been just perfect only moments ago was now overpowering.

Mac shut off the engine, leaving them cocooned together with only the soft hiss of the rain and the distant traffic noise for company. The silence grew and she turned her head slowly, almost reluctantly.

The warmth of his gaze made the heater superfluous. If she had been standing in the middle of Antarctica wearing nothing but a bikini, she was sure that just one look from him would have been enough to heat her blood to a fever temperature.

Holly was helpless to protest as his long fingers slid into the hair at the back of her neck and he eased her gently toward him. She let him pull her across the seat without a murmur of dissent. In fact, she was conscious of a vague gratitude that he'd had the foresight to own a car without a gear console. Her hands were dwarfed by the the broad strength of his chest.

"Holly." Her name was a mere breath, a prayer, a sigh of recognition. Her eyes fluttered shut as his mouth touched hers and the world tilted. The kiss was a startling contrast to the gentle pressure of his hands in her hair. His lips did not ask her response; they demanded it. This was not an exploratory first kiss; it was a kiss between two people who had been lovers forever. After a moment of stunned surprise, Holly met the demand eagerly, her lips parting to capture the invading thrust of his tongue, her short nails digging into the front of his shirt.

The soft thickness of his mustache rubbed across her upper lip, setting her nerve endings on fire. She arched toward him and her tongue came up to join his, twining together in an erotic love duet.

His hands tightened on her shoulders and she felt the shudder that went through him a moment before he lifted his mouth from hers. Her eyelids quivered briefly before she could raise them. She felt as if she had been on a long journey, one that had changed her life forever. She stared into the hooded darkness of his eyes. Beneath her palms, she could feel the steady beat of his heart, its accelerated pace matching her pulse.

His gaze was piercing, asking questions she didn't understand, demanding answers she didn't have. Tentatively, her fingers crept up to his face, running delicately over the rough surface of his jaw. With a groan he twisted his face away and his hands tightened on her nape before his mouth came down on hers with a demanding pressure that stopped just short of being hurtful. His lips slanted across hers, his tongue surging past the barrier of her teeth and plunging deep into her mouth before withdrawing, only to surge inward again.

The erotic implication set Holly's slight frame humming with need. A warm liquid feeling gradually spread outward from the pit of her stomach to encompass her entire body. Her small hands slid into the ruffled darkness of his hair as she strained to get closer.

She stiffened in surprise as his hand suddenly cupped her full breast. For an instant she was frozen. She could almost feel the hard, callused palm against her soft skin. She could imagine the pad of his thumb stroking her nipple. With a moan she dragged her mouth away from his and stared up at him, the wild look in her dark eyes telling him of her disturbance.

Outside the car everything was the same but Holly knew that she was changed. A soft flush heated her cheeks as she stared at him, and the small hands that lay on his chest pushed slightly. He let her go without protest and she eased herself a few inches away, still unable to break the spell of his eyes on hers.

"I want to see you again."

His husky voice broke the last remnants of the spell, and her eyes jerked away, the color in her face darkening. Holly couldn't remember the last time she had kissed a man with such abandon. She drew a shaky breath and began to fumble on the floor for her purse and tote bag.

An involuntary shiver raced through her when he touched her shoulder and she straightened up, helpless to resist the urge to look at him.

"Mac, I...I don't want to go too fast...." She let the sentence trail off. So many men expected a woman to fall into bed with them right away. She wanted to make sure that he didn't expect that of her.

His mustache tilted upward in that lazy smile that wreaked havoc on her pulse. "We'll take it as slow as you like, love.

We're not working on a deadline. I'd just like to see you again. One step at a time.''

"I'd like that, too," she admitted, wishing her voice didn't sound so breathless.

He walked her to her apartment door, despite her assurances that hers was a very safe neighborhood. At the door she turned, shrugging off the leather jacket he had once again wrapped around her. His features were shadowed by the dark canvas hat and she shivered lightly. He looked dark and mysterious. But there was nothing mysterious about the solid warmth of the brief kiss he gave her.

"I'll call you."

She leaned back against the closed door, listening to his swift steps echoing on the pavement before fading out of hearing. She put her fingers up to her tingling mouth, and a tiny smile of anticipation curved her lips.

Chapter Three

When she finally managed to drag her mind away from Mac and look at a clock, Holly was surprised to find that it was still early. It was only three hours ago that Baby's recalcitrant engine had refused to start. There was still plenty of time for her to wash her hair and then work on the projects for tomorrow's class.

By ten o'clock, when Maryann's key was inserted into the lock, Holly had managed to accomplish at least part of her program. Her hair had been washed and towel-dried until it lay in fluffy dark curls against her head. But the notebook open in front of her, waiting to be filled with ideas for the entertainment and education of her students, was filled with nothing more earth-shattering than several meaningless doodles and the name "Mackenzie Donahue" written in various forms.

Maryann dropped her purse on a chair and strode to the refrigerator, giving Holly a casual greeting as she passed. She rummaged through the refrigerator, coming up with a package of sliced ham and some mustard.

"How was your day? Did you murder any of the little monsters?"

Holly grinned but drew her brows down in a ferocious scowl. "My students are not monsters. They are well-behaved children with a thirst for learning."

Maryann sliced her thick sandwich in half with a deft stroke of the knife and offered Holly a sardonic smile. "Pull the other leg, Holly. I've worked in the children's ward, remember? I know exactly what your sweet little students are like." She gestured warningly with a carrot stick as she leaned back against the counter. "My advice to you would be, don't turn your back. You never know when one of the little darlings is going to turn up with a hand grenade that he whipped up out of Play-doh and Lego pieces."

Holly laughed and shook her head. "I've given up trying to convince you that children aren't constantly on the lookout for ways to sabotage the adults in their life."

Maryann nodded agreeably. "You're right. They're not plotting all the time. Even *I* acquit them of making devious plans while they're sleeping."

"Just wait until you have kids of your own," Holly warned her. "Then you'll regret all your unfounded accusations."

"The only thing I'll regret is that I was dumb enough to get pregnant. *I'm* not the woman who daydreams in baby shops. You're the one who's in for a rude awakening. You wait until you have one of the little beasts underfoot twenty-four hours a day and then tell me that you love kids."

Holly gave up the argument with a smile. "So, how was life in the big city hospital today?"

Maryann shrugged as she reached up to pull the pins out of her thick auburn hair. She gave a sigh of pleasure as it fell around her shoulders, framing her rather ordinary features like a soft cloud.

"Dr. Johnson was on the prowl again tonight. I swear that man needs surgery to detach his hands from his libido. I may just provide the knife," she added darkly, as she unbuttoned her prim uniform and kicked off her shoes. She continued to talk as she walked into her bedroom, leaving the door open while she changed clothes and raising her voice so that Holly could hear her.

She wandered out into the kitchen a few minutes later, her slim figure swathed in a voluminous flannel nightgown. Holly was still seated at the kitchen table, her knees drawn up to her chest and her expression dreamy. Maryann let her voice trail off in midsentence, moving over to stand behind her roommate and stare down at the notepad that lay on the table.

"Who's Mackenzie Donahue?"

Holly jumped and her hand flattened against the paper as if trying to hide a guilty secret. Maryann circled around the table and sat down opposite her, looking at her quizzically. Holly flushed beneath her interested glance, dropping her feet to the floor and turning over a new sheet of paper.

"Who's Mackenzie Donahue?" Maryann repeated the question, letting Holly know that she wasn't going to let the question slide.

Holly shrugged. "Just a guy I met today." Her tone said that he was no one important.

Maryann let her brows go up just a fraction of an inch, the slight movement expressing her disbelief. "The last time I remember your doodling a guy's name all over the place, it was Dick Orman's name."

Holly flushed deeply and tossed the other woman a glance that spoke volumes. "That was eleven years ago in high school and I had a crush on him."

Maryann let her smile deepen to an annoying depth. "Exactly. So the last time you filled a notebook with a guy's name, you had a terrific crush on him. And this time, it's a guy you just met?" She shook her head gently. "Tell it to someone who hasn't known you as long as I have."

"I knew it was a mistake for us to share an apartment," Holly grumbled. "One should never move in with someone who thinks she knows you. It's worse than if I were living with my brother."

Maryann shook her head. "You're not going to distract me, Holly. Come on, spill it. After all, you told me all about Dick Orman," she coaxed.

"That was different," Holly wailed, knowing that she was fighting a losing battle. "I was infatuated with him. You always tell your best friend when you've got a crush on somebody. This isn't like that."

Maryann sobered slightly. "So tell me what it is like. Who's Mackenzie Donahue? I can't remember your ever mentioning anyone with a name like Mackenzie, except that guy who helped you in Tijuana last month. Wasn't his name Mac or Mick or something like that?"

Holly nodded, keeping her eyes focused on the table.

"That's a coincidence, meeting two men with names like that in the space of a month," Maryann went on. "Mac could be short for Macken—" She stopped and stared at her friend's bent head. There was a moment of charged silence, and when she spoke again, her voice had dropped to an incredulous croak.

"Holly Reynolds, tell me I'm nuts. Tell me that this Mackenzie Donahue that you 'just met today' isn't the guy from the bar in Tijuana."

Holly maintained a stubborn silence. Maryann's voice rose to a stunned squeak. "Do you mean to tell me that you're looking all starry-eyed over some giant pimp?"

"He's not a giant," she protested mildly, keeping her eyes down so that Maryann could not read the amusement in them. She hadn't decided definitely to tell Maryann about Mac, but since the decision had been taken out of her hands, she was going to have fun with it.

"He's not a giant!" Maryann all but shrieked. "I don't care if he's Tatoo or the Jolly Green Giant. The point is that he's a pimp. Do you know what that means? How can you live with what he does for a living?"

Holly shrugged, her wide mouth tucked into a repressed smile as she struggled to keep the laughter out of her voice. "As long as he doesn't try to enlist me, I don't feel I have any right to make judgments." She managed to put just a hint of anguish in her words, trying to convey the impression that she was willing to set aside her morals to accept him.

Maryann all but tore at her hair. "Holly, you're not thinking like a rational person. I know you said he was attractive, but think of what kind of person he must be to be able to use women like that. And even if that doesn't bother you, consider the fact that prostitution is illegal. How are you going to feel if he gets arrested? How is your family going to react? For Pete's sake, James is a diplomat. What kind of effect could this have on his career?"

She broke off as Holly raised a laughing face. "I'm sorry, Maryann. I shouldn't have led you on. It's just that I so rarely get to put one over on you."

Her friend was so relieved she forgot to be upset. "I should have known better than to think you could be attracted to a pimp.''

Holly flushed and shifted a little in her seat, remembering how hard it had been to tell Mac that she couldn't accept his line of work. Her conscience had won out in the end, but not without a battle.

Maryann got up and moved into the kitchen to fill the teakettle. ''I shouldn't be drinking tea just before going to bed, but after the shock you just gave me, I need the caffeine to calm my nerves. Now tell me who Mackenzie Donahue is.''

''He's the guy who came to my rescue in Tijuana last month.''

The teakettle hit the stove with a thump. Water splashed out the spout and hissed angrily against the open flame of the burner. Maryann ignored this minor flood and spun around to look at Holly. She fixed her friend with a stern look in her gray eyes. It was a look that had been known to make recalcitrant patients spring to do her bidding.

Holly held up her hand defensively. ''Don't look at me like that. I'm telling you the truth. He really is the guy from Tijuana, the one I thought was a pimp.''

''From your description of his clothes, I don't see how you could have been mistaken. He's either a pimp or he has the world's tackiest taste.''

''Neither one, actually. He's a cop and he was on a job down there. Well, he could hardly go into that area in uniform,'' she snapped in answer to Maryann's skeptical look.

''Great. You went to Tijuana to get my grandfather's watch and you come back without the watch but manage to pick up some guy who's nine feet tall, who dresses like a pimp and claims to be a cop. Just great!''

The kettle whistled urgently and Maryann turned away to pour steaming water over two tea bags in a pair of mugs, carrying them over to the table. She sat down at the table and began to dunk her tea bag, her attention on her roommate.

''How do you know he's a cop?''

''He told me he was. And I believe him. And he's not nine feet tall.''

Maryann shrugged. ''You don't have to bite my head off. If

he told you he's a cop and you want to believe him, that's entirely
your business. I just don't want to see you hurt." She scooped
sugar into her mug with a generous abandon that Holly envied as
she sipped her unsweetened tea.

"I'm not going to get hurt. He showed up after school today.
And it's a good thing he did, because Baby wouldn't start again.
He showed up, offered me dinner and a ride and then brought me
home. That's all there was to it." Her casual tone dismissed the
evening as nothing out of the ordinary. She wondered if the word
"liar" was emblazoned across her forehead or if it just felt that
way.

"Are you going to be seeing him again?"

"He said he'd give me a call." She patted her hand over her
mouth to stifle a yawn and made a production out of noticing the
clock. "Good heavens, it's getting late. I'd better get to bed if
I'm going to make it to work on time."

Maryann didn't try to detain her and Holly escaped to her bedroom. Despite the late hour, she didn't fall asleep immediately.
Every moment of the evening had to be taken separately and
examined again in the light of Maryann's skepticism. Had Mac
lied to her about being a cop? Was she a fool for believing him
without proof? With a sigh she decided that she didn't have to
worry about it unless he called again. And there was no guarantee
that he would.

But she fell asleep with a furtive prayer and her dreams were
once again filled with his presence.

HOLLY'S PRAYERS WERE ANSWERED even sooner than she could
have hoped. As she got ready for work the next morning, she was
in a less than perfect mood. She was going to have to walk to
school. The rain had stopped and the sun was shining with a fitful
brilliance that was typical of Los Angeles in March. The weather
was perfect for a walk but her legs still felt as if they'd been run
through a grinder, and walking was the last thing she felt like
doing.

She had just managed to find a pair of shoes that actually
matched each other in the tangle of footwear that littered the
bottom of her closet when the doorbell rang. Muttering impre-

cations directed toward anyone who might be within hearing, she hurried across the living room, patting vainly at her hair, which looked as if it had battled with a tornado and come out on the losing side.

She flung open the door, ready to explain to the manager that Maryann would be giving her the rent check as soon as she woke up, and then gaped at the apparition on the doorstep. Mac had one hand braced on the top of the door jamb, his long body leaning casually against its support.

He gave her a slow smile that made her bones feel like butter left in the sun. "I thought you might need a ride to work this morning since your car is out of commission."

"I...I...as a matter of fact, I could use a ride. I was going to walk but then I couldn't find my shoes and I burned the toast and—" She broke off and smiled at him, letting herself bask in the warmth of his azure eyes. With an effort she broke away from his mesmerizing gaze. "Let me put my shoes on and comb my hair and I'll be right with you. Would you like to come in?"

She backed away as he nodded and stepped into the apartment. Immediately the room seemed to shrink. Holly stood in front of him uncertainly, feeling as if the two of them were all alone in a tiny compartment. She swallowed hard and forced her feet to move away from him.

"I'll only be a second," she murmured breathlessly before she disappeared into her bedroom. Alone in the room, she hurried over to her vanity and gave a moan of despair as she took in her tousled hair and the warm sparkle in her eyes. "You look like a scarecrow," she muttered to her reflection. "You not only look like a refugee from Oz, you also look like someone who's just met Prince Charming. If you don't learn to look a little less star-struck, you're going to scare the poor man to death." Her stern words did not still the bubbling feeling in her stomach, but they did serve to bring a more sober expression to her face.

It didn't last. As soon as she stepped into the living room and saw Mac, Holly could feel her mouth turning up in an inane smile. The only thing that made it bearable was the knowledge that his expression was only a shade less fatuous, though more restrained.

Walking out to his car, she was vividly aware of the light

pressure of his hand on the small of her back, and she had the urge to look down to see if her feet were still touching the ground. They certainly didn't feel as if they were.

She hesitated momentarily when she saw the slim figure leaning against Mac's car but Mac urged her forward. The man turned and she came to a dead stop three feet away from him, her face reflecting her surprise. He grinned at her, revealing a full set of perfect teeth.

"Hi, Lady. Been in any good brawls lately?" The grin was irresistible as was the twinkle in his hazel eyes.

"I'm sure you remember Ken Richardson," Mac murmured dryly.

"How could I forget the only person who's ever given me a cocker spaniel's nickname? You look a little better than you did last time I saw you," she told the smaller man. She shook her head. "I suppose you're a cop, too."

He glanced questioningly at Mac, his eyes intent, and then the expression was gone so quickly that Holly wondered if she had imagined it.

"Sure. Mac and I have been partners for a long time."

"And I suppose your missing teeth were all done with makeup, just like Mac's scar?"

"Well, not exactly. I'm afraid a gentleman with no sense of humor knocked them out a few years back. It was easy to take the bridge out. I thought it gave me an appealingly adventurous look."

"You looked as if you'd just crawled out of a sewer," she told him flatly.

He grinned again and opened the passenger door for her. "That's what I said. I looked adventurous."

Holly got into the car, sliding over into the middle as Ken got in next to her and Mac walked around the front. Even Ken's presence didn't serve to soften the impact of Mac's hard thigh brushing against hers. She kept her eyes straight ahead as the car pulled away from the curb. She wondered if he could feel the tremor that ran through her each time his arm touched hers. She was grateful when Ken spoke, giving her something else to think about on the short drive to the school.

"Mac says you teach kindergarten. I have a niece about that age." He gave an exaggerated shudder. "I don't know how you can stand a whole classroom full of them." He emphasized the last word.

Holly smiled, trying not to notice when Mac's leg shifted to rest more firmly against hers. The soft tie of her wraparound dress suddenly felt unbearably tight. Her voice was slightly breathless when she answered Ken.

"You sound like my roommate. Maryann thinks that small children are related to pit vipers and should be treated with equal caution. I like kids and I enjoy teaching them. They can be a bit of a handful but I can't imagine another job as satisfying. Of course, there are days when I'd gladly trade all of my students for a wooden nickel," she said, laughing. "But that's the exception."

Mac pulled his car into a parking place next to the Fiat and got out. He reached a hand in to assist her and Holly hesitated for only an instant before placing her small fingers in his palm. The tingling shock wave that raced up her arm was expected but still disconcerting, and she knew he couldn't help but feel her reaction to his touch. His fingers tightened over hers and her eyes flew to his face. Her heartbeat grew erratic as she saw the warmth in his eyes. He didn't release her hand even when they stood next to her car.

"Do you have plans for tonight?" His husky voice was pitched low so that only she could hear him.

Holly shook her head, mesmerized by his eyes. "It's Friday," she said, unconcerned that the comment was totally irrelevant.

"Have dinner with me." It was not quite a request and not yet a command.

"I'd like that," she told him honestly.

He lifted her hand to his lips, turning it over to press a kiss into the palm. His mustache brushed softly against the sensitive flesh and she shivered as she felt the tip of his tongue flick along the soft mound at the base of her thumb.

She was as breathless as if he had possessed her mouth. When he pulled back, Mac closed her fingers around his kiss before releasing her hand.

"Eight o'clock?" he asked huskily. She nodded. In her current state she would have agreed to anything. He pressed the back of his hand lightly against her flushed cheek. "Dress up. I want to take you somewhere with candlelight and flowers."

She leaned back against the side of the Fiat as he got into his car and backed out of the parking slot.

Ken leaned out of his window and waved. "Nice to see you again, Lady." He watched her in the mirror on his side of the car. She was still leaning against the Fiat when they turned out onto the street.

Ken turned bright, inquiring eyes on Mac. "A cop, huh?"

Mac shrugged, keeping his gaze firmly on the road in front of them. "I had to tell her something. She thought I was a pimp and she started trying to explain very politely that she didn't think she could be comfortable with my line of work."

"So you told her you were a cop." The words were flat, without intonation.

Mac threw him an irritated look that held more than a trace of guilt. "What was I supposed to tell her? 'No, I'm not a pimp. I'm here to spy on your brother.'?"

Ken raised his hands in surrender. "Don't jump down my throat. Did I say anything?"

"You didn't have to," Mac told him sourly. "I didn't lie to her...exactly," he added defensively.

"I'm not saying a thing." Ken was all innocence.

"Well, stop thinking it," his friend growled unreasonably.

"My mind is a blank."

Mac's grim expression lightened involuntarily. "Now *that* I can believe."

Chapter Four

Holly smoothed her hands over her soft silk dress and then twisted at an impossible angle to check that the seams of her stockings were straight. It felt wonderfully wicked to be wearing a lacy garter belt and sheer nylons with fine seams up the backs of her legs. The garter belt and stockings had been a Christmas present from Maryann and this was the first time she had worn them.

She turned back to face her reflection, meeting sparkling brown eyes that reflected her inner excitement. She had long since given up trying to subdue her anticipation. She was looking forward to seeing Mac, and it showed. Her dark brows came together in a faint frown. It was a little scary to realize just how much she was looking forward to this date. She didn't want to get in too deep too fast.

The doorbell rang before she had a chance to follow the thought any further. She gave one last pat to her hair and turned away from the mirror. Something about her radiant reflection made her uncomfortable.

MAC RESISTED THE URGE to tug at his tie after he rang the doorbell. His fingers tightened around the small bouquet of flowers. He was surprised to find that his palms felt clammy. Damn. He hadn't been this nervous about seeing a woman since...since last night, when he had been waiting outside Holly's school. His mustache lifted in a mocking smile. He had been in more life-and-death situations than he cared to remember and here he was, sweating like a schoolboy on his first date.

What was there about Holly Reynolds that stirred his senses so? Each time he saw her, he was torn between the urge to hold her and protect her and the need to make passionate love to her, burying himself in her warmth until he forgot everything but the feel of her, until he forgot that he was supposed to be probing for information about her brother.

He looked up as Holly opened the door, her breath catching at the dark turbulence in his eyes. For just a moment she was frightened. This was not the warm and gentle man she had gone out with last night. This was someone larger and more threatening. But his expression vanished so swiftly that she half thought she had imagined it. Any lingering uncertainty disappeared beneath the warmth of his smile.

"Hi. Come on in. You're right on time." *Boy, was that a brilliant conversational gambit,* she chided herself.

Mac stepped into the apartment and she gave a soft gasp of pleasure as he held out a delicate bouquet of yellow roses and baby's breath. "Oh, how beautiful. Thank you."

He put a hand over his heart and bowed. "They pale to insignificance before your beauty." She laughed, but there was enough sincere admiration in his eyes to draw a faint flush of pleasure to her cheeks.

"Let me put these in water."

He followed her into the kitchen. The draped neckline of the royal-blue dress left her upper back bare, and she could feel his eyes trailing the vulnerable skin.

"Would you like something to drink?" She spoke quickly, more to distract her own wayward thoughts than anything else. Without waiting for an answer, she placed the flowers on the counter and opened one of the cupboards.

"We've got some brandy that Maryann bought for a fruitcake and some Scotch that was supposed to go into a pie."

Mac looked at the dusty labels doubtfully. From the looks of the bottles, they had been sitting in the cupboard for several years. In fact, he wouldn't have been surprised to find out that she had inherited them from her grandparents. He shook his head.

"I'd better not. We have reservations at the restaurant."

Holly shut the cupboard door, hoping that her relief wasn't

obvious. No one knew how old those bottles of booze were. She had a vague memory of James suggesting the last time he visited that she donate them to a museum.

With a practiced gesture she hooked one foot around a small step stool and pulled it beneath the cupboard where the vases were stored. It was still a stretch to reach the top shelf and her fingers had almost made contact with a crystal vase when a long, masculine hand appeared and lifted it easily off the shelf. Her heels hit the stool with a thud.

Mac was a warm presence along her back, not touching but so close that her nerve endings quivered. Her eyes followed the movement of his hand, watching as he set the vase gently on the counter. Time hung suspended; even her breathing stopped, waiting. His breath touched the back of her neck an instant before his mouth tasted the vulnerable flesh exposed by the careful upsweep of her hair. A shiver rippled up her spine and every bone in her body seemed to dissolve.

His hands caught her at the waist, supporting and turning her until she faced him. She gave a breathless laugh.

"I should have warned you about what kissing the back of my neck does to me. It's ridiculous the way it..." Her voice trailed off as his head bent and his teeth nibbled gently just beneath her ear. Only his hands held her upright. Without their support she would have collapsed in a boneless heap.

"Umm. Kissing you under the ear seems to have the same effect." She could hear the smile in his voice. His tongue tasted the pulse that fluttered at the base of her throat. Her nails flexed against his shoulders.

"Mac." His name quivered with need but there was also a shaky protest in it. His mouth stilled. He heard the need and his body tightened in answer. But he also heard the protest. His head came up slowly, reluctantly relinquishing the sweet territory that he knew could be his.

But it wouldn't be fair to force a decision so soon. The chemistry between them was explosive and, like dynamite, it needed to be handled with respect and caution. He could lift her in his arms and carry her to bed and she wouldn't struggle, but something precious might be forever lost: her trust.

Her lashes fluttered open and the dazed passion in her eyes was almost his undoing. She looked so warm and willing. He forced a smile, letting his lids drop to conceal his expression.

"I guess that's not taking it slow, is it?"

Holly shook her head, trying to control the wild pounding of her heart. How could he look so calm when her entire body tingled? Tension quivered between them, alive and beckoning.

"I guess I'll have to confess that I have a fatal weakness when it comes to women standing on stools." Mac hung his head, the very picture of contrition.

Holly blinked. Desire had slowed her mental processes to the point where, for an instant, she actually tried to make sense of his absurd statement. But only for an instant.

"Have you tried therapy? I understand they can do marvelous things these days." If her voice was slightly breathless, Mac didn't seem to notice.

He winced. "You're a hard woman." He stepped back and glanced at his watch. "We'd better hurry if we want to use our reservations." And the atmosphere eased.

The restaurant was dim but not so dark that flashlights were necessary to read the menu. The service was quiet and efficient. The food was excellent but it was secondary to the pleasure of Mac's company. If it hadn't been for the tingling feeling that lingered along her spine, Holly might have wondered if she had imagined those intense moments in the kitchen.

"You really enjoy working with kids, don't you?" She glanced up from her grilled salmon and smiled.

"I love it."

"It's been a while since I met someone who admits to liking children. It seems to be unfashionable at the moment. Even people who have them don't like them."

"They can be a handful but they're so incredibly alive. There's a vibrancy about a child that makes the whole world look brand-new. They get so much out of life. Sometimes it makes me realize how seldom adults let themselves just sit back and take pleasure in little things."

She broke off and laughed self-consciously. "Maryann could

have warned you not to get me started on kids. She thinks they should all be put in cages and visited with extreme caution.''

Mac took a sip of wine and studied her over the rim of the glass. He wondered if she had any idea how vibrant she was, so much like the children she described. She had such zest for life.

"I'm surprised you don't have a houseful of kids of your own,'' he commented.

"I will have one of these days. I promised myself that by the time I'm thirty, I'll either have a child or I'll be less than nine months away from having one.''

"It usually takes two for what you've got in mind,'' he pointed out dryly.

"I know. I suppose I'll just have to capture some poor helpless male of the species and ravish him,'' she declared theatrically.

"I doubt if he'll struggle too hard. I know I certainly wouldn't.''

A faint flush rose in her cheeks as she met the electric blue of his gaze. It was an effort to hang on to her composure. "But we've already established that you have a weakness for women standing on step stools. Who knows what other flaws you may have.'' She shook her head sadly. "Today it's step stools, to-morrow it could be ladders. It's all downhill from here.''

"If I promise to try and control my weaknesses, do you think you'd be able to consider me as a candidate?'' His tone was comically serious.

"I'll keep you in mind,'' she promised lightly. She hoped that her voice didn't betray her inner agitation. The thought of him fathering her child brought mental images that were both explicit and disturbing.

She pushed the pictures away. "What about you? Ever been married? Any children?''

"I've never been married. I came close once but it didn't work out.'' For a moment his expression was so bleak and filled with pain that Holly wanted to reach out and soothe the lines from beside his mouth.

"What about your family? Brothers? Sisters?''

He shook his head, his expression easing. "No brothers and

sisters. My mother died when I was a kid and my father died when I was twenty.''

''That's a rough time to lose a parent,'' she murmured sympathetically.

''Yeah, I suppose it is. We didn't get along very well, but I guess he did the best he could by me.''

Holly swallowed the last bite of salmon and looked at him thoughtfully. The product of a loving family, she was still close to her parents and her brother, not to mention the assorted aunts, uncles and grandparents that went along with them. It was difficult for her to conceive of being without close family.

''What did you do after he died? Were you in college then?''

''Yeah. I finished school and then joined the marines. Seemed like a great way to see the world.'' His mouth twisted ruefully on the words.

''When did you decide you wanted to be a cop?''

''That didn't come until later.'' He shifted restlessly and lifted a hand to signal for the waitress. ''How about dessert? This place is famous for their chocolate mousse pie.''

Holly hesitated for only a moment. ''I'll regret it in the morning but I can't resist it tonight.''

The pie was justly famous and she savored it down to the last tiny bite. Mac grinned at her empty plate. ''I guess I don't have to ask whether or not you enjoyed it.''

''Just as much as you did.'' Holly cocked her head at his equally clean dish. She sat back in her chair, replete.

That feeling of completion lasted almost all the way home. It was only when he stopped the car outside her apartment building that tension coiled inside her. If he kissed her now in the warmth and intimacy of the car, she would have a hard time holding on to her equanimity.

The car had barely rolled to a stop before she was opening the door. Mac arched one brow as he left the car at a more leisurely pace. He didn't ask why she was in such a hurry.

Holly kept up a stream of meaningless chatter all the way to her apartment door. The moment the words left her mouth, they were forgotten. They were just a convenient means of filling up the silence with something safe.

She stopped outside the door and turned to look at him. "I'd ask you in for a drink but Maryann is working a late-afternoon shift right now and she probably just went to bed. I had a wonderful time. The meal was wonderful and the restaurant was won—"

He put his fingers over her mouth. "I know. The restaurant was wonderful, too," he said with such gentle amusement that she couldn't be offended. His hand slid from her mouth to cup the back of her neck.

"I didn't mean to babble. It's just that..."

"It seems like a little too much, too soon," Mac finished for her.

"Yes." The word was little more than a sigh. She leaned her cheek against his wrist, feeling the rough brush of hair. Her eyes half closed. "When I'm with you, I forget all the good, practical rules I've laid down for myself," she admitted.

His thumb stroked the tender skin behind her ear, his eyes intent on her face. "It's the same for me. I won't push it, Holly. I think we could have something important together. It's worth waiting for."

She let her hands rest on his chest. "I don't know if I'm glad to hear you say that or sorry. There's a part of me that would love for you to sweep me off my feet."

Mac groaned, tugging her up onto her toes as his head dipped. "Don't say things like that. You make it hard to be a nice guy."

"You don't kiss like a nice guy," she murmured a few minutes later, her voice dreamy.

"Maybe I should practice some more."

Holly laughed and put her fingers against his lips. "I think you've had more than enough practice."

She eased out of his arms and he let her go without protest, watching as she unlocked the door. "I'll call you tomorrow." It was half a question and Holly nodded.

"I'd like that."

He bent and dropped a hard kiss on her mouth, a promise for the future. "Sleep tight."

Holly eased the door shut behind her, listening to his quiet footsteps until they faded into silence. A silly smile curved her wide mouth. He was going to call tomorrow. And that was just the beginning.

MAC DID CALL the next day. In fact, for the next month not a single day went by that Holly did not either see him or talk to him. March and April were cool and unusually damp for Southern California, but as far as she was concerned, the weather had never been more exquisite, her students had never been more cooperative and her life had never been more perfect.

Even Baby was in a good mood. It was almost as if the little Fiat felt that it had done its part by giving Mac an opening that first night and now there was no need to throw tantrums. All through the rains of March and the drizzle of April, Baby purred. For Holly it was just one more item to add to her list of good things that had happened since Mac came into her life.

The only dark spot on her horizon was Maryann's pessimistic attitude.

"You're moving too fast, Holly. You're asking to get burned. What do you really know about Mac?"

Holly suppressed the urge to scream and continued to run the iron gently over the emerald silk blouse she was going to wear that evening. Maryann was genuinely concerned and Holly appreciated that but she was tired of hearing all the dire warnings.

"I know that he's tremendously nice; he's sexy; he likes me; he's sexy; I like him; he's sexy; he hasn't pushed me; he's—"

"I know, I know: He's sexy!" Maryann was sitting cross-legged on Holly's bed, stabbing a half-eaten banana in the air for emphasis. "That's precisely my point. You're so caught up in how sexy he is. That could be blinding you to all sorts of faults."

"Like what?" Holly turned the blouse and began pressing the back. Maryann really was sweet, if overprotective. She spoke as if she were six years older than Holly instead of six months.

"Anything." The banana waved wildly. "What if he gets mean when he drinks?"

"He almost never drinks."

"Maybe he hates dogs."

"I'm not too fond of dogs myself."

"Maybe he has a secret wife and six kids hidden somewhere."

"He's never been married."

Maryann pounced. "How do you know?"

"He told me." There was no arguing with that simple statement.

"What about his job? Being a cop is hardly in the same category as sitting at a desk all day. What if he gets hurt or..." She trailed off, biting her lip. "I'm sorry, Holly. That was hitting below the belt."

Holly shook her head, forcing a smile. "It's not something that I can ignore. I won't say it doesn't bother me but I'm not going to dwell on the bad possibilities. Remember to whom you're talking." Her smile widened. "This is the woman who was voted 'Most Likely to Believe the World Is Perfect.' I count on you to blow a little fresh air on my fantasies once in a while but I'm still going to look on the bright side.

"Now what other hideous faults do you perceive in Mac? Is he a chocoholic? A secret needlepoint fanatic?"

Maryann accepted her lead, keeping her tone stern but staying away from potentially hurtful subjects.

"He could be a closet pervert for all you know." The banana punctuated the end of the sentence.

"Is that someone who has a thing for closets?" Holly threw her exasperated friend a grin. "You don't have a single concrete thing to say against him and you and I both know it."

"And you can't tell me a single concrete fact to support your theory that he's perfect."

"I don't think he's perfect." Holly slid a hanger into the blouse and laid it across the ironing board to carefully button the neck. "I'm not an idiot, Maryann. I'm being cautious. But for the first time I've met someone I can imagine spending the rest of my life with. I'm not going to throw that away just because he doesn't come with the *Good Housekeeping* Seal of Approval."

"I still think you're risking an awful lot of hurt but you always have been pigheaded. Just remember that I'm going to say 'I told you so' if he turns out to be an ax murderer."

"If he turns out to be an ax murderer, then I suspect you'll be saying that at my funeral, which should make it doubly satisfying for you."

"You're impossible!" Maryann gestured one time too many with the banana. This time the abused fruit popped out of its skin with the force of her exasperation. The two women watched as the soft fruit sailed through the air and landed with a squishy splat...right on Holly's newly ironed blouse.

Holly stared at the mess for a moment before lifting her gaze to Maryann. The other woman looked from the ruined blouse to the empty banana skin still clutched in her fingers and then up at her friend. She shrugged weakly.

"They just don't make bananas like they used to."

IT WOULD HAVE MADE Maryann feel better if she had known that her words were not falling on totally deaf ears. Though Holly easily dismissed any thought of Mac's having a wife and children, she could not quite so easily set aside his job. That was real and right in front of her any time she chose to look.

So far she had been dealing with it by not looking, but sooner or later she was going to have to face the issue. Could she cope with loving a cop? Maybe it was too late to be asking that question. Wasn't she already in love with him?

She stopped, the mascara brush suspended halfway to her eye. Was she in love with Mac? She stared blankly at her reflection for a moment before shaking her head. No. It was too soon. She wasn't going to be in love with him yet. And if she *was* by some bizarre mistake already in love with him, she didn't have to face it yet. She would just put it out of her mind for now.

Maybe it was time Maryann got to know Mac. Then she'd see for herself how nice he was and she'd stop predicting disaster. She finished stroking mascara on her lashes and then smiled at her reflection. Yes, that was definitely the thing to do. Maybe she would invite Mac to dinner and Maryann could get to know him a little. Of course, she'd have to browbeat Maryann into showing up but Maryann owed her one after throwing that banana on her best blouse.

"HURRY UP, MARYANN. They're supposed to be here in ten minutes and you aren't even dressed yet."

Maryann gave her friend a sour look. "This is a stupid idea," she said flatly. "It's a stupid idea and it's *your* stupid idea. I'm going along with it, but don't expect me to smile while I do it."

"It's not a stupid idea," Holly defended. She handed Maryann a simple black dress that made the most of her friend's pale skin and richly colored hair. "This is called killing two birds with one stone."

"Not to mention ruining a good friendship."

Holly went on as if nothing had been said. "Ken wanted to have dinner with us and I wanted you to meet Mac. This way, you get to meet Mac *and* Ken..."

"Oh, boy, I can hardly contain my excitement."

"I get to see Mac..."

"It's been at least a whole day since you did that."

"...and we both get a nice dinner in pleasant company."

"That remains to be seen."

"Stop grousing. You haven't been out on a date since Jason left and it's about time you stopped mooning around, thinking about him."

"I have not been thinking about that shifty little weasel." Maryann turned to glare at Holly. "I've been busy at the hospital. You know that."

Holly moved until she could reach the back of Maryann's dress again and began to zip it. "All I know is that I had to threaten you with dismemberment to get you to agree to a simple double date. What's the big deal? Nobody's asking you to fall in love with Ken, just to go out with him. He's nice, he's fun, he's attractive. What more could you ask for on a casual date?"

"The whole thing is ridiculous. Everybody knows that people always hate each other when their friends force them into blind dates. Blind dates—even the term is ghastly. It's going to be a disaster. I can feel it."

"Now who's being stupid? Of course it's not going to be a disaster. We're going to have a lot of fun and you'll be sorry you made such a production out of the whole thing."

Perhaps it was inevitable that everything would go wrong. If Maryann's pessimistic attitude wasn't a clue, then the weather should have been. During the afternoon clouds had gathered and by evening it was raining, not a light drizzle, but a heavy down-pour that looked as if it was settling in for a long stay.

Holly's umbrella was not to be found and Maryann's had de-veloped a hole that allowed the rain to trickle icily down the neck of whoever was lucky enough to be standing under it. Mac and Ken were late, and when they showed up, Mac presented them with the news that his car refused to run, so they had used Ken's. That wouldn't have been a problem except that the manufacturer's idea of a back seat did not allow for passengers with legs.

Maryann rolled her eyes before climbing into the back seat. The short drive to the restaurant was easily filled with idle chatter about the weather, but the atmosphere between Ken and his "date" could not have been any cooler if he had been the wolf who had just eaten her grandmother.

As Mac helped her out of the car, Holly wondered if she should come down with an attack of acute appendicitis. Something told her that the evening had already reached its high point and it was only going to get worse. After all Holly's talk about what a won-derful, warm person Maryann was, what a great sense of humor she had, Mac had to wonder if this was an android sent to take the real Maryann's place.

Maryann and Ken walked ahead of them, their icy silence doing little to dispel Holly's already chilled mood. She glanced at Mac, almost afraid to see his expression. He caught her look and grinned, rolling his eyes comically.

"I should have warned you that Ken hates blind dates. He met his ex-wife on a blind date and he's never quite gotten over it."

"Maryann isn't exactly being a model of sweetness and light," Holly admitted.

Mac looked at the couple ahead of them and then glanced around the parking garage. His fingers tightened around Holly's and he gave her a conspiratorial look. "If we hurry, we could lose ourselves in here. They'd never find us. I can hot-wire a car and we can make our escape."

Holly sighed. "Too late. They've seen us. Besides, if we let them get into the elevator alone, they'd probably be like the ging-ham dog and the calico cat and tear each other to pieces. We'd never be able to come back here."

Both Maryann and Ken turned to look in the direction of the laughter, their expressions making it clear that they didn't find anything amusing. With a sigh Holly released Mac's hand and tucked her arm through Ken's, pulling him into the elevator.

"Tell me what Mac's really like. All I ever get to see is his good side."

Ken grinned, the look in his hazel eyes telling her that he was well aware of her motives. "The problem is, Lady, that Mac doesn't have any interesting vices. He's disgustingly wholesome. I've been trying to corrupt him for years."

The rest of the evening could not be called a success, but it was not the disaster it could have been. Holly made it a point to keep the conversation under control, changing the subject whenever it looked as if Ken and Maryann were going to lunge for each other's throats. Mac for the most part sat back and watched, his eyes dark with lazy amusement.

It seemed they couldn't agree on anything. Maryann ordered a steak, Ken ordered a vegetarian platter. She accused him of trying to make everyone else feel guilty and he called her a carnivore. It didn't seem to matter what their companions ordered. They argued about every subject that came up. She was a liberal, he was a conservative. She liked classical music, he liked jazz. They couldn't even agree to differ.

The final cap to the evening was when the waiter bumped Ken's drink and spilled wine all over Maryann's lap. She made all the right noises, saying that, of course, it wasn't his fault, but her frigid tone got across a different message.

Naturally, the evening came to a grinding halt. Maryann could not sit around in a wet dress. There was a general feeling of relief that the evening was almost over. Mac had other plans.

He smiled genially as they all rose. "I'm sure you can manage to see Maryann home without our assistance, Ken. I promised Holly a long walk in the rain," he lied calmly. "It was nice meeting you, Maryann. I hope your dress isn't ruined. Holly and I will pick up a cab later. See you tomorrow, Ken."

Holly hesitated when she caught Maryann's frantic expression. It was a look that clearly said she didn't want to be left alone with Ken. But Mac's arm wrapped gently around Holly's shoulder. With an apologetic smile at her roommate, Holly let herself be led away. She waited until the elevator doors had shut behind them before she spoke.

"I will never, ever arrange a date for anyone again. Nobody told me that it could be so dangerous. What happened?"

"I think it was a case of hate at first sight. I just hope they don't kill each other before they get home."

He opened his umbrella and stepped out into the rain, putting one arm around Holly's shoulders to hold her close. "I know a nice little place about a block away where we can stop and have a drink."

"I feel guilty about abandoning Maryann like that."

"Ken will get her safely home. He's got some odd habits but attacking women has never been one of them. Besides, they deserve each other after what they put us through."

She snuggled her head against the hard strength of his arm. "I could use a few minutes of quiet."

The rain was heavy enough to discourage all but the most determined of pedestrians, and they had the street to themselves. They had gone perhaps half a block when Holly came to a stop. Mac looked down at her questioningly.

"Do you know what my favorite movie is?"

He raised his brows. "Is there a reason that we have to stand in the rain while you tell me?"

"It's *Singin' in the Rain*."

He met the mischievous smile in her eyes and shook his head, the beginnings of a smile tilting his thick mustache. "No. I absolutely refuse to dance in the streets like Gene Kelly. I could get arrested."

She pulled the umbrella away from him, folding it with a snap and leaving them both standing in the downpour. "This is Los Angeles, home of strange things and even stranger people. Nobody will even notice."

She spun on her toes, her arms thrown out, face tilted to the sky. "After the evening we just spent, I need to rinse away the dust of battle."

"You go ahead. I'm not going to dance in the street." But he made no move to put up the umbrella.

"Just one little bitty step?" she coaxed.

He shook his head, his teeth gleaming beneath the mustache. He followed her as she hopped from puddle to puddle. "You're ruining your shoes," he pointed out.

"They're only shoes," she dismissed grandly.

"How many glasses of wine did you have?"

"I'm not drunk," she said indignantly. "I'm just enjoying the weather. After all, this could be the last rain we have until fall."

"So you're going to absorb as much water as possible to see you through the coming drought?"

She had thrown open her coat and was skipping her way down the sidewalk, kicking up water with total disregard for her clothes. Watching her, Mac was reminded of a little girl playing hooky from school, delighted with the slightly illicit freedom. She spun giddily around a lamppost, her laughing face catching the light as she invited him to share her pleasure.

She gave a startled gasp when his arm caught her around the waist, lifting her off her feet and pulling her against the hard length of his body. One of her shoes slipped off and fell in the gutter to drift unnoticed and unmourned on the small river that rushed along the street.

She caught a brief glimpse of his eyes, darkly blue and glittering before his mouth crashed down on hers. Her soft moan was lost beneath the hungry pressure of his tongue. Mac's arm was a steel bar at her back, holding her against his frame. His other hand came up to cup the back of her head, tilting her face to allow his mouth better access.

Desire rose turbulently between them. Holly tilted her head back as his mouth moved gently against her throat, letting the rain fall like a warm benediction on her face. The light from the lamppost created a pool of watery brilliance that encapsulated them in a tiny, private world all their own.

The short beep of a car horn pulled them apart. Mac's eyes met hers as he let her slide slowly to her feet. Water plastered his hair to his head and sleeked his skin.

"I lost my shoes." Her voice was breathless.

He looked down at the one dark pump that lay forlornly on the sidewalk. "So you did. Where's the other one?"

"I think it went in the gutter. You're all wet."

"Who's idea was it to dance in the rain?" he asked mildly. He bent to pick up the discarded umbrella and hooked it over his arm. "I think it's a little late for this to do any good. Come on, I'll see if I can find a phone and call us a cab."

She let him lead her down the street, his arm a welcome weight on her shoulders. "I thought we were going for drinks."

"I don't think anybody's going to let us in. You don't have any shoes and we both look like drowned rats. Of course, we could always go back to my place for a drink."

She hesitated, caught between common sense and desire. Common sense won, but not without a battle. "I have to go to work tomorrow."

"Pity. I was really looking forward to showing you my collection of old bottle caps."

"I'd love to see them some other time," she murmured softly. The light conversation carried stronger, deeper meanings and her words were a promise.

His arm tightened around her shoulders. "I'll polish them up for you."

Chapter Five

The double date that had started on such a bad note yielded more than a romantic walk in the rain. Maryann did stop suggesting that Mac might be the next worse thing to Attila the Hun. Holly would have appreciated it more if she could have thought that it was because her roommate had discovered just how nice Mac was. Unfortunately, Maryann had simply found a new target. Mac was forgotten in the barrage of ammunition she now aimed against Ken.

He was a rude, overbearing, egotistical, smart-mouthed male chauvinist and "pig" was too nice a word to add to the end of the list. All Holly's attempts to find out just what Ken had done to deserve such a sweeping condemnation met with Maryann's unswerving assertion that he hadn't done anything; it was just obvious. And if Holly hadn't been so determined to like Mac's friend, she would be able to see for herself his true colors.

Holly gave up. At least she wasn't being forced to defend Mac. She wasn't going to replace that with defending his friend.

Besides, there were so many other things to think about. There was less than a month left to the end of the school year and she had to decide what to do with her summer. In the past she had taught in a summer program. This year she had tentatively planned to go to Europe. Her brother had told her that she could use his apartment as a base if she wanted to stay with him and launch her travels from there.

There was no question of leaving for Europe now, not as long as Mac was still in L.A. She had already written to James and told him that her plans had changed and she would be staying in the States. She frowned slightly. She hadn't heard from James in almost a month. Usually he wrote or called every two or three weeks. Still, if something was wrong, her father would have known, and he hadn't said anything when she talked to him the previous week.

Holly dabbed on an extra bit of perfume and gave her reflection a satisfied look. She was no Raquel Welch, but she didn't think Mac would have any complaints. The soft yellow dress was right out of the fifties. Strapless, with buttons down the front and a swirling skirt that fell to her knees, it was sexy but subtle, a salute to the feeling of spring that filled the air.

Tonight was going to be special. She could feel it in her bones. Mac had invited her to have dinner at his home and the wonderful tingle of excitement that ran down her spine had nothing to do with the thought of his home cooking.

They both knew it was only a matter of time before their relationship moved to a more intimate level. But not quite yet, not tonight. She didn't want to take that step yet. She wanted to savor the anticipation a while longer.

MAC STUCK HIS HANDS in the pockets of his jeans and then pulled them out again. Damn, he was nervous. Ridiculous. It wasn't as if he hadn't entertained a woman at his home before. Craig Claiborne didn't tremble when Mac walked by but he could turn out a pretty fair meal. Besides, he had everything organized. Nothing was going to go wrong, he thought as he waited in Holly's apartment for her to finish getting ready.

The phone rang and he glanced over at Holly. She was twisted at an impossible angle, trying to buckle her sandal. "Shall I get that?"

"Could you? I just found the buckle and if I let go now, I'll never get the strap through."

He smiled at her muffled words and moved toward the phone. "You could just wear tennis shoes."

"Not with a dress. It would look tacky."

He picked up the phone on the second ring. "Hello?"

There was a long pause on the other end and he could hear the static hum that identified it as a long-distance connection.

"Hello?" The voice was male, surprisingly clear and obviously uncertain. Mac felt his stomach muscles tense. "I may have a wrong number. Is this Holly Reynolds's home?"

"Yes. Here she is now."

He moved slightly away as Holly took the receiver, shrugging in answer to her questioning look. He didn't want to know who it was.

"James!" Holly's delighted exclamation gave him the answer he had feared. He turned away, afraid that his expression might give away his inner rage. Damn! Why now? Just when he had almost managed to forget the damned assignment.

He closed his ears to her end of the conversation. Tonight he didn't want to be an agent. He didn't want to think of his duty. All he wanted was to be an ordinary man having dinner with a woman he was falling in love with. He was going to have to drop this assignment. He'd tell Daniels that he couldn't handle it. Let Daniels assign someone else to do his dirty work. And then, of course, Mac would have to strangle the other man.

His hand was clenched and he forced himself to relax the fingers one by one, slipping them casually into his pocket as he turned to face Holly, automatically listening to her end of the conversation and sorting the words into potentially useful information.

The fact was that no matter how much he hated it, the job was going to get done, whether he did it or someone else did it. And if someone was going to bring Holly's world crashing around her ears, he would rather be the one to do it. At least maybe he could shelter her from some of the pieces.

Holly hung up the phone and turned a beaming expression on Mac, unaware of his inner torment. "That was my brother, James. If I'd known it was him, I wouldn't have had you get the call. I had to answer a catechism of who you were and what you were doing here. Sometimes he acts as if I'm eight instead of twenty-eight." There was affectionate exasperation in her words.

"I guess it's always hard to let someone grow up," Mac murmured noncommittally.

"I suppose so."

"How are things going in Europe?" *Good, Mackenzie. That's a nice casual question. Nothing there to make her suspect that you're out to get her brother.*

"Pretty good. He likes his job and says the country is gorgeous." She picked up her purse. "I guess I'm ready to go. I hope James's call didn't mess anything up with your dinner."

Mac glanced at his watch, surprised to see that she had been on the phone for almost fifteen minutes. Funny how time flies when your guts are being twisted. He shook his head.

"No problem." At the moment he couldn't even remember what he had planned to cook, so it wasn't exactly a lie. He waited until they were in his car, headed toward his house, before he opened the conversation again.

"Your brother has been in Europe quite a while now, hasn't he?"

"It's almost a year now. He was home for a while in February."

"How does he like working outside the country?" *Boy, I make myself sick. How can I sit here, pumping her for information that may help to send her own brother up the river?* His fingers tightened on the steering wheel.

"James has spent a lot of time out of the country. I think he's almost more at home in Europe than he is in the States. He seems pretty happy. He isn't crazy about his boss." She frowned slightly. "Actually he sounded a little strained."

"Umm?" *That's it. Sound nice and sympathetic. Offer her a friendly ear. Let her pour out all her worries to me. After all, I'm not going to tell anyone but the United States government.*

"I had written to tell him that I wouldn't be spending the summer in Europe and he sounded almost relieved. He said it was probably just as well that I wasn't going to be coming over because he was going to be really busy and he wouldn't have much time to spend with me. He knows he doesn't have to entertain me."

"Maybe he just didn't want you to feel guilty about canceling the trip." *Or maybe he had other things to do this summer, things that an inquisitive sister might get in the way of.*

Mac pulled the car into the driveway and got out. That was enough business. He had done his duty and he wasn't going to think about it anymore tonight. Tonight was for the two of them. His job was not going to intrude.

Holly looked around curiously as he led her into the house. It was the first time she had been to Mac's home and she wondered what it would tell her about him. It was too dark to see much of the outside, just a vague outline of a one-story house in a quiet residential area.

The interior of the house was revealing. Pale gray with accents of rich russet created an atmosphere that radiated calm. The furnishings had been chosen for comfort: huge overstuffed chairs and a sofa, a plush carpet that looked thick enough to sleep on and a fireplace of brick and stone.

She turned suddenly, catching Mac's eyes, an unaccustomed hint of anxiety in their depths. *He's really concerned about what I'll think,* she realized in amazement. The unexpected vulnerability added warmth to her smile.

"It's beautiful. Not quite what I expected from a swinging bachelor, though. Where are the lights that dim automatically, the bearskin rug and the soft music that spills from invisible speakers?"

He reached out and flipped a switch and the lights dropped to a seductive level. Holly giggled softly. "What about the rug and the music?"

He turned the lights back up and shrugged apologetically. "Sorry, they were all out of bearskins and mood music when I dropped by Bachelor World."

"Bachelor World?"

"Sure. That's where all we swinging bachelors shop. You can get everything from the latest aphrodisiacs, guaranteed to turn your date into a raving nymphomaniac, to a plastic blow-up date for those nights when you'd rather not have to make conversation but you don't want to be alone."

"A blow-up date?" She giggled.

"Certainly. Something every man should have stashed in his closet. She's guaranteed to listen to stories even your best friend doesn't want to hear again. She never spills her wine, doesn't complain about the food and doesn't notice if you drip spaghetti sauce on your tie.''

"Sounds like a real paragon. Doesn't she have any faults? I mean, I've got to know my competition.''

He frowned. "Well, she doesn't like fireplaces; if she sits too close, her makeup melts. And if you drop your steak knife on her, she does tend to hit the ceiling.''

"Right before she goes flat?''

He shook his head sadly. "I've lost more good dates that way.''

The faint tension was banished by the silly conversation and Holly wondered why she had been concerned. Mac wasn't going to turn into a raving maniac just because he had her alone. It was going to be a wonderful evening with a nice dinner and a quiet glass of wine afterward. Maybe she would talk him into starting a fire in the fireplace. A perfect evening...

ALAS. THE BEST-LAID PLANS of mice and men, et cetera. The steak Mac had put in a spicy soy sauce marinade the night before might have been nicely flavored and tenderized if he had remembered to put the marinade in the pan with the steak. Instead, the steak lay in solitary splendor in the refrigerator and the marinade sat forlornly on the counter, waiting to be added to the steak.

"Don't worry about it. We'll just heat the marinade and serve it on the side.'' Holly gave him an encouraging smile. "I do that kind of thing all the time.''

"The problem is that this cut isn't all that tender unless you marinate it.''

"Who needs tender meat? I've often thought that one of the problems with today's youth is that they don't even have to worry about chewing their meat. Think how much better off we were in the days before tenderizers.''

Mac smiled reluctantly. "I hadn't thought of it that way. As long as you promise not to sue me for any dental work that results from trying to get through this.''

"I promise.''

She leaned her elbows on the breakfast bar that separated the kitchen from the dining room, cradling a glass of wine between her palms. She would never have thought that Mac would fall to pieces over a minor kitchen disaster.

Mac turned on the water to boil for the rice while he prepared the fresh broccoli that would be lightly steamed. By the time he finished readying the broccoli, it was time for the rice to go in. He dumped the polished grains into the boiling water and put the lid on, making a mental note of the time so he would know when to start the meat.

"Is there anything I can do to help?"

"Nope. I think everything is under control." He leaned against the counter opposite her and lifted his wineglass. "I probably should have just picked up some nice gourmet take-out food and served that."

"Why? Everything is going just fine. The marinade looks delicious."

"I think I wanted to show you how domesticated I can be," he admitted.

"I'm very impressed." Her wide mouth was held primly serious but the dimple in her cheek quivered slightly.

"I can tell."

"No, really." She protested her sincerity. "Of course, I would have been even more impressed if you had served me an avocado and pink tofu salad with grapefruit and goat cheese dressing."

"Sorry. I only make that on alternate Thursdays."

He reached across the breakfast bar and kissed the laughter from her mouth, tasting the warmth of her response, feeling it reach deep inside and melt away some long-held barrier he hadn't even known existed. He drew back and their eyes met.

The sparkling humor in her eyes faded, leaving them a gentle brown. Her hand came up to touch one lean cheek, tracing the softness of his mustache.

"You have the most beautiful eyes," she murmured, almost to herself. "If I never saw you again, I could never forget your eyes."

He turned his head and pressed his mouth to her palm. "And I could never forget yours. There's so much joy. You're always looking forward to the next moment as if something exciting might happen."

"Something exciting *might* happen." He leaned toward her and her voice dropped.

"Like what?" he asked huskily.

"Like—" Angry hissing interrupted her, accompanied by a loud metallic rattle. Mac spun around and then reached the stove in one long stride, grabbing hold of the pot of rice and jerking it off the burner. White foam oozed down the sides of the pan as the lid subsided to a sullen mutter.

"Like the rice might boil over," Holly finished her sentence, though not quite as it had started out.

"I forgot to turn the heat down."

"That's okay. Just set it on a very low heat and it will be all right."

Shaken, he obeyed her instructions, turning the flame so low that it was in danger of going out. He grabbed his wine and took a fortifying swallow. "Well, at least nothing else can go wrong," he said lightly.

Mac put the still-damp broccoli into a saucepan and turned the heat on, carefully checking to make sure the flame was not too high before he turned on the broiler to preheat for the steak. He poured the forgotten marinade into a small saucepan and set it over a low flame. He got out plates and silverware and set them on the breakfast bar, giving in to Holly's insistence and letting her set the table.

Everything was under control as he carefully slid the unmarinated steak into the broiler, checking his watch again so that he would know just when to turn it. The rice simmered gently on a back burner and the marinade was starting to send out tantalizing scents of soy sauce and garlic.

"Is something burning?" Holly asked as she picked up the plates. Mac glanced at the stove but everything seemed all right.

"No, everything is fine."

She shrugged and carried the plates into the dining room. A few moments later she was back. Her nose wrinkled slightly. "Mac, are you sure nothing's burning?"

He took a deep cautious breath, inhaling the acrid scent of incipient disaster. He lifted the lid on the rice.

"The rice is okay. The marinade is doing all right." He bent down to peer into the broiler. "The steak looks okay. That leaves—"

"The broccoli," she finished for him.

"But that's impossible. The heat is really low. There's no way it could burn...unless I forgot to put the water in it." His voice trailed off and he gave her a pleading look that made her want to tell him that that wasn't the case.

He lifted the lid off the pot and stared down at the blackened bottom. The broccoli lay in olive-green misery, surrounded by the smoking steamer. "Dammit!" He snatched the pot off the stove and turned to drop it into the sink.

Holly's cry of warning came just a moment too late. Steam rushed up as overheated metal contacted water. There was a loud, metallic ping and the bottom of the saucepan bowed upward, declaring silently that it had cooked its last meal. Mac stared at the ruined pot for a long moment, wondering what he had ever done to deserve such a fate.

"The steak!"

The words made him turn around, but not quickly. He was resigned to his fate now. Even before he saw the smoke pouring out of the broiler, he knew what had happened. He grabbed a box of salt out of the cupboard and pulled open the broiler, dumping the salt over the charred steak, dousing the flames that had been happily consuming the meat.

Holly didn't say a word as he left the broiler pan and lifted the lid on the rice. He gave the pot a desultory stir. "The rice is stuck to the bottom of the pot," he announced without inflection. He turned to look at the saucepan that held the marinade as if expecting to find that it had erupted or boiled dry or given rise to the creature from the Black Lagoon. "The marinade is nice and hot."

She didn't say a word, taking in the smoking steak, the warped pot, the mess on the stove where the rice had boiled over and then looking at his stunned expression. Her mouth twitched and then was still.

"I'm really not all that hungry anyway. Why don't we just have a glass of wine and maybe some cheese and crackers or something?"

He stirred the marinade. "Maybe I could make a salad."

"I know a place that has great pizza and they'll deliver," she offered.

He dropped the spoon onto the dirty stove and arched one eyebrow in her direction. "I get the feeling that you think I'm not safe in the kitchen."

"Oh, no. I'm sure you're a terrific cook. It's just that tonight doesn't seem to be your night for making dinner."

"Maybe you're right. It's a good thing I just bought ice cream for dessert. Otherwise, I'd probably have managed to ruin that, too."

"Maybe we could pour the marinade over the ice cream," she suggested, earning herself a stern look.

He pulled open the freezer to check on the one element of the meal that he could still depend on.

"Well, at least the ice cream is still all right," he muttered forlornly.

"See, the dinner isn't a total loss."

Mac pulled his head out of the freezer and gave her an enraged glare. "Are you laughing?"

She shook her head, biting hard on her inner lip. "Of course not. Why would I be laughing?"

He slammed the freezer door shut and took a threatening step toward her, causing her to scoot off her stool and back a step away.

"You *are* laughing! Do you know what I do to dates who laugh at me?"

"I'm not laughing *at* you, Mac. I'm laughing *with* you," she offered unsteadily.

"Do you see me laughing?"

"I'm sorry." Holly backed another step as he advanced. "It's just that your face was so funny."

"A polite date would have pretended not to notice that anything was wrong. She would have eaten the meal and never said a word."

"Don't you think that maybe the steak might be a little too salty?" She backed out of the dining room, trying to keep one eye on Mac's advancing figure and another on the floor behind her. "Of course, maybe if we poured the ice cream over it, it would cut the saltiness a bit."

"You are an ingrate. I slave over a hot stove to cook a meal for you and you complain about a little too much salt."

"I'm sorry. You're quite right. Maybe you could feed it to your plastic blow-up lady. I'm sure she'd appreciate it much more than I do." She backed around the sofa. With his long legs, he could have caught her in an instant but he was allowing her to prolong the chase, enjoying the game as much as she was.

"I think you need a thorough beating," he decided, rounding the sofa after her.

"Oh, please don't beat me; I promise to be good. I won't make fun of your cooking anymore." Holly was laughing so hard she could hardly get the words out. She turned her head to see where she was going. Out of the corner of her eye, she saw him lunge toward her. With a shriek she dodged the other way and scurried around the sofa.

She faced him across the rust-colored back, her eyes bright, her face flushed and excited. There was something exhilarating about this mock chase scene. Adrenaline pumped through her veins, making her feel breathless and incredibly alert at the same time.

"It'll go worse for you if you don't come along peaceably," he warned her.

"You'll never take me alive, copper." She hurled the corny line at him and then gasped and darted around the sofa as he rounded the end of it. Now he stood behind the sofa and she stood in front of it, the fireplace at her back.

"I always get my woman." The words were said in jest, but to hear him call her "his woman," even in play, sent an atavistic shiver down Holly's spine. Something deeply buried responded to the possessiveness in his voice.

His eyes gleamed suddenly and that was all the warning she had as he put his hand on the back of the sofa and leaped over it, landing in front of her before she had time to do more than gasp. She turned to run and found herself firmly caught and held as his arms locked around her back.

She raised accusing eyes to his face. "That was cheating!"

"All's fair in love and war and chastising ungrateful dates."

"I'm not ungrateful."

"You sounded pretty ungrateful to me." He tugged her a little closer, enjoying the feel of her soft curves brushing the hard planes of his chest.

"I honestly thought you were trying to make me laugh. I didn't think anyone could cause that many disasters accidentally."

"That does it." Mac lifted her and tossed her lightly over his shoulder. "I'm going to have to resort to drastic measures."

He strode out of the house and across the back lawn, ignoring her muffled pleas and apologies. The apologies lost much of their effect by being choked with laughter.

He stopped next to the pool and shifted her so that she lay in his arms. Holly took one look at the water and threw her arms around his neck, clinging desperately to him.

"I'm sorry, Mac. I didn't mean to laugh. I'll never laugh again. Honest."

He let her dip slightly over the water and she shrieked and tightened her hold, a reaction that didn't displease him in the least.

"Your apologies would be a lot more effective if you weren't laughing so hard while you're making them."

Holly tried to swallow the laughter but couldn't. "It's hunger," she offered anxiously. "I always laugh when I'm hungry."

Mac tilted his head to look down at her. In the soft darkness that blanketed the yard, she could just make out the gleam of his eyes. She tried to make her expression as innocent as possible, biting fiercely on her lip to hold in the laughter.

"Hungry, huh?" He appeared to consider the idea and then nodded. "Okay, I'll buy that. I'll order a pizza and feed you." He turned and headed back to the house. "But don't think you're getting away scot-free. Sooner or later, you're going to have to pay a forfeit."

Chapter Six

An hour and a half later, Mac lifted the empty pizza box from the floor between them and set it out of the way on a side table. Holly leaned back against the sofa and lifted her glass of wine and clinked it gently against Mac's. In front of them, the fire hissed and popped a soft accompaniment to their conversation.

"I told you Dominic's had the greatest pizza in town."

He nodded, stretching his legs out in front of him and pulling a pillow off the sofa to tuck behind his back. "It was a great pizza, all right."

A comfortable silence settled between them. Holly couldn't remember the last time she had felt so utterly content with life. She wanted to freeze this moment in a time capsule so that she could take it out and look at it later.

She looked around the restful room before letting her eyes settle on her host. He looked as relaxed as she felt. Thick dark lashes shielded his eyes. His long body looked completely free of tension.

"I really like your house."

"Thanks." His lashes lifted and his eyes skimmed the room. "Ken says it puts him to sleep the minute he walks in, but his place is decorated in modern eclectic in every color and style he can lay his hands on. I wanted something a little more solid-looking."

"It suits you."

His mustache quirked upward. "Solid and dull?"

"No. Warm, stable, honest, straightforward."

Mac seemed to wince. He lifted his glass and drained the wine from it in one swallow. "Honest. Straightforward. I don't think those are terms that apply to someone who tells lies for a living." There was an underlying bitterness in his voice that she had never heard before.

"Sometimes you have to tell lies to do something good. I don't think it has any bearing on the kind of person you are. It's your job."

His eyes pinned her, an oddly intent expression in them. "My job. Is that really how you think of it?"

"Yes. I don't think you'd ever do something you thought was truly wrong. I trust you to do what's right, Mac."

His mouth twisted. "You trust me," he murmured almost inaudibly. "I wish I had your confidence."

Holly stared at him uncertainly. It was obvious that something was bothering him. Should she ask questions or just leave it alone? Maybe it was something he couldn't talk about. Before she came to a decision, he shook off the brooding atmosphere that had threatened to envelop them and smiled at her.

His hand closed around her upper arm and tugged her closer. "I seem to recall that there's still that matter of finding a suitable punishment for you." She let him take her glass from her and set it next to his, her mouth relaxing into a coaxing smile.

"I thought we were going to forget all that. You have to admit that it was pretty funny, Mac. Besides, I was weak from hunger and hardly responsible for my actions. And I did come up with Dominic's. You admitted it was a terrific pizza. That should make up for a lot."

He shook his head, a decidedly predatory gleam in his eyes. "I'll give you a few points for the pizza but that wasn't enough to make up for the terrible blow to my ego. I told you I was going to have to teach you a lesson on how a good date behaves."

"I have been a good date," she protested, hanging back against his hand. "How many of your dates would have helped you clean up the mess in the kitchen? Mac!" His name came out on a breathless shriek of surprise as he captured her hand, his free arm sweeping around her back as he pulled her onto his lap.

Holly lay across his thighs, her back supported by the steel hardness of his arm. Her dress had twisted beneath her and she was vividly aware of the roughness of his jeans against her nylon-clad legs.

Their eyes met and suddenly the playful mood was gone, replaced by something more dangerous. Holly licked her lips nervously, drawing his eyes to her mouth. She wasn't ready to take the next step yet, she reminded herself but the reminder seemed faint and far away.

His head dipped slowly and her pulse fluttered at the look of hunger that darkened his eyes to midnight blue. The very air that surrounded them seemed to thicken and shimmer. The fire popped quietly but the sound was distant, unconnected to the world that Holly was floating toward.

Her lashes dropped as his mouth found hers. It was like setting a torch to dry chaparral: instant combustion. An explosion of the senses that swept through her with irresistible force. The past weeks of gentle kisses and restrained caresses had left her with a deep hunger that matched his.

Her fingers found their way into the thick darkness of his hair, curling around his skull, to hold him to her. Not that Mac showed any signs of leaving. His mouth slanted across hers, demanding and receiving access to the honeyed warmth of her. She could taste the tang of the wine on his tongue. Or was it on hers? It didn't matter. They twined together in a ritual as old as time, seeking, probing, demanding.

Mac's fingers skimmed across the front of her dress, hardly seeming to touch, yet the buttons that ran down the front fell open in his path. Holly moaned a protest as he drew away, her fingers sliding reluctantly from his silky hair. He shifted, easing her back onto the thick rug and leaning over her as he opened the dress, spreading it out on the gray carpet. It framed her body in a soft swirl of pale yellow.

Mac groaned and her eyes fluttered open. In the firelight his features were more shadowed than revealed. The hard line of his jaw counterbalanced the soft flicker of his eyes as they skimmed over her. A gentle warmth flooded her cheeks, a warmth that had nothing to do with the fire.

Mac groped desperately for his self-restraint as he looked down at Holly. He hadn't intended to take things so far. What had started out as a game had rapidly escalated into something he couldn't control. It wouldn't be fair to go any further when she didn't know the full circumstances.

Even as he told himself that, a groan that held a note of pain tore itself from his throat. He was lost. Some distant part of his mind shouted that it wasn't too late. He could still call a halt with no harm done, still stop things before they went any further. But the voice was muffled by the rapid beat of his pulse.

Holly lay beneath him, her body flushed with firelight, her eyes languorous and wanting. As if from a distance, he watched his hand come out, touching the delicate thrust of her chin, trailing onto her throat. His fingers barely skimmed her breasts, feeling the flutter in her breathing as he brushed across the taut peaks. He let his thumb settle against her navel, his hand fanning out across her stomach.

"Holly." Her name was ragged, half question, half plea. Her eyes opened slowly to meet the burning warmth of his gaze. With an effort his mouth twisted in a smile. "How do you expect me to keep my head when you wear something like this?" His hand brushed lightly across the tiny panties and lacy garter belt, trailing down to trace the line of one garter across her thigh to the top of her stocking.

For a moment the mists parted and Holly saw clearly that this was her moment to choose. If she wanted him to stop, now was the time to tell him. Her eyes searched his face, seeing hunger and the iron control that held it in check. But she also saw need, a need that was not just physical.

Mac moved away as she sat up slowly, holding his breath as her breast brushed against his arm, braced on the carpet beside them. She bent one leg in a graceful, feminine move and reached beneath it to unhook one lacy garter. Mac hardly dared to breathe as she unhooked the other garter and rolled the stocking down her slim leg in a gesture so sensual and alluring that his entire body tightened in response. The nylon was tossed carelessly toward the sofa.

"It's much easier if someone else does it." The words were a throaty invitation. His eyes swept to her face for an instant, reading all the desire he had hardly dared to dream of, with just a flickering hint of uncertainty. This was not a woman who was accustomed to offering such blatantly sensual invitations. That Holly wanted him enough to do so added to his already inflamed senses.

His fingers trembled slightly as he reached down and unhooked the delicate fabric, rolling the other stocking down the smooth length of her leg and tossing it toward its mate.

Her fingers shook against his chest as she maneuvered first one button of his shirt and then another through buttonholes that seemed too small. He sat patiently until the last button surrendered and she was able to push the shirt off his shoulders. Her palms ran over his chest, her fingers curling into the thick mat of hair that covered its muscular strength. She brushed across a masculine nipple, lingering in response to his indrawn breath, her head lifting until she could see his face.

Mac's patience melted and vanished beneath her delicate touch. With a groan he swept her back down onto the carpet, his broad chest crushing her breasts with controlled power. His mouth took hers with avid hunger.

Mac's fingers moved rapidly, ridding himself of his jeans and stripping the last tantalizing bits of fabric from her willing body. Holly's hands were not still. She explored the rigid length of his spine, tracing each rippling muscle that spanned his back.

She gasped as he kicked his jeans away and his naked body came against hers. His hard arousal was a heated brand along her hip, a promise. His mouth left hers and brushed past her throat to find the silken weight of her breasts. Her nails dug into his shoulders as his lips closed around one swollen nipple and began a deep tugging motion that sank to her very core. Her hips arched in unconscious echo of that movement.

His hand slid across her stomach, his fingers finding the silky dark curls that sheltered her femininity. His body jerked in response to the waiting warmth he found there. Mac's forehead felt feverish as he rested it between her breasts, fighting for some semblance of control.

But if Mac was struggling to stem his passion, Holly was too far gone even to remember the meaning of the word "control."

Her body was on fire. She felt as if she lay in the very midst of a bed of smoldering coals and it would take only the lightest of touches to make her burst into flame. The fire that burned beside them was nothing compared to the burning heat inside.

Mac's chest heaved with the effort of thinking. His mind was filled with the sight and sound and scent of her. But there was something he needed to do, something he had to ask. He forced his spinning mind to vague coherency.

"Holly, are you protected? Is it safe?" The words were muttered against her breast and they came to Holly in a meaningless jumble.

Words. She didn't want words. What was he waiting for? She ached. She burned. She needed. Her whole body was on fire. Safe? Did he think he would hurt her?

"Mac, please." Her head tossed restlessly, her body straining toward his. His fingers curled deeper into her warmth and she whimpered. "Yes! Yes! Please, Mac, now!"

"Oh, Lord, I want you!" His legs moved between hers. He tested himself against her, felt her readiness and surged deeply inside her. Time stood still for a moment as they lay locked in the most intimate of embraces, savoring their closeness.

Mac slid one palm beneath her, his hand almost spanning her buttocks as he tilted her upward and began to move. Holly's nails bit gently into his back, her body arching to receive his, her entire being concentrating on the sensations that rioted through her. Such was the intensity of their involvement that it could not last long.

Mac felt the delicate tightening of her body around him and he moaned deep in his throat. Her eyes flew wide and she stared at him for a long moment, her entire body taut and quivering as she met the wild darkness of his gaze. Her eyes fell shut and her fingers bit deep into his muscular buttocks as she drew him even closer, catching him in the sweeping force of her climax.

His body arched heavily against her. A long shudder racked him as he followed her into swirling ecstasy, her name a hoarse mutter against her neck.

THE FIRE CRACKLED SOFTLY, feeding on the last of the wood. The flames that had leaped so high earlier had sunk to flickering shadows. The two figures who lay entwined in front of its fading glory were still. Mac's arms wrapped Holly close against his side, his face was buried in her hair, his eyes closed in utter contentment.

He nuzzled her ear softly, eliciting a soft giggle from her limp form. Pleased, he tightened his arms and let his tongue trace the convolutions of her ear. This time, she purred throatily and tilted her head, directing his mouth to the sensitive area behind her ear. He shifted his hand to cup her breast, his thumb brushing softly over the tip, feeling her response.

"What are you doing?"

"This is called foreplay," he told her without pausing in his gentle assault.

"Foreplay?" She laughed, tilting her head out of his reach and grabbing his marauding hand to control its wandering. "I thought foreplay was supposed to come before."

Mac rose up on an elbow until he could look into her face. "Usually it does, but we didn't take time for it earlier and I didn't want to miss out on any of the steps, so I just thought I'd throw it in now."

Her fingers combed lightly through his chest hair, her eyes resting there rather than on his face. "I don't usually act like that," she murmured.

"Like what?" He brushed the tousled curls back from her forehead.

"Umm." Holly searched for the right word. "Demanding. I mean I hardly gave you time...."

The chuckle started deep in his chest and she felt his breath brush her forehead as it broke from him. "Isn't this a bit of a role reversal? I thought I was the one who should be apologizing."

Her flush deepened and he dropped a kiss on the end of her nose. His voice was tender. "You are without a doubt the most magnificently sensual woman I have ever known. If we rushed things, then I deserve a share of the responsibility. I wanted you so much, Holly. I felt like a boy again. I couldn't have slowed things down if I'd wanted to...which I didn't," he finished firmly.

"I just didn't realize I could be so...so aggressive," she confessed.

Aggressive? He hid a smile at the word. Did she really think she'd been too aggressive? "You were perfect," he told her with certainty. He got to his feet, bending down to scoop her up in his arms. "And just to reassure you, this time we'll take it real slow."

Holly linked her arms around his neck, enjoying the deliciously helpless feeling of having him carry her so easily. "This time?" she questioned as he left the living room and walked down a hallway.

Mac angled her through a doorway and into his bedroom. She had only a fleeting glimpse of heavy drapes and a bed that seemed endless before he dropped her lightly on the mattress and leaned over her, his expression unreadable in the dim light that filtered through the hall.

"This time we'll take it so slow that you'll beg me to rush it. We've got all night and I'm going to use every minute of it."

Her hands tugged him down. "I hope you don't expect me to protest."

"No, just enjoy."

"Is IT SAFE? Are you protected?" The words mumbled their way into her dream and Holly stirred restlessly, her forehead wrinkled. "Is it safe? Are you protected?" Safe? Safe! Her eyes snapped open and she sat up in bed, her breathing harsh as if she'd been running.

"Oh, good Lord." She muttered the words out loud and then turned to look at the bed next to her, her shoulders sagging when she saw that she was alone. "Safe. Protected. My Lord, what did I do?"

Mac hadn't been afraid of hurting her! He had been asking about birth control! And she had said yes. Her fingers knotted in the sheet. What was she supposed to tell him now? "Gee, Mac, I'm sure sorry that we had this little misunderstanding. I'll let you know if you're going to be a father."

"Idiot!" But castigating herself wasn't going to do any good now. It was over and done with. The chance had been taken. Now she had to decide what to do about it. Was she going to tell Mac?

Of course she was. He had a right to know. *But why worry him unnecessarily?* a little voice whispered. *You won't know for weeks. What if you aren't pregnant?* What's it going to do to the relationship if he spends the next few weeks worrying for nothing?

But it wouldn't be fair, she argued with herself. Is it fair that he should have to worry (perhaps without need) because she took a stupid chance? This way she'd be saving him a lot of suffering. Her fingers tightened on the sheet until her knuckles whitened. She couldn't tell him. She just couldn't.

She heard the front door slam and the sound put an end to her self-questioning. Whether she told him or not, she definitely did not plan to be waiting in his bed, looking eager for him to join her. Last night might be forgiven as a stupid mistake, but she didn't have that excuse this morning.

MAC FROWNED at the empty bed. When he left, Holly had looked as if she might sleep until noon. He had been looking forward to finding her curled up against the pillows, waiting to be awakened by a kiss. His mustache quirked upward. Maybe Ken was right. He *was* a romantic at heart.

His head tilted as he heard the shower come on in the bathroom that adjoined his room. He crossed the floor and put his hand on the knob, then hesitated. The mental image of Holly in the shower, her body all sleek and wet, tempted him. He could almost feel the dampness of her skin beneath his hands.

He dropped his hand and turned away, going to the closet to get a change of clothes. He had to keep in mind that their relationship was still very new. He didn't want to push for too much intimacy too fast. She had taken a big step by sleeping with him last night; he'd let her have her privacy now. There'd be other mornings, other showers.

When he entered the bedroom again, he was freshly showered and dressed in worn jeans and a dark T-shirt. Holly was just stepping out of the master bathroom, her movements almost furtive as she glanced around the door. She jumped when she saw him, and her fingers tightened their death grip on the big towel that was wrapped around her body.

"Hi." His voice was soft, his smile an intimate reminder of the night before.

"Hi." Her eyes skipped restlessly around the room, oblivious to the warm gray-and-burgundy tones. Mac came forward and she had to forcibly control the urge to back away. He set his hands on her shoulders, frowning inwardly at the tension in her muscles. What on earth was wrong with her?

She stepped away the moment the kiss ended and Mac felt a cold chill run up his spine. Something was definitely wrong. She looked like a prisoner about to take the last walk. Her skin was pale ivory, without a trace of color, and her lips showed a tendency to quiver. Her eyes avoided his as if she was afraid of what they might reveal.

"Holly?" Her gaze met his with visible reluctance. He gave her what he hoped was a reassuring smile, trying to still the panic in his chest. "Is something wrong?"

The uncertainty in his eyes reached her as nothing else could have. She strove to swallow the hysteria that threatened to overwhelm her. She was acting like a fool. No wonder Mac was looking at her as if he was considering calling for the men in white coats.

She forced herself to give him a natural smile. "I'm always a little dazed before breakfast. Don't pay any attention to me."

His smile relaxed, though his eyes retained a hint of wary appraisal. "In that case, maybe I'd better see that you get fed."

It seemed as if years went by before he dropped her off at her apartment and Holly was free to fall to pieces. She had done her best to act naturally but she knew she hadn't really succeeded. She managed to mumble some excuse when he suggested getting together later in the day.

She knew he was concerned by her behavior but she couldn't find words to reassure him. She settled for giving him a fervent kiss and a promise to have dinner with him on Tuesday night. By Tuesday she hoped she'd be able to look him in the eye without feeling like a criminal.

When Maryann came home from the gym two hours later, Holly was curled up on the floor next to the coffee table, listlessly dealing out a hand of solitaire. Maryann dropped her gym bag on the sofa and sat down next to it.

"You missed the black four on the red five."

"Thanks. How was your workout?"

"Just fine. How was your date?"

Holly's head bent over the cards. "Just fine. We had pizza."

"You didn't come home last night." It wasn't a question. It was a statement that held out an invitation to talk if that was what Holly needed. It was an offer of a shoulder to cry on and right now that was what she needed more than anything else.

Tears welled up in her eyes, spilling over her lashes and trickling slowly down her cheeks. "I've done something awful." She dropped the cards on the table and buried her face in her hands, her shoulders shaking with suppressed sobs.

Maryann came around the table and knelt beside her, hesitating for a moment before she reached out to put her hand on the other woman's arm. In all the years she had known Holly, she had never seen her so distraught. For all her apparent volatility and scatterbrained behavior, Holly was one of the most emotionally balanced people Maryann had ever known.

"What happened?" Her voice was hushed. Visions of Holly having murdered Mac flitted through her mind.

"I went to bed with him." The words were muffled but understandable, and Maryann's frown deepened.

"What's wrong with that? I could see weeks ago that was where the relationship was headed. You must have—" She broke off, her fair skin paling until the dusting of freckles stood out starkly. "Did he... Holly, did he...hurt you?"

"No. He was wonderful. He was tender and gentle and he even...he even...asked me if I was protected." She finished on a wail of anguish.

Exasperated, Maryann took hold of Holly's arms and gave her a gentle shake, forcing her roommate to look at her. "Then why are you so devastated? You wanted him, didn't you? He wanted you, didn't he? You made love and it was a terrific experience. Why are you crying as if your dog had just died?"

"He asked me if I was protected and I said yes."

Maryann frowned. "I don't think I get the point. He was responsible enough to be concerned and you..." Her words trailed off. Her eyes widened and Holly nodded slowly. "You lied?"

"I didn't lie exactly. I didn't realize what he was talking about until this morning."

Maryann tugged absently on a loose strand of her hair. "But you knew this was coming. Why weren't you prepared?" She waved away the answer. "Never mind. It's none of my business. Oh, Holly, what did Mac say when you told him? Was he angry?"

Holly got to her feet, crossed to the window and tugged on the curtain. Behind her Maryann stood up.

"I didn't tell him." The words came out more emphatically than she felt. There was a firm sound to them that surprised her.

"But you've got to tell him. It's not fair to keep this from him."

"I don't see any reason to worry him when there might not be anything to worry about." Funny, how weak that argument sounded when she voiced it out loud.

"That's a cop-out."

Holly turned to look at her, her small chin set at a defiant angle. "Well, I'm not going to tell him."

"You're not being fair and you know it. You're the one who's been telling me what a wonderful, understanding guy he is. You made a mistake; you didn't commit a crime. Tell him."

"I don't know that I did make a mistake." The words were hardly above a whisper and the defiance fell away to show the agony she was feeling. "What if I did this deliberately? What if I planned it?"

"You're getting hysterical." Maryann's calm tones cut through the rising pitch of her voice and Holly drew a deep, calming breath before trying to explain herself. Her fingers twisted together.

"I can't tell Mac because I don't think I could look him in the eye and tell him this was an accident. You know how much I've always wanted a child. What if I did this deliberately because I wanted to get pregnant? I checked my calendar and I couldn't have chosen a worse time to do something like this. What if I planned it? What am I supposed to say to him, Maryann?"

"Stop it! Come over here and sit down. I'm going to make some tea and we're going to have a nice, rational discussion about this, and if you try to get hysterical, I'm going to throw a glass of water on you."

The stern words had the desired effect. Holly sat at the kitchen table and let the soothing familiarity of Maryann making tea wash over her. The other woman had spent three years in England with her parents when she was young and she had picked up the British attitude that a cup of tea could help any situation.

When Maryann set the cup in front of her, Holly reached for the sugar bowl. This was no time to be thinking of calories. Right now she needed all the help she could get.

Maryann fixed her with a serious look and Holly managed a strained smile. "You remind me of my aunt Margaret. She used to look at me like that when she found out I'd been snitching cookies. Of course, Aunt Margaret wouldn't have been caught dead in a bright blue leotard with black stripes."

"And I bet your aunt wouldn't have been distracted any easier than I'm going to be. Holly, if you don't tell Mac and you *are* pregnant, how is he going to feel when he finds out? You said yourself that the timing made it likely."

"I didn't say it made it likely," Holly protested weakly. "I just said it was a likely time. Look at all the women who spend years trying to get pregnant. Just because you make love at the right time of the month, that doesn't mean it's going to happen."

"I'm a nurse, remember? I know all about the problems people can have getting pregnant. There's no reason to think that you're one of them. You've spent so many years dreaming of having one of the little animals, you've probably psyched your body into getting pregnant at the drop of a hat," she finished glumly.

They were silent for a few moments. Holly wrestled with her conscience and came up with the same answer. She should tell Mac but she couldn't. She just couldn't do it. She absently spooned another teaspoon of sugar into her tea.

"I know you're right. I *should* tell him but I just can't do it. I'm so afraid that I did this deliberately, Maryann. Looking at it from a purely practical point of view, I couldn't have chosen anyone better to father a child. He's intelligent, healthy, he's even a nice guy. What if that was in the back of my mind last night?''

"He's not going to hold you responsible for what your sub-conscious might have been thinking."

"But *I* hold me responsible. *I* took the chance. I should be the one to do the worrying and I'll be the one to take the responsibility if I am pregnant."

Her friend sighed and finished the last of her tea. "All right. It's your decision. I think you're making a mistake but I'll support you in your stupidity. That's what friends are for, I guess."

Holly reached across the table to clasp her hand, her eyes sparkling with moisture. "Thanks. I don't know what I'd do without you."

"Probably a lot worse," Maryann told her gruffly, her own eyes suspiciously bright. She pulled her hand away and lifted the teapot to refill their cups. "Okay. What's the next step?"

"I need you to find me a doctor who'll work fast. I took a chance last night that might be forgivable, but I don't want to take any more chances."

Maryann nodded. "That seems reasonable. You're going to have to be careful. If you are pregnant, you don't want to use anything that might endanger the baby."

"And it's got to be something that I don't have to tell Mac about. And I've got to have it by Tuesday night because Mac is taking me out to dinner and I want to be able to go home with him if he asks me."

"You don't want much, do you?" her friend asked dryly. "Well, no problem. Supernurse is here and I just happen to know a very nice doctor who's at the hospital right now and he owes me a favor. Brush your hair and wash your face and we'll go talk to him."

"Thanks, Maryann. I really appreciate this."

"Sure. Just don't tell Mac I was party to this deception. I don't think my insurance covers dismemberment."

"Maybe I'll be lucky. Maybe I'm not pregnant." Holly left the room, ignoring her friend's cynical muttering.

"I have a nasty feeling that's too much to ask for."

Chapter Seven

Mac leaned against the wall and closed his eyes. He drew a deep breath, knotting his hand into a fist and then slowly relaxing each finger, concentrating on the movement and shutting out the soft click of typewriter keys. It didn't work. His muscles were still tense.

He opened his eyes and stared at the bland office walls, wishing that he was almost anywhere else. Holly would be just finishing up at school. She would soon be going home to take a nice long bath. He didn't have to close his eyes to picture her sitting in the tub. She would be surrounded by heaps of bubbles, her hair would be caught in a wild mass of curls on top of her head and her skin would be dewy with moisture. And she would give him that slow smile that made his blood simmer.

Only he wouldn't be there to receive that smile. He would be sitting in the chief's office, trying to explain why he didn't have more information about Holly's brother.

"Relax. Remember you're supposed to be the calm half of this partnership."

Mac looked over at Ken and smiled, forcing his body to relax. "I am relaxed."

"Sure you are. Why don't you stop clenching your fists, then?"

Mac's smile faded as he looked down at his taut hands. With a conscious effort he spread his fingers out and then eased them into a natural position.

He stood away from the wall and then leaned back against it, controlling the urge to pace back and forth across the small office.

He was aware of Ken's eyes on him, their look quizzical but with an underlying concern in them. The other man opened his mouth but before he could say anything, the door to the inner office opened and Livvie was waving them through.

Mac went through first, and as he entered the office, Chief Daniels turned away from the window and limped toward them. Mac was reminded of the last time he had been called into Daniels's office.

"Donahue. Richardson." Daniels nodded briefly to each of them as he sat down behind the desk. "Have a seat." He waited until the two agents were seated across from him before speaking again.

"There hasn't been much progress on the Reynolds case." The words and tone were both mild. He might have been commenting on the weather but both men sat a little stiffer.

"There hasn't been much to report, sir," Mac said.

Daniels nodded. "True. We haven't been able to pinpoint any new shipments and Reynolds—if he's the one we're after—has been lying pretty low." He paused and shifted some papers on his desk. He picked up a photograph and studied it.

"Holly Reynolds." Mac stiffened, catching Ken's glance from the corner of his eye. Daniels let the name hang between them for a moment and then his eyes swept up to meet Mac's. "She's a very attractive woman."

Mac said nothing, his eyes a cold blue as he watched the older man. He would trust Daniels with his life—and had on a number of occasions—but when it came to Holly, Mac trusted no one. Not even himself.

Daniels dropped the photo and linked his fingers together, his elbows on the desk. "I understand that she's pretty much living in your house. Is her apartment being fumigated?"

"No, sir."

"I hadn't heard of any mud slides in that part of town."

"No, sir."

Daniels met Mac's unwavering gaze and seemed to give a sigh. "You're very stubborn, Donahue. That's a good trait in an agent. You and Richardson are one of our best teams. One of the reasons I gave you this assignment was that it wasn't moving real fast.

This kind of thing can go months without much happening. I felt the two of you could use the break. Your interest in Ms Reynolds seemed to make it that much easier. Now I'm not so sure.''

"Are you pulling us off the case?" Ken asked the question.

Daniels frowned. "I don't want to. That kind of thing is always untidy. Too much paperwork and too much time lost while we try to get someone else in. The two of you have done a fine job. Richardson, you've managed to pass yourself off as an art collector who doesn't much care where your acquisitions come from, and you've gotten close to Reynolds's sister, Mac. I'm not saying you haven't done a good job.''

"Then what are you saying?"

If Daniels heard the ice in Mac's tone, he ignored it. "Conflict of interest. It's obvious that you're personally involved with Ms Reynolds. How is she going to react if you're instrumental in putting her brother away?"

"She'd hate my guts. But we don't know that her brother is guilty.''

"We don't know that he isn't, either," Daniels returned. "Are you going to be able to continue your job without letting personal feelings influence you? Because if you can't, I'd rather pull you off the case now than see you ruin a good record by blowing it later.''

Mac appeared perfectly relaxed. His fingers rested lightly on the arm of the chair; his lashes drooped lazily over his eyes, concealing their expression. Only the muscle that ticked in his jaw revealed inner turmoil.

"If James Reynolds is the man we're looking for, he's dealing with the kind of people who wouldn't think twice about using his sister as leverage against him. I'll do whatever is necessary to put him away.''

Daniels's eyes traveled searchingly over the other man's face and then he nodded. "All right. I'll accept your word on it. The two of you can get back to work. See that you make your reports as scheduled.'' He waited until they were at the door before he spoke again.

"Richardson, be careful how you spend the department's

money. Six hundred dollars for a pair of boots seems a little excessive,'' he finished with a sardonic smile.

NEITHER OF THEM SPOKE until they were seated in a dim lounge a few blocks away from the agency office. Mac slid his fingers around the short glass and lifted it to his mouth, taking a hearty swallow before setting it down on the table with a faint thud.

"Six hundred dollars?" He raised one brow as he looked at his partner.

Ken grinned. "Lizard skin. There's this guy down in Texas who makes them special order."

"Six hundred dollars?"

"Well, I'm trying to pass myself off as a wealthy art collector. I've got to look the part."

"It's a good thing you decided to go into law enforcement. I hate to think how much damage you could have done as a master criminal."

"I know. I think of all the money I could have made." He shook his head regretfully. "It does seem a bit of a waste. But when your dad is a cop, it's hard to get the right angle on being a crook."

"Your talents haven't gone completely to waste. You could always get hold of the most amazing things in Saigon and you can't tell me that you didn't do a bit of fancy footwork occasionally."

"What can I say? When you've got it, you've got it."

Mac's smile gradually faded and he took another swallow of Scotch, signaling to the waitress for a refill.

Ken's eyes moved over his friend with shrewd understanding. "Kind of reminds me of that bar in Tijuana. Of course, it's safe to drink the booze here and it's a bit cleaner."

Mac said nothing and Ken waited until the waitress had replaced Mac's empty glass with a full one before speaking again.

"How's Holly?"

"Fine. She's planning on roping you in to help with the school athletic program in a week or two. She says she's sure you're a natural when it comes to kids."

"Sadistic, isn't she. I suppose it won't kill me. Besides, I've already figured out that it doesn't do any good to argue with Holly once she's determined that you're going to do something.''

"She does have a way of getting what she wants."

Again silence fell between them.

"It isn't going to be easy."

"Nope." Mac signaled for another drink.

"It's a hell of a position to be in."

"Yup." He swallowed some of the new Scotch. There was a pleasant buzzing in his ears that seemed to help muffle the pain in his chest.

"Are you worried that I'm not going to be able to support my end of things because I'm involved with Holly?"

"No-o-o." Ken drew the word out, turning his glass between his fingers as he considered the question. "No, I know you won't let me down. You never have and we've been in situations tougher than this."

He finished his whiskey and signaled for another one. "But this is a lousy time to be falling in love and I don't see why you had to fall in love with the chief suspect's sister."

"I know. Bad planning all around." Mac swallowed the last of his drink as the waitress brought Ken his second. "Bring us two more, please."

Ken looked at him, his brows raised, and Mac gave him a smile from which alcohol had erased all but the smallest traces of pain.

"You don't intend to let me get drunk alone, do you?"

"Is that what you're planning on doing?"

"You bet. Tonight is a great night to get drunk. We should celebrate."

Ken was amenable but curious. "Sounds fine to me. What are we celebrating?"

"We'll drink to a full moon. If it isn't full now, it will be one of these days."

IT WASN'T A FULL MOON, a fact that Holly could have told Mac if he'd been there to ask. She knew it wasn't a full moon because she spent a lot of time looking out the window, waiting for him to come home.

It was a little after ten the last time she checked and she let the curtain drop with a sigh. He had told her not to expect him at any particular time and she had asked no questions. That was one thing she had promised herself. She would never ask questions when it came to his work.

She wandered into the kitchen and poured herself a cup of lukewarm tea, grimacing at the strong bite of it. She would never learn to make tea like Maryann. It was either too weak or too strong. Maybe she should just go back to her own apartment and have a nice cup of tea with Maryann and go to sleep in her own bed and put Mackenzie Donahue out of her mind, at least for tonight.

She sighed and swallowed some more of the tea. The problem with that was that Maryann was working the night shift again and she wouldn't be home. Besides, the apartment they had shared for the last four years no longer felt like home.

She carried her cup into the living room and sat down to stare into the empty fireplace. The trouble was that right now, she wasn't sure just where home was. This house felt like home when Mac was here.

Mac. She leaned back and closed her eyes. Where was he right now? Was he safe? She swallowed a lump in her throat and forced the question away. Holly had already learned that she couldn't think of what might be happening to Mac when he was away from her. He never spoke of his job but it didn't take a genius to realize that there was a certain amount of danger that went along with being an undercover detective.

He kept his job and his personal life separate and she couldn't fault him for that. She wasn't sure whether it would be better or worse to actually know what he was doing. Sometimes she thought that her imagination conjured up worse demons than anything he could present her with, but then she was afraid that if she had actual confirmation of her worst fears, she wouldn't be able to deal with them anymore.

It was nights like this that were the worst. She sat in the house that was not quite a home and she had nothing to do but think of what might be happening. She sat up straight and took a deep breath. She was not going to spend another minute worrying. Mac had a lot of experience in his line of work and he was still alive to talk about it.

In less than two weeks the school year would be over and she was going to have a whole summer to play. She would have three months with no commitments and nothing to do but concentrate on Mac and the relationship they were building. Her face relaxed into a faint smile.

As she drew nearer to thirty, Holly had begun to have occasional pangs of regret for roads not taken. It was not that thirty was such a great age, but each decade marked a significant new watershed in a woman's life. Some of her friends from college were married, had children, and were working their way up the corporate ladder. She hadn't envied those friends with high-powered careers. She admired their dedication and accomplishments but that wasn't what she wanted out of life.

She had sometimes wondered if maybe she should have settled for something less than a passionate love and married one of the nice men she had gone out with during the last few years. She would have a nice home, a nice husband and children. She shivered now, thinking of what it would have been like to have her nice husband and her nice home, with perhaps a child and *then* to have met Mac—to love him and know that she could never have him because she had taken a safer road long before they'd met.

Of course, if she'd taken that safer road, chances were she would never have known Mac. But she couldn't help but wonder if she wouldn't have known what she was missing. Somewhere inside, there would have been something that said she could have had so much more.

She laid her hand lightly over her stomach. Of course, there was no saying that she was home free yet. As the weeks passed, it was becoming more likely that she was pregnant. Her period was already late but it could be just the emotional tension that went with worrying about it. She was faithfully using the diaphragm that Maryann's doctor friend had prescribed. It didn't seem quite fair that she should get pregnant from that one night's carelessness.

She refused to dwell on the possibilities. She was either pregnant or she wasn't and worrying about it wasn't going to change it. Mac must have thought she was crazy, considering the way she had acted after their first night together, rushing him out of the house and then making lame excuses not to see him for two days. But she had made it up to him. A light flush came up in her cheeks as she remembered just how she had made it up to him.

Starting that night, it seemed as if her belongings had started sprouting wings and flying off to Mac's house. She honestly couldn't remember how so many of her things had come to have places in his home. Her clothing hung next to his in the closet. Her toilet articles jostled his for space on the bathroom counter. Somehow she seemed to have moved in with him without planning it.

Holly opened her eyes as the front door closed quietly. Mac came to a halt just inside the living room and leaned against a wall. He smiled slowly when he saw her.

"Hello. Are you waiting up for me?"

"Not exactly." She stretched the truth slightly. "I was just sitting here thinking. I didn't realize how late it was."

"Were you thinking of me?" There was a boyish wistfulness in the question that was as charming as it was uncharacteristic.

She stood up and moved toward him, her eyes narrowing slightly as she studied him. "As a matter of fact, I was thinking about you. I didn't hear you pull into the driveway."

"I took a cab."

"Why?"

"Why what?" He blinked owlishly down at her as she came to stand in front of him.

"Never mind," she muttered disgustedly. "You're drunk!"

He frowned and considered the accusation before his mustache lifted in a smile that was almost beatific. "You're right. I'm a success. It's nice to know that I'm a success in at least one area. Where're we going?"

Holly shook her head and tightened her hold on his fingers as she led him through the house. "I'm taking you to bed."

"I love an aggressive woman."

He stopped, drawing her to an abrupt halt and spinning her into his arms. Holly had barely a moment to draw a breath before his mouth came down on hers. Her toes dangled a few inches off the floor as his forearm slid beneath her bottom to lift her up against his hard frame.

Hard, but not aroused, Holly realized dazedly a few minutes later. Mac's mouth nibbled distractingly beneath her ear and her body hummed. She arched her hips forward in automatic reaction and gave a sharp gasp when she felt his cold belt buckle against her stomach.

She dragged her hands out of his hair and pushed irritably against his shoulders. "Put me down, you idiot!"

He set her down instantly, a vague look of hurt in his eyes. "There's no need to get nasty."

Her eyes sparked. She had been sitting up, worrying about him and he had the nerve to come home perfectly safe and loaded to the gills. How dare he worry her for no reason?

"You're lucky I don't just let you pass out in the hall and sleep it off." She took hold of his hand and tugged him into the bedroom. "You're too drunk to be starting anything so just get your clothes off and get into bed and, if you're lucky, I won't wake you with a trumpet blast in the morning."

He obediently started unbuttoning his shirt, shrugging it off his wide shoulders and tossing it onto a chair. Holly swallowed hard and turned away as he reached for his belt. He was drunk and she was irritated with him but the sight of that muscular chest was still enough to speed her pulse.

She heard the thud of his jeans hitting the floor and turned back to look at him. He stood in the middle of the floor, his pants in a heap next to him, white cotton shorts his only covering and his expression a mix of sleepiness and hope. He looked like a small boy who'd just accomplished a difficult task and was hoping for a pat on the head in reward.

Despite herself, she smiled. "Get into bed before you pass out, lush." A few minutes later, she crawled into bed beside him and reached out to flip off the lamp. Immediately his hands sought her out in the darkness and pulled her against his body. His mouth nuzzled in her hair and his fingers cupped her breast.

With a sigh she captured his fingers in hers. "Mac, you're too drunk to start anything. Take my word for it, you won't be able to finish it."

He let her push him onto his back, sighing heavily as he realized the truth of her words. His mind wanted her but his body was slipping into sleep. "Maybe you're right," he mumbled into her hair.

She settled her head into a more comfortable position against his shoulder. "I know I am. Now just go to sleep and in the morning, you'll feel much worse."

"Heartless, aren't you."

She giggled softly. "Serves you right." But her only answer was a soft snore.

HOLLY SQUINTED against the bright sunlight and looked across the football field. She could just make out Mac's tall figure patiently dealing with a bruised knee. She smiled and sat down in the bleachers again, hardly aware of the hard seat.

If she had ever wondered how Mac would deal with children, she was getting her answer today. She had been a little hesitant about asking him to help with the school's mini Olympics. What if it turned out that he hated children and wanted absolutely nothing to do with them? A stern voice had reminded her that if that was the case, it was better to find out now than later.

He had agreed easily. Ken hadn't shown up yet but Mac had arrived bright and early. In the time since then, he had been endlessly patient with the trials and tribulations of the budding athletes. He had congratulated winners, consoled losers, wiped noses and controlled overexcited children without ever looking in the least bit ruffled.

Holly smiled, leaning her elbows on the seat behind her and tilting her face to the sun. She was taking a much-needed break and enjoying every moment of it. She felt as if all was right with her world. She was in love with Mac and he was in love with her. The words might not have been spoken but the feeling was there. By the end of summer, she'd be willing to bet that she'd be planning a wedding.

And maybe a baby shower. She brushed aside the niggling thought. Mac would accept their baby, if she was pregnant. She no longer had any doubts about that. He might be upset at first, but he'd get over it. They loved each other. Anything else was secondary to that.

"You look like the cat that just ate the canary." She opened her eyes and blinked against the dazzling sun for a moment before she found the source of the voice.

"Ken. I see you managed to time your arrival beautifully. We're going to be wrapping this up in an hour or so."

He shrugged and sat down next to her, giving her an engaging grin. "I ran out of gas," he offered.

"Sure you did." Her disbelief was obvious but there was no heat behind it.

"Where's your friend?" He scanned the field in front of them, looking for a head of bright auburn.

"Maryann is running the nurse's station." Holly pointed toward the far end of the field and Ken could pick out the rich red glint he had been looking for. "Why do you want to know?"

"I want to know which end of the field to avoid." He shrugged in answer to her frown. "I'm just looking out for my personal safety. If I get near her, I'm likely to be needing medical attention and she's not likely to dole it out after she's torn me limb from limb."

Holly's frown deepened as she stared toward the small tent that had been set up for Maryann. She couldn't argue with his assessment. Maryann had been unfailingly hostile toward him. After the debacle of the double date, she hadn't tried to throw them together but they had bumped into each other once or twice and her friend had been cold enough to freeze Vesuvius.

With a mental shrug Holly abandoned her speculation. She was just going to have to chalk it up to fate. It was a pity, because she liked Ken, but if Maryann didn't like him, there wasn't anything she could do to change it.

She switched her attention to Mac, her face relaxing in a tender smile as she watched him gently pick up and dust off a small girl who had just fallen down. Ken didn't have to turn his head to guess whom she was watching. The look in her eyes said it all.

"He's always been good with kids," he commented idly.

"He's wonderful with them. He seems to have such endless

patience. He never loses his temper. I'm beginning to think he doesn't even have a temper.''

"Oh, he's got one all right. Luckily he doesn't lose it often.''

Holly dragged her eyes away from Mac's tall figure and looked at her companion. "Have you seen him lose his temper?" Ken had known Mac a long time and it occurred to her that she might gain a lot of insight into Mac's sometimes enigmatic personality by talking to his best friend.

He nodded. "A time or two. That was enough.''

"What happened?''

"Once was in 'Nam. We were in Saigon and he found out that an officer in another unit had brutalized a young Vietnamese girl that Mac and I knew. She was a prostitute but she was just a kid, probably not more than fifteen or so. A cute little thing. Mac used to keep chocolate in his pocket to give her when we saw her in a bar. She worshiped Mac and I think he was checking into ways to get her out of the country.''

He was silent for a long moment, his eyes dark and far away, seeing things Holly could only guess at. Just when she thought he wasn't going to continue, he seemed to remember where he was and went on.

"Anyway, this guy had all but killed her and Mac found out about it. He went to visit her in the hospital and when he came out of there, it was like looking into the face of death. He didn't even hear you talking to him.

"A couple of us followed him. I don't think he knew we were with him. He dragged the guy out of bed and asked him if he was the one who'd attacked the girl. I think he might have been able to control it if the guy hadn't sneered and asked why Mac cared about a cheap little slut.''

"What happened?" Holly's voice was hushed.

Ken shrugged. "Mac beat him half to death. It took four of us to pull him off the guy before he killed him. I got a black eye and one of the others lost a tooth. We had him pretty well under control when the MP's showed up and hauled him off to the stockade. Luckily, Mac didn't break any of the other guy's bones. And since neither one of them was in uniform when it happened and the guy was a known troublemaker, Mac spent a few days in the stockade and got a slap on the wrist."

He shook his head, reminiscing. "Take my word for it, you don't want to see Mac lose his temper." He smiled crookedly. "It's like trying to handle an angry grizzly bear."

"What happened to the girl?"

Ken's smile faded. "The hospital took a hit while Mac was in jail. She was killed."

Holly shivered, rubbing her hands up and down her arms in an attempt to warm a chill that the hot summer sun couldn't touch. Ken leaned over to touch her lightly on the back of the hand.

"The thing to remember about Mac is all that control of his takes its toll. The kind of work we're in is high pressure. A lot of guys crack. Some of them deal with vermin for so long that they become vermin themselves. You've got to have a way to handle it. I cope by refusing to take life seriously. Mac copes by distancing himself from it and putting on that sleepy facade. But he's a crusader at heart and it eats at him that we can't help every sad, unhappy junkie and hooker that we meet.

"Don't lose sight of the vulnerability underneath the strength. He needs you. Remember that, no matter what happens."

Holly searched the unaccustomed solemnity of his face. "What could happen?"

But her whispered question was destined to go unanswered, even if Ken had had an answer for her.

"I see you managed to arrive after all the work was done." Mac's deep tones broke the tense silence. His dark-blue eyes shifted from one to the other, an unasked question in their depths. Holly's tongue seemed to be glued to the roof of her mouth and she couldn't think of a single coherent sentence.

Ken got to his feet and swung down off the bleachers, giving Mac a grin as he landed in front of him. "I ran out of gas. I can't tell you how devastated I am to think that I might have missed all the fun."

Mac smiled lazily. "That's okay. I knew you wouldn't want to miss everything so I figured you could help with the cleanup."

Ken groaned theatrically as the two men started across the field together, leaving Holly alone. She hugged herself. Why did it suddenly feel as if the sun had gone in and wouldn't be back out for a long time?

Chapter Eight

Holly stretched and rolled over, presenting her back to the sun. The soft canvas cushion that covered the redwood lounger smelled hot with faint traces of suntan oil. She turned her head to the side, closing her eyes and letting the burning rays soak away every care she'd ever had.

Ten days. Ten luxurious days since she'd last been in a classroom. Much as she enjoyed her job, she had to admit that she relished the time away from it. Her smile deepened as she heard the patio door slide open. Of course, she had to admit that this summer vacation was different from any she'd had before. This year she had Mac.

The cushion sank near her left hip. "You're beginning to look like a very pale lobster."

"Why don't you put some lotion on my back, since you're just sitting there doing nothing."

"Look who's talking about doing nothing," he jeered mildly. "I have a couple of steaks marinating for dinner tonight."

"Did you remember to put them in the marinade this time?" she asked without opening her eyes.

His palm came heavily on her bottom, startling a yelp out of her. "Don't get nasty, Ms Reynolds. You're in a rather vulnerable position at the moment." He unhooked the back of her bikini to emphasize the point.

"Brute." But the word died on a sigh of pleasure as his hands, slick with suntan oil, came down on her heated back. He stroked his palms over her shoulders, applying just the right amount of pressure to turn her into a quivering mound of jelly.

"I went over to see Maryann today and I picked up my mail. There was a letter from James." His hands stopped moving for a moment and there seemed to be a waiting stillness about him.

"How is he?" His hands began to move again and Holly dismissed the odd impression.

"Okay, I guess."

"You don't sound too sure."

"I don't know. It wasn't anything specific. He just seemed a little upset. The sentences were disjointed, and he kept saying that this assignment wasn't anything like what he'd expected. He sounded worried or excited or something. Maybe he's met a beautiful European countess who's offered to make him a kept man."

"Mmm, maybe. I know I'd certainly jump at the chance." His hands continued to stroke her back for a few more minutes and the subject of the letter was dropped.

"If you don't watch out, you're going to become permanently attached to that lounger, which is going to make it difficult to buy clothes. I don't think you've moved since school ended."

Holly rolled onto her back, clutching her top as she did so. She gave him a mock-indignant glare. "How can you say that? Who was it who made me give up my hard-earned rest and go to Disneyland? You dragged me all over the park yesterday. And if I'm tired, you've got no one to blame but yourself. I think we went on every ride at least twice, and you fed me enough ice cream and junk food to ruin my diet for the next six months."

He lifted his shoulders, his face the picture of innocence. "What can I say? I like Disneyland. Besides, I didn't hear you do much complaining. Who insisted that we go on 'Pirates of the Caribbean' the third time?"

She sniffed haughtily and lay back, closing her eyes. "I'm a good sport. Naturally, I didn't want to spoil your fun."

"You're just too nice to me." His hands, still slick with oil, came to rest on her bare stomach. He stroked his palms upward, sliding under the loose bikini top to cup her breasts and then sliding away before she could do more than gasp.

"Mac! What are you doing?" She couldn't sit up without risking losing her top. His broad frame, blocking the sun, was surrounded by a dazzling halo. He smiled down at her, his palms resting lightly against her sides.

"Well, since I have this oil on my hands, I've got to do something with it, and we certainly don't want to risk your burning something important."

"I'm hardly likely to burn 'something important' when my bathing suit covers...Mac!" His name was punctuated by the soft plop of Holly's bikini top hitting the surface of the pool. Her hands came up automatically to cover her breasts but his fingers caught her wrists and drew them away.

"Mac, what if someone sees us! It's broad daylight, for heaven's sake."

"The hedges are very high. Nobody can see us. But if it bothers you..." He stood up, lifting her easily into his arms, and carried her across the lawn to where a small Victorian gazebo stood, its white paint sparkling in the sun.

He laid her on a sofa, catching both her wrists in one hand, stretching her arms over her head and pinning them gently against the cushions. Holly's pulse accelerated madly. There was something wild and pagan about lying beneath him as she was.

His free hand came to rest just beneath her breasts. She could not drag her eyes from his face. His features were shadowed—mysterious planes and angles. The sun that streamed through the sides of the gazebo found copper highlights in his hair and seemed to catch in the blue of his eyes. He was all bronze and blues: the darkly tanned skin of shoulders and chest, the thick brown pelt of hair on his chest, tapering to a narrow line that disappeared into his electric blue trunks that matched the mesmerizing glint of his eyes.

His finger brushed soft as a butterfly's wing over the tip of her breast. His eyes never left her body as he repeated the caress until she finally arched upward, a soft moan catching in her throat as she sought to deepen the caress.

"You're such a good sport. I can see that you just don't want to spoil my fun." His hand left her body and she bit her lip to hold back a groan of frustration. But Mac was only changing the angle of his assault. He had brought the suntan oil with him and picked up the bottle, hot from lying in the sun, and flipped open the cap with his thumb.

"I wouldn't want you to burn." He tilted the bottle and a thin stream of warm oil slid across her taut nipple causing her to gasp. It seemed to pool in the pit of her stomach, a burning liquid weight that pulsed with life. Mac repeated the gesture on the other breast and her stomach tightened.

She closed her eyes against the dazzling light and gave herself up to the magic only he could create. His palm spread the oil over her breasts in a slow circular motion, stroking the excess down across her stomach and coming to a halt at the top of her bikini bottom. His fingers slid just beneath the band, feeling the fluttering pulse that beat there.

He hesitated a long, tense moment until Holly thrust her hips upward, arching against the restraint of his hand around her wrists. Her breath left her in a sob as his fingers eased down to cup her femininity. His head dipped and he caught one swollen nipple between his lips, rolling his tongue around it and then nibbling gently with his teeth.

Holly tugged demandingly against the hand that manacled her wrists, and his fingers slid away, allowing her to bury her hands in the thickness of his hair and pull him closer. He obligingly took her into his mouth, his cheeks flexing in a rhythm that tugged at her breast and echoed deep in her belly.

She was whimpering helplessly when his mouth left her breasts and moved across her stomach, nibbling and tasting along the way. His tongue explored the indentation of her navel as he sank to his knees beside the sofa, his fingers locking around the bikini bottoms and tugging them over her hips and down her legs.

Holly felt as if she were on fire. Every inch of her body burned. The sun created a hazy red glow inside her closed lids as Mac's teeth nipped gently at the soft flesh of her inner thigh. Her legs fell apart with abandon as his tongue soothed the sensuous tingle.

His fingers touched her lightly and she shuddered with reaction. "You're so hot," he whispered huskily, so close that his breath brushed over her. Her own breath caught, only to leave her in a rush as he tasted the honey of her desire. Her body went rigid, her fingers clawing against the sofa fabric, trying to hold on to some reality in a world that was suddenly spinning madly around her.

"Mac, Mac, Mac." His name became a breathless litany as he forced her to climb endlessly upward, her body totally under his control. She opened her eyes as his mouth left her, hearing her own whimpering protest as if from a great distance. His huge shadow blocked out the light and she caught a glimpse of the hungry glitter in his eyes before his body came down on hers, seeking and finding entrance.

Her body arched convulsively as he surged inward. He had brought her to such a fine pitch that rippling contractions seized her immediately. Her nails bit into his hips as she shuddered with fulfillment.

Mac held himself still, beads of sweat breaking out across his naked back as he reined his own passion to savor hers. His eyes were fierce on her rapt expression. As the last delicious shudder ran through her, he lowered his torso until she could feel the furred muscles of his chest gently crushing her breasts.

His mouth caught hers as he began to move within her. Holly's hands moved frantically up and down his sun-hot, sweat-slicked back. So sensitized was she that each movement sent shock waves of pleasurable agony through her. His lips twisted hungrily over hers, his tongue slipping inside to mate with hers. Her scent filled his mustache, adding another element to the smell of hot sun, suntan oil and sweat.

She brought her legs up to twine around his hips, urging him still deeper, her fingers biting deeply into the taut muscles of his buttocks. With a groan, Mac tore his mouth from hers, burying his face against her shoulder, his huge body shaking with endless waves of pleasure.

Minutes—or was it hours?—later, Mac stirred at her side, his arm heavy against her stomach. Her fingers were threaded through his hair and she felt as if she could lie just where she was for the next century or two. A warm breeze flicked playfully across their bodies and Holly opened her eyes, suddenly aware of the fact that the gazebo was hardly as secluded as their bedroom. She shifted uncomfortably. Now that their passion was spent, she was uneasy. Mac was right. The hedges were very high and nobody could possibly see in, but she was still uneasy. What if someone came to read a meter or something?

Mac stirred reluctantly, lifting his head as she started to slide out from under his arm. "Where are you going?" She was struggling with the bikini bottom, which had twisted itself into an uncooperative rope.

"Someone might see us."

"You weren't too worried about that a few minutes ago." He yawned, running his fingers through his tousled hair as he leaned on one elbow and watched her fumbling attempts to untangle the bikini and keep an eye on the surrounding yard.

"A few minutes ago I was busy defending my virtue and I had other things on my mind."

His brows shot up. "Defending your virtue? If that's the way you defend it, I'd like to see you when you surrender it."

The look she shot him was tinged with roguish humor, her dark eyes twinkling as she finally succeeded in getting one foot into her bikini. She fluttered her eyelashes. "What could I do against a big, strong man like you? I didn't dare resist."

"You were very brave." He got to his feet and stretched, magnificently unself-conscious. Despite herself, Holly couldn't help the feeling of possessive pleasure that took hold of her as she admired the ripple of muscles beneath his skin.

He caught her eyes on him and his expression softened to such tenderness that she felt as if her heart would stop.

"I love you." The words didn't need to be thought out. She didn't weigh the pros and cons. She just said them quietly, asking for nothing in return.

His eyes had an arrested look, followed by a look of joy that was almost frightening in its intensity. He cleared the sofa in one long step and caught her in his arms, causing Holly to forget completely about their nakedness.

"Oh Lord, Holly, what am I going to do with you?" The words were thick and muffled against her hair.

"I think you've already done it." She tried to lighten the atmosphere a little, though her eyes sparkled with unshed tears.

He bent and swung her up against his chest, carrying her toward the house. "You are the most beautiful, giving woman I have ever known."

She wound her arms around his neck and let him carry her into the bedroom, content. It was only much later that she realized he hadn't actually said that he loved her, and she wondered about the shadow of pain that had darkened his eyes.

THE FIRST WEEK IN JULY was hot, so hot that at times even thinking seemed like too much of an effort. Holly brushed the hair up from the back of her neck and considered the advantages of having her head shaved. Even her short, casual curls felt heavy and uncomfortable. She pulled the last of the clothes out of the dryer and carried the basket into the bedroom.

At least the bedroom was cooler. Dumping the laundry onto the bed, she sat down with her back to the cool draft coming from the air conditioner and lifted the hair off her neck. Pleasant goose bumps came up on her arms as the cold air blew across hot, damp skin. The halter top and shorts she was wearing were designed to cover as little as she could legally get away with, and it still felt like too much.

With a sigh she dropped her hair and reached out to pick up a pair of Mac's jeans. Her thoughts wandered as she sorted and folded clothes. She picked up a shirt and her smile deepened as she remembered that Mac had been wearing it the night they had gone on that disastrous double date with Ken and Maryann. Funny, how two people that she liked so much could take such an instant dislike to each other. She would have thought that they'd have a lot in common. They each faced life with a similar air of genial skepticism.

Holly flushed as she realized that she was rubbing the shirt against her cheek, and then she laughed softly. She was pretty far gone when she started mooning over Mac's clothes. She tossed the shirt onto the pile of things to be hung up and picked up the next item. Any doubts she might have had about the state of her feelings disappeared when she realized that she was actually enjoying keeping house.

Whether she planned it or not, she seemed to be living with the man. In the past month she hadn't been back to the apartment she shared with Maryann for anything but to pick up more clothes. She wouldn't want to cook and clean house forever, but it was a novelty for now and she intended to savor it until it grew old. Besides, Mac was so gratifyingly appreciative of her efforts.

Holly picked up his swimming trunks and flushed lightly, remembering the episode by the pool the day before. Her fingers lingered over the smooth fabric and her eyes grew dreamy. He loved her. She didn't doubt it, though he had yet to say the words. But the words weren't vital, not when she could read the emotion in his eyes.

She set the trunks down and touched her fingers lightly to her stomach. There hadn't been a chance to use the diaphragm the day before but she was rather sure it didn't matter. She hadn't had the tests yet, but she didn't have any real doubts. She knew she was carrying Mac's child and a doctor's confirmation could wait.

Her smile wavered. Would Mac be happy? Would he understand that she hadn't done it deliberately but that she was thrilled by the thought of having his child? She was going to have to tell him sooner or later. But not quite yet. She wanted a little more time with him.

Holly shivered as she got off the bed and began putting things away in drawers and closets. There was something a little frightening about being so happy, about having so much to lose. She shook off the dark thought. There was no sense in being superstitious.

A few minutes later, everything was on hangers or in drawers except a stack of her lingerie and soft cotton tops. She glared at them for a moment and then sighed. She had rearranged the one drawer Mac had cleared for her more times than she could remember, and that stuff was simply not going to fit. She hesitated, then knelt next to the dresser. Mac had told her to clear out whatever space she needed. The bottom drawer was probably the one he would miss least.

The drawer was full of sweaters. He certainly wasn't going to need these for the next few months. She lifted things out and carefully set them on the floor. The last garment didn't lift out easily and Holly didn't tug too hard because if the fabric was caught, she didn't want to snag it. She reached into the drawer and felt along its bottom until she found where the sweater was caught. Her tongue stuck out slightly as she worked gently to loosen the soft wool, and then she gave a sigh of pleasure as she lifted the sweater out. The garment was obviously old and well cared for—it would be just her luck to ruin some precious memento from Mac's past.

The sweater was unharmed and she put it neatly with the others before returning her attention to the drawer. If there was a loose splinter of wood, she didn't want to put her things on top of it. She pulled the drawer out as far as possible and ran her fingers lightly along the bottom. Her fingertips caught on a raised edge and she frowned slightly. It felt as if an entire board was loose. She tugged experimentally and then gasped in shock as the entire bottom of the drawer came up with it. It was so unexpected that she fell back on the carpeting with enough force to draw a wince from her.

Holly scrambled onto her knees, staring at the dresser in consternation. She lifted the drawer bottom, thinking that maybe it would settle neatly back where it belonged, but then stopped, staring down into the drawer.

It wasn't broken at all. It was a false bottom! Beneath the visible drawer there was a shallow compartment the same width as the drawer that lay above. Neat stacks of paper sat in one corner of the area. Next to it lay a small gun and a sheathed knife. Why would Mac keep a gun in the drawer? There were two other handguns that she was aware of and he kept them in the study. And what were the papers?

She forced down her curiosity. It must have something to do with Mac's work, and he wasn't likely to be terribly pleased if he realized she'd found out about this hiding place. She could debate the merits of telling him that she'd found it at a later date. Right now, all she wanted to do was cover it back up again. She felt chilled by this reminder of the kind of work he did. It made her realize how easily she could lose him.

"Holly A. Reynolds." The name seemed to leap off the paper at her as she lifted the false bottom and started to slide it into place. She stared at it for a long moment without moving. A premonitory chill ran up her spine. Her face was totally blank as she set aside the drawer bottom and lifted the folder with her name out of its hiding place. She was unsurprised to find that her fingers were trembling slightly as she got to her feet and carried the folder over to the chair by the window.

MAC SHUT THE FRONT DOOR behind him and tossed his suit jacket onto the sofa as he entered the living room. Wearing a suit in one-hundred-degree heat was not his idea of fun and comfort. But Mr. Reginald C. Naveroff's financial consultant would certainly never consider wearing anything less. He tugged on the knot of his tie and sent it to join the coat. He shook his head. Watching Ken put on the persona of a newly rich poor boy from Louisiana, who'd struck it rich in oil and now wanted sophisticated artwork to complete the picture, had at least been good for a laugh.

In his role as financial adviser, he'd had to do nothing more than look pained at some of his client's more blatant gaffes and shuffle financial statements in his briefcase. He had to admit that Ken really got into his role. The owners of the gallery where they'd gone to check out the paintings might have winced at Ken's faux pas—or "fox passes," as "Reg" called them—but they had stumbled all over themselves to show him their offerings. Unfortunately, as far as the two agents could tell, they didn't have anything they shouldn't have—no lost works by any of the great masters.

Mac stretched as he entered the kitchen and got a beer out of the refrigerator. Twisting the top off the bottle, he tilted his head slightly. The house was quiet, but Holly's car was in the driveway. He took a long swallow of icy beer as he headed for the bedroom. She was probably out by the pool. His eyes darkened with memory. Maybe he could go out and interrupt her sunbathing as he had done yesterday.

The warmth left his face abruptly as he stepped into the bedroom. The lowest drawer of the dresser was open; his sweaters lay to the side and the false bottom leaned carelessly up against the chest. Someone had searched the house. His left hand tightened on the neck of the beer bottle and his right reached automatically for the shoulder holster he wasn't wearing.

The movement was halted before it was half begun as his eyes found Holly. She was seated in a chair across from him, a file folder open on her knees. She hadn't heard him come in and, for the moment, her attention was on the folder. He set the bottle down with a faint thump, and she looked up slowly, as if unsurprised to find him there.

Mac's heart twisted in pain. He wanted to run across the room and snatch the folder away. He wanted to wipe the stunned look from her face and tell her that it was all a mistake, that he didn't know anything about the information contained in the file. Instead, he slid his hands in his pockets and looked at her without saying a word, waiting for her to make the first move.

Holly stared at him, trying to make her dazed mind accept the fact that he really was there. He was real. All six feet four inches of him, dressed in a pale-blue silk shirt, unbuttoned at the top, and gray linen slacks. What had he done with the tie? she wondered. That morning before he left, she had tugged on that tie, using it to pull his head down so she could kiss him. She had laughed and said that she'd never realized how handy a leash could be.

That morning. A million years ago. Before she had opened that damned drawer. Her fingers tightened on the manila folder. A slow rage began to build inside her, replacing the numb agony that had swallowed up every other emotion.

"Who are you?" Her voice shook with the words and she swallowed, trying to subdue the anger that threatened to fly out of control. "Just who the hell are you?"

"Holly..."

"You're not a cop, are you? Are you? Answer me, dammit!"

"I'm not a cop. At least not in the sense you mean."

"Not in the sense I mean? Now that's a clever piece of weasel wording. You mean not in the sense you led me to believe. Who do you work for?"

"I'm with the FBI." His expression was blank, a perfect blank that added to her anger. How could he stand there looking so unmoved when her world lay in splintered pieces at her feet?

"FBI? You've been spying on me for God knows how long,

taking notes as if I were a laboratory specimen. What are you looking for?''

"Holly..."

She gestured sharply, cutting him off. "It doesn't matter. Nothing matters. You're a damn spook and that's the most important piece of information." She flicked her fingers against the crumpled pages in the folder. "It's got something to do with James. I can figure that much out. You got to know me to see what you could get out of me about my brother. Damn you!" She came to her feet, throwing the folder across the room, papers scattering onto the carpet like dry leaves. "Damn you! You've been using me to try to hang my brother."

"Holly, we're not trying to hang James. We're trying to prove his guilt or his innocence. Nobody's out to get him."

"Guilt or innocence of what? What is he supposed to have done?"

Then she hadn't read the file on her brother. The agent in him breathed a sigh of relief. The case might still be salvaged. But that was the only thing that was likely to be salvaged, he acknowledged, looking into her furious face.

"I can't tell you that."

"You can't tell me a lot of things today, can you?" She spun on her heel and started for the dresser. "Maybe I'll just have to check in the magic drawer and see if it can tell me all these things that you can't talk about."

His hand closed around her upper arm with gentle but implacable strength. "I can't let you do that. I'm sorry you found the damned drawer, but I can't let you look at any more." His agony was audible in the roughness of his voice, but Holly was too wrapped in pain to hear it.

"You're trying to destroy my brother and you've used me to help you and all you're sorry about is the fact that I found out about it." She didn't try to throw off his light hold and she didn't turn to look at him. "Was it all a setup? Even in Tijuana? Was that planned, too?"

"No. Holly, when I saw you in that bar, you were like a bright flower in the middle of a dump. After you went home, I couldn't get you out of my mind. I started trying to find you, and then the case came up and I didn't have any choice but to take the assignment.''

"You could have turned it down."

"If I'd turned it down, someone else would have been assigned to it. I couldn't bear the thought of that."

"No, I don't imagine you could. After all, then someone else would have been getting what you wanted. A nice gullible schoolteacher who's good for a quick roll in the hay." She felt a vague satisfaction when his fingers tightened around her arm.

"You were never that to me."

"Let go of me," she ordered flatly. "It makes me sick to feel your hands on me."

Instead of releasing her, Mac turned her to face him, trying to penetrate the wall of pain.

"Holly, we can get through this. You said you loved me. Are you going to throw that away?"

Her hand came up and connected with his cheek. The crack of sound echoed in the suddenly quiet room. Mac's fingers didn't leave her arm and he didn't lift his free hand to explore the handprint that was beginning to show red on his cheek. His eyes were steady on hers.

"I love you."

Her breath sucked in audibly. "You don't know the meaning of the word. It's interesting that it only occurs to you to say it now that your damned case is in danger of blowing up in your face."

She closed her eyes, her breathing rapid as she struggled to regain control. "Let go of me." The flat tone got her the desired response and his fingers slowly left her arm.

"Holly, you have to listen to me. I do love you. I didn't say the words before because I knew this whole mess was still between us. We can work through this."

She drew a deep, shaking breath. She had to get out. She couldn't take much more without falling to pieces, and she was damned if she was going to let him see how badly he had destroyed her. She had to put an end to it now.

"You're right. We probably could work through it if we tried.

The thing is, it isn't worth trying. You were using me and I was using you. We'll just call it a draw and leave it alone.''

Mac stiffened. ''What do you mean you were using me?''

She forced her voice to be level, almost casual, hiding the pain that was tearing her to pieces. ''Remember I told you that I'd sworn to have a child or be pregnant by the time I'm thirty? Well, thirty is creeping up on me and artificial insemination is so impersonal.''

''Shut up, Holly.'' She felt a twinge of vicious satisfaction at the hoarse sound of his words. Good. She wanted him to feel at least a fraction of the pain she was feeling.

''Actually, when you look at it logically, Mac, you're perfect material for fathering a child. You're healthy, intelligent, the right age. What more could I ask for? I liked you and you're a dynamite lover, which was a nice side benefit.'' She suppressed a twinge of remorse as she took in his dazed expression and looked around for her purse. It was lying on the foot of the bed. Lord, she had to get out right away.

''But you told me you were protected,'' he muttered hoarsely. ''I asked you and you told me you were safe.''

''I lied. I guess that makes us even. I lied to you and you lied to me.'' She took one step toward her purse. All she wanted was to put this scene behind her. She gasped, her eyes widening as he grabbed her arm, spinning her back to face him, his hands clasping her shoulders in an unbreakable grip.

His eyes burned with blue flame as he drew her up on her toes, his fingers digging into her flesh. She felt dizzy with a mixture of anger, fear and pain. She wanted to put her head on his shoulder and beg him to make things right again. She wanted to pass out and wake up to find this had all been some terrible nightmare. And she wanted him to hurt as terribly as she did.

''Let go of me. I can't stand to have you touching me.'' Her voice rose and she could feel her control slipping.

''Are you pregnant?'' He ground the words out, barely moving his lips.

She lied instinctively, giving him the only answer that would make him let her go. ''No. I guess we're even there, too. I didn't get what I wanted and you didn't get enough to ruin my brother. Now let go of me.''

His fingers loosened slowly and he stared at her as if he wasn't quite sure who she was and how she came to be there. Holly backed away from him, groping behind her on the bed until she found the strap of her shoulder bag. Her hand knotted until the leather bit into her palm.

"I'll send someone to get my things." She edged toward the door. There was a quality in his stillness that frightened her, and she remembered Ken's words about not wanting to see Mac lose control. "Just stay away from me. I don't ever want to see you again."

Mac didn't turn as she left the room. He didn't move even when he heard the front door slam and then the distant sound of the Fiat starting. His chest hurt with the effort of breathing. No. It couldn't happen this way.

"No!" The echoes of the word died in the room. Pain lanced up his arm to his shoulder and he looked at his hand, vaguely surprised to see that he'd put his fist through the wall. He pulled his hand away, unaware of the shattered plaster that fell in a powdery dust. The false drawer panel caught his eye, and in an instant it was hurled across the room.

Fifteen minutes later he sank onto the bed and buried his face in his hands, his huge shoulders shaking. Around him the room was in shambles. Blood oozed from his torn knuckles, trickling down to stain the cuff of his shirt. He didn't feel the pain; he was oblivious to the destruction he had wrought.

All he knew was the desolating sense of emptiness. He was alone as he had never been before.

Chapter Nine

The essence of a good friend is the ability to know when to ask questions and when to offer silent support. When she came home from the hospital to find Holly curled in a ball on the sofa, her face streaked with tears, Maryann didn't ask for explanations. With gentle insistence, she chivied the smaller woman into a warm shower and then a soft cotton robe. She ignored Holly's mumbled protests and sat her down in front of a bowl of canned chicken soup, all but spoon-feeding it into her.

Once Holly had something in her stomach, Maryann led her off to bed. Holly swore she could never sleep. Maryann agreed but said that she would feel better in bed, and Holly didn't have the energy to argue the point.

Maryann turned out all the lights except one near the bed and sat down in a comfortable chair, a cone of crochet cotton and a half-finished tablecloth in her lap.

"You don't have to baby-sit me," Holly protested.

"Who said I was baby-sitting? The place has been empty the past few weeks. I'm just enjoying the company." She began to crochet, adding a motif to the delicate cobweb in her lap.

"How long have you been working on that thing?" Holly stifled a yawn.

"Almost a year."

"What are you going to do with it when it's done?"

"Put it in a drawer and start another one. I don't do it to have the finished product; I just enjoy making it. There's something very soothing about the rhythm that you pick up."

"Hmm." Holly's eyes followed the silver hook as it slid through a loop and pulled a strand of ecru cotton after it. "Mac and I broke up." Her voice was flat. All the emotion had been drained out by an afternoon of weeping.

"What happened?" The hook never paused and Holly found it difficult to pull her eyes away from the flash of steel.

"He lied to me."

"You haven't been totally honest with him," Maryann pointed out.

"I know. But that wasn't intentional. At least not at first."

"And Mac lied intentionally?"

"The whole thing was one big lie. It was all part of a job he was working on. The fact that I thought I was in love with him was just a big fat bonus." Her words dripped bitterness, and Maryann's eyes skimmed over her friend, seeing the pain that lay beneath.

"I'm sorry it didn't work out."

"So am I."

Holly lay back against the pillows and closed her eyes wearily. She was so tired. Three solid hours of crying had left her with a sore throat, eyes that burned and an empty space inside where all her emotions had been.

She opened her eyes again. "I think I'm pregnant."

The crochet hook stilled and Maryann's eyes swept up to Holly's face, worried but unsurprised. "Have you seen a doctor?"

"No, but I don't really need to, at least not to have it confirmed. I'm ninety-nine percent sure already."

"How do you feel?"

"Before this afternoon, I felt wonderful. Now I don't feel anything at all."

"Did you tell Mac?"

"Of course not." Holly stirred, her eyes restless. "I was too busy throwing him out of my life. I'm not going to tell him, either," she added defiantly, anticipating the other woman's next question.

Maryann returned her attention to her crocheting. "Doesn't seem quite fair, but it's your business."

"What he did to me wasn't fair, either," she muttered broodingly.

"So turnabout's fair play?" Maryann arched one brow to emphasize her doubt.

Holly flushed. "It's not really that. I just don't want to see him again. And I certainly don't want to share my baby with him."

"It's none of my business, but it seems to me that the more lies you tell, the more tangled things become. Mac lies to you, you lie to Mac. Pretty soon, it's difficult to separate the truth from the lies."

"I know you're right. I should tell him but I just can't." She rubbed her hand across her forehead. "I feel so tired and worn and angry. I just can't stand to see him again." Her voice rasped with exhaustion. "I just can't," she whispered.

"All right."

The room was quiet, with only the sound of late-evening traffic breaking the stillness. The two women were silent for several minutes, each wrapped in thought. The crochet hook caught the light with each smooth movement.

"Have you given any thought to what you want to do now? Are you going to stay here?"

Unspoken between them was the thought that Mac would come looking for her. Holly had thought of little else once the tears had ceased. Remembering the look on his face when she left him, she wanted to put some distance between them.

"I don't want to stay here. I can't go stay with my parents, not until I've decided what to tell them."

"What about James?"

Maryann's auburn head was bent over her crochet so she missed the flash of pain that went over her roommate's face. The mention of her brother brought back one horrible scene in vivid detail.

"No. I don't want to go to James. He's busy with his job right now and he'd demand all kinds of explanations. Besides, I don't want to leave the country."

The other woman nodded as she lifted her head and let her hands fall idle. "I don't think that would be a good idea. One of the nurses at the hospital comes from Michigan. Her parents are going to Africa for the summer and they've been looking for someone to house-sit their home. They wanted Nancy to do it, but she doesn't want to leave L.A. right now. They were pretty upset about it. They seem to think that it's her duty to drop everything and run home to baby-sit their mansion. I'd tell them to buzz off, parents or no. But Nancy's agonizing over what to do.

"If she could provide them with a respectable house sitter with impeccable references, it would solve her problems and their problems and your problems all at once."

Holly hadn't thought she had any tears left, but she had to blink back moisture as she looked at Maryann's slightly freckled features. "It sounds perfect. Mac couldn't find me even if he wanted to."

Maryann was kind enough to keep her doubts about that to herself. She folded up her crocheting and got to her feet. "Good. I'll call Nancy in the morning but I don't think there'll be any problem. You can probably be on your way in a couple of days."

"The sooner, the better," Holly muttered fervently. "What would I do without you?"

Maryann turned in the doorway and gave her a cynical smile that failed to conceal the warm friendship. "Probably a lot worse."

Dear Holly,

I suppose you're enjoying weather intended for human beings. Something under a thousand degrees with perhaps an occasional breeze to keep things bearable? The weather here has been beautiful, if you happen to be a Venusian native who doesn't need water to survive.

One of the other nurses bought a sunlamp so that she could get a tan without spending hours in the blazing sun. She left it with me while she went to Mazatlán for two weeks and I succumbed to temptation and tried it. Suffice it to say that I burned portions of my anatomy that were never intended to see sunlight. Serves me right for bowing to the current myth that a tan is essential to beauty. I suppose you're sprawled out in the sun feeling smug as you read this. I knew there was a reason we shouldn't be friends.

I'll try to write more later. Right now I'm rushing off on a hot date with a ninety-year-old doctor who thinks the discovery of penicillin is still big news. We're going to have lunch together and he's going to catch me up on the latest techniques.

Drop me a note when you get a chance.

Love,
Maryann

Holly folded the letter with a smile. Maryann knew her too well. She stretched her legs out on the lounger and closed her eyes, letting the sun pour over her. She'd make it a point to answer the letter tonight. There was nothing on television and she owed her parents a letter, too.

And James. She hadn't written to James since she got to Michigan a month ago. Maryann had forwarded a letter from him almost two weeks ago and it still sat on the desk, looking at her reproachfully each time she saw it.

From James her thoughts skipped inevitably to Mac. The two had become inextricably intertwined in her thinking. Thoughts of one led to the other, and she resented it. Part of her screamed that she had to warn her brother, to let him know that he might be in danger. But her fingers always fell short of dialing the phone. What could she say? She didn't really know anything. Mac had said they were trying to prove him guilty or innocent, but she didn't have any idea what he stood accused of.

And much as she hated to admit it, there was a little part of her that said that telling her brother what little she did know would be a betrayal of Mac. Consciously she insisted that she owed Mac no loyalty, but the conflict held her back. She tapped Maryann's letter idly against the arm of the lounger. She couldn't put it off any longer. If she didn't warn James and he fell into some trap, she would never forgive herself.

If Holly had hoped that the overseas phone call would answer all her questions, she was disappointed. James seemed at first stunned, then furious, then oddly wary. She was thankful that he didn't question her sources but worried by his unaccustomed preoccupation. She would have expected him to demand details of exactly how she had come by the information.

She put down the phone, feeling more uneasy than ever. James was hiding something. She could hear the reserve in his voice. He had asked why she was in Michigan when earlier she'd told him she'd be spending the summer in California, and she had muttered her excuse about taking care of the house for a friend. He had accepted that without question, which was unlike him. Being almost six years her senior had given him a lifelong conviction that he had the right to the details of her life.

She ran her hands lightly up and down her arms as she left the desk and crossed to the French doors that opened onto an expanse of green lawn. It was twilight, and she could hear the crickets starting up their evening chorus. The air was still, with just a tiny breeze rustling through the leaves of a nearby tree. The dusk still carried a lingering warmth from the sun but Holly felt chilled, even in the soft cotton sweater she wore over her jeans.

What if James was guilty of whatever crime Mac was investigating? She tried to push the thought away but it refused to disappear. She couldn't deny that her beloved older brother was capable of an occasional streak of ruthlessness but she couldn't believe he would do anything illegal. Even if he was tempted, surely he would never risk his entire career.

HOLLY WAS NO CLOSER to an answer a month later. Two months in Michigan hadn't given her the peace of mind she had been seeking. By mid-August she was restless and edgy, and by the end of the month she felt lonely and desperate. She pounced on Maryann's letters, reading them over and over again. She devoured any tidbit about mutual friends. But what she hungered for most was news of Mac. The problem was that she had made Maryann promise not to mention his name. She hadn't wanted to know if he'd come looking for her. So she reread the letters, trying to read between the lines.

When she had left Los Angeles in such a hurry, she'd had every intention of forgetting Mackenzie Donahue. She would erase him from her mind as if he'd never existed, and she hoped that all the hurt would go with him. Two months later, she had to admit that things hadn't worked out quite like that.

She opened the refrigerator and peered listlessly inside. She had to eat something, if only for the baby's sake. She pulled out a package of sliced roast beef and set it on the counter. A roast beef sandwich would be simple and nourishing.

Holly's hands came to rest on the bulge of her stomach and her eyes softened dreamily. Would it be a boy or a girl? She'd told the doctor she didn't want to know ahead of time. There was a certain delicious tension in the wondering.

Her baby would be a little girl with her heart-shaped face and Mac's eyes or a little boy with Mac's stubborn chin and those brilliant eyes. Funny, she was so sure that the baby was going to inherit Mac's eyes.

She layered the roast beef lavishly on whole wheat bread and poured herself a huge glass of milk. What would Mac say if he could see her now? Would he be pleased about the baby? She swallowed a bite of sandwich that tasted like sawdust and doggedly took another bite.

Two months had given her a different perspective on things and she found that her rage and pain had greatly mellowed. It still hurt to think that he had used her, but some of the things he had said during that horrible scene had taken hold. If James was being investigated by the agency Mac worked for, it was logical that someone would be assigned to see what she knew. If it hadn't been Mac, it would have been someone else.

Did it make it better or worse that it had been Mac who took the assignment? The betrayal hurt more because she cared about him. She had a sudden memory of Mac's face and she knew that he hadn't done what he had without paying a heavy price for it.

Holly got to her feet and rinsed off her dishes. The problem was that she was still in love with him. No matter how much she wanted to hate him, she loved him. And she hurt for him. She winced, remembering his face when she had told him that she'd been using him so that she could get pregnant. She'd hurt him badly with that.

She left the kitchen and climbed the stairs, her movements slow and heavy. Coming to Michigan had been a childish reaction. It wasn't quite as bad as running away to join the circus but it ranked a close second. She had spent two months rattling around in the huge old home and she'd had nothing to do but think.

In some ways it had been good for her. She'd gained distance from the situation, distance that enabled her to see that the faults had not been all on Mac's side. She should have told him right away about the possibility of a pregnancy. Her talk about not worrying him had been a way for her to avoid taking responsibility for her actions.

She undressed and crawled into bed, snapping off the light. Looking up at the darkened ceiling, she swallowed hard against tears. She'd had a right to be angry when she found those files, but had it been her own guilt that made her react so violently? She could have asked for a rational explanation instead of blowing up and saying things that should never have been said.

The truth was, she loved Mac and, no matter what he had done, she couldn't stop loving him. She might hate his career and the things he did for that career but she still loved him. She threw an arm across her eyes, blotting the tears. She felt so alone.

Holly cried herself to sleep and woke up the next morning with eyes that burned, a headache and a thorough disgust with herself. She was behaving like a girl of eighteen instead of a woman of twenty-eight, mooning around and crying when she should have been putting her life back together.

A long shower did a lot to restore her physically though the headache lingered. She fixed herself a hot breakfast and ate every bite of it before carrying a glass of orange juice onto the brick patio and sitting down. A huge elm tree shaded the patio, filtering the sun into dappled patterns on the brick.

She drew a deep breath and forced her shoulders straighter. She had lost a great deal. Mac was gone as surely as if he had died. That last look he had given her had contained something very close to hatred. And she couldn't even blame him. No matter how justified her anger, the things she had said to him had been vicious. He had used her, but it hadn't been by his choice.

Okay, she had counted the losses; now it was time to look at the positive side. She rested her palm against the roundness of her stomach and felt peace steal over her. She was carrying a child, Mac's child. If Mac was lost to her, she still had this and it was no small thing. In a few months she would hold a tiny baby that would forge an unbreakable link with Mac, even if he didn't know about it.

Holly smiled, absorbing the pleasure of that thought. She could never look on her relationship with Mac as a loss when she held this precious gift. Mac was part of the past, and no matter how much she wished that things could be different, she knew he would stay there.

The decision faced and made, Holly found the next week, if not happy, at least not miserable. She began to look toward the future, avoiding thoughts of the past with almost grim determination. She had to make plans for the new school year that was to start in just a couple of weeks and she had to calculate when she would have to take maternity leave.

Financially, the picture was brighter than it was personally. She had a few thousand dollars in savings, money that her grandfather had left her that she had kept aside as an emergency fund.

All in all, the future looked reasonably good. No future could look wonderful without Mac, but once the baby was here maybe she wouldn't miss its father so much. And if she repeated that often enough, she just might come to believe it.

HAVING MADE SO MANY firm and wonderful decisions, Holly was quite shocked to open the door one afternoon and find Mac standing on the other side, his expression grim. She could only cling to the door and stare at him, her mind spinning with so many questions that she couldn't get any of them out. His name was all she could manage.

"Mac!"

Chapter Ten

Holly had spent so many weeks coming to terms with the fact that she would never see Mac again that she couldn't really believe in his presence. Her gaze went over him from the top of his thick dark hair to the scuffed boots that covered his feet. She must be delirious. She couldn't remember Dr. Grant mentioning that delirium was a symptom of pregnancy, but that was the only possible explanation.

"We need to talk. May I come in?" The slow drawl, more clipped than she remembered, broke into her distracted thinking, making it clear that he was not a figment of her imagination. Still, she could only cling to the door and stare at him, her wits scattered by his presence.

"Holly? Are you all right?"

She shook her head, hoping to shake some sense loose. "I'm fine," she told him huskily. She cleared her throat and stepped back. "Come in. It's a surprise to see you. How did you know where to find me?"

He followed her into the living room, his gaze skimming over the beautiful antiques that filled it before settling on her. "I've known where you were since you got here."

"Oh." There didn't seem to be much to say in answer to that. Mac shook his head in response to her gesture toward one of the chairs. He stood facing her and she was made vividly aware of his size. He loomed over her, filling the big room with his presence. She ran out of words and just stared, drinking in the sight of him. She didn't want to know why he had come or why he hadn't come weeks ago. Not right now. Because right now, all that mattered was that he was here.

Her eyes started at his feet and traced a hungry path over faded denim that clung to long legs and a dark-blue T-shirt that molded the heavy muscles of his chest and shoulders. His face looked older than she remembered. New lines etched his forehead and bracketed his mouth. The summer sun had deepened his tan, and the vivid blue of his eyes stood out against the warm brown of his skin.

Holly realized that he was studying her with every bit as much interest as she had shown in him and her hand went instinctively to the gentle swell of her stomach, which was concealed beneath the gauzy maternity top. His eyes darkened at her gesture before lifting to meet hers.

"You got what you wanted. You're pregnant. Is it mine?" She drew in a sharp breath of pain, the cool indifference of his voice as wounding as his question.

"Of course it's yours!" Her eyes were wide with hurt and indignation, but Mac shrugged as if the question were perfectly natural.

"Well, you were so damn set on having a baby, how was I to know that you didn't find somebody else to give you what you wanted?"

She swallowed hard, keeping her voice level. "I thought you said you've known where I was."

He shrugged again. "I knew where you were; I didn't know every move you made. And you did tell me that you were not pregnant."

She winced, remembering that lie, among others. "It's your baby," she said flatly.

He stared at her in brooding silence for a moment and Holly returned the look uncertainly. What did he expect from her now? His hand came out to press lightly against her belly, feeling the slight rounding that cradled his child. She held her breath as his fingers moved over her. Shock waves of sensation moved through her body. With just that light touch, Mac brought back so much that she had been trying to forget.

"When are you due?" She stifled a sigh that was half relief, half regret as he withdrew his hand, pushing it into one of his pockets as if to keep from reaching out to her again.

"The doctor says around the middle of January, give or take a week." His eyes narrowed and she wondered if he was calculating that she must have gotten pregnant one of the first times they made love. Should she tell him what had happened? Her eyes flickered over his face and she decided that now was not the right time; he was obviously not ready to listen.

"Are you well?" She almost smiled at the odd formality of his question.

"I'm healthy as a horse."

He nodded, his eyes drawn to her stomach again, as if fascinated. She was intensely aware of his scrutiny, and she tried to appear nonchalant as she sank down onto the arm of a softly overstuffed chair. She didn't want to advertise the fact that her knees were reluctant to support her weight.

Silence built between them and he seemed in no hurry to break it. Finally Holly spoke. "Why are you here, Mac?"

He ignored the question and asked one of his own. "Why Michigan?" He turned away from her as if it bothered him to look at her, focusing his gaze out the window.

She hesitated a moment and then shrugged. There was no reason not to answer him. "I thought I needed to get away for a while. Maryann knew about this house-sitting job and Michigan seemed as good a place as any."

She looked at his wide back, noting the bunched muscles in his shoulders. "Why are you here, Mac?" She repeated the question, almost afraid to hear the answer. He turned to look at her before answering.

"We're going to Las Vegas."

She frowned. "Las Vegas? What are you talking about?"

"You're going to marry me." The statement was flat, without emphasis, but Holly felt exactly as if she had been kicked in the solar plexus.

"What?" She shook her head, trying to figure out what she must have missed, but he repeated himself in the same flat tone.

"You're going to marry me. I've got reservations for a flight that leaves this afternoon. We're flying to Las Vegas and we'll be married there.''

"Have you gone crazy?" she asked incredulously. "You can't just walk in here out of the blue and announce that we're getting married.''

There was not a trace of warmth in his blue eyes. They were cool and hard with determination. "I'm not crazy and I'm not joking. That's my baby you're carrying and you're going to marry me.''

"You can't show up and start giving me orders." She was sputtering with surprise and indignation, and her protest did not sound particularly original or effective, but she couldn't come up with anything better in her stunned condition.

"I'm not going to argue with you, Holly. You're coming with me, even if I have to haul you out of here bodily. And don't think I wouldn't do it.''

She slid off the arm of the chair and into the seat with a bump, staring up at him disbelievingly. This was not the easygoing man she had known in Los Angeles. This was a hard-eyed stranger whose attraction held a touch of fear.

"You're actually threatening me?" She could not reconcile this with the man she thought she knew.

He gestured impatiently. "I wouldn't hurt you. I wouldn't have to. I could take you out of here without putting a single bruise on you. But I'd rather you didn't force it to that. It would be better if we could start our marriage off on a more amicable note.''

"More amicable! Good Lord, you don't ask for much, do you?" Her eyes darkened with anger as she looked up at him. She wanted to get up and face him on a more even level but the trembling in her legs told her that she would be better off staying where she was. "You walk in here and coolly announce that you're going to marry me and that if I don't agree you're going to use brute force to make me and then you talk about starting our marriage off on a more amicable note!" Her voice rose in disbelief.

"You're nuts," she added flatly.

"That's my baby you're carrying, Holly." His eyes blazed with the words, and she realized that his calm exterior was a paper-thin facade. Beneath it Mac was seething with emotion.

"You used me to get that child and I'm damned if I'm going to just walk away and forget about it. I'm going to have a say in my child's future. You will marry me."

"Even if you did force me to go with you, what good will it do? You can't force me to say 'I do' once you get me to Las Vegas." Despite her best intentions, her voice quavered slightly.

"You'll agree. Your own conscience will force you to say 'I do.' You owe me this baby."

The whiteness of her face seemed to touch a core of gentleness in him. He dropped to one knee in front of her, but he did not reach out to touch her.

"I wouldn't hurt you, Holly." His husky voice softened, but it failed to conceal the iron determination behind his words. "That's my baby. You got what you wanted out of our relationship; all I want is a right to my child. I'm not thinking in terms of something that will end once the baby is born. I'm willing to try and shape a workable marriage with you. I won't make any demands on you, but that's my baby and it will have a father."

Her eyes searched his face, trying to read something in his features that she could not hear in his voice. He spoke of wanting the baby. Did he want her, too? Or was she nothing more than a vehicle to give him access to his child? Had he loved her? He hadn't said the word—except when faced with losing her the day she found that file—but there had been so many times when she had seen the emotion in his eyes. Or had that been only wishful thinking?

Mac knelt before her, saying nothing, letting her consider his words. His outward calm ran barely surface-deep. Inside, he was such a mass of confusion that he felt almost sick. It had taken him almost two months to decide that he didn't have any option but to come after her. Almost two miserable months during which he had all but destroyed his record at the agency.

He'd had himself pulled from the Reynolds case immediately. Not only had his prime target—Holly—disappeared, but he couldn't even try to keep his professional distance on this one anymore. Ken had worked himself in deep enough that he stayed in his persona as Reginald C. Naveroff, art collector with flexible morals.

Mac had been given a two-week vacation and then assigned to a desk, the only relief coming when he was called out to back up Ken. He understood and appreciated Chief Daniels's reasoning. He still had enough wits left to realize that he was in no condition to be functioning as an agent. But paperwork gave him too much time to think. And thinking was the last thing he wanted to do.

In a short time Holly had managed to destroy the calm, impenetrable cloak he had been pulling around himself ever since Vietnam. He had survived the jungles of Southeast Asia and the cement jungles of Los Angeles for as long as he had by never letting anything get too close. When people got close, somebody ended up getting hurt.

After Holly dropped her verbal bomb and left him, he had found himself barely able to function. Nightmares interrupted his sleep, dreams of Holly carrying a tiny blanket-wrapped infant lost in jungles both natural and man-made, endlessly calling his name. He could never get close enough to touch her. She would fade away as his tired feet drew near, only to reappear somewhere else, calling to him and holding out the child. The cycle would repeat itself until he woke, sweating and exhausted.

Ken had shown up a week after Holly left, concerned that Mac had missed two appointments. He had done a good job of concealing his reaction to the unshaven, unkempt man who greeted him with a snarled command to get out. It had been Ken who had forced him to pull himself together.

Sitting at a desk, doing endless reams of paperwork, Mac had gradually begun to think that he could survive this. If he had survived everything else, he could handle this. And then he began to question what had happened. And the more he thought, the more he found it hard to accept the idea that Holly had cold-bloodedly used him to father a child.

She had been hurt when she found out he was investigating her brother. He couldn't blame her for that. What if she had just lashed out instinctively, wanting to hurt him as she'd been hurt? She had no way of knowing just how effective her particular choice of defense would be with him.

The more he thought about it, the more sense it made. He felt as if a huge weight had been lifted from his shoulders. Hurt, even a deep hurt such as she'd been dealt, could be healed if he could just talk to her, make her see that he'd done what he had to do, that there hadn't been an option.

He had accessed her files from the computer, looking for her current address, and found the notation that the subject had been seeing an obstetrician on a regular basis. The words had danced in front of his eyes. She hadn't been lying. She really had been using him. Rage such as he'd never felt before had boiled up inside him. He was not going to lose this child.

He dragged his thoughts back to the present when she spoke.

"You say you want to marry me because you want the baby to have your name, but there's more to a marriage than just being a parent. And if there's hostility in the rest of the relationship, that's not going to make for a very stable home for a child." She glanced up into his face before dropping her eyes back to where her hands lay clasped in her lap.

She couldn't believe that she was actually considering this insanity!

"I've already told you that I'm willing to work to make it a good marriage. We got along well enough until you found out what I do for a living."

"You mean before I found out that you were investigating my brother!"

He shrugged. "Whatever. I don't see why we couldn't get along again. I make a reasonably good living." He stood up and ran his fingers through his hair, half turning away from her. "I spend a fair amount of time away from home. I can make it a point to spend even more. I can't promise to stay out of the way once the baby's born, Holly. I want this child every bit as much as you do and I'll want to spend time with him or her." His short laugh held bitter humor. "Who knows, in my line of work, I may not be around long enough for us to drive each other crazy." He didn't look at her as he spoke, so he missed seeing the color drain from her cheeks. "If it reassures you any, I'm not working on your brother's case anymore. I'd become too personally involved with it. I lost my objectivity."

"What are they investigating him for?"

"I can't tell you. He's not suspected of murder, and that's all I'll say." He gestured sharply with his hand, swinging around to pin her to the chair with the harsh brilliance of his eyes. "I don't want to talk about your brother. I want to have your decision. We can make it work, Holly. Say yes."

Why, he really cares what my answer is, she realized, feeling a flicker of warmth unfold at the thought. For all his tough talk and his obvious anger, he wanted her to say yes without a fight. He cared, at least a tiny bit.

She dropped her eyes away from his serious expression, unconsciously stroking her hand over her stomach as she tried to think clearly. She had been concerned about the gap being fatherless would leave in her child's life. Mac was offering not just a name, but a real father for the baby. He would be a good father, one who cared.

But there was more to consider than the child. Could she live with Mac without knowing what he felt for her? Could she bear it if the day came when she had to accept the fact that he could never love her as she loved him? On the other hand, he had said that he was willing to work at making their marriage a good one. Could she turn her back on the chance that, once they were married, they could work their way through the obstacles between them and develop a relationship all the stronger for having been tested?

Really, what was there to debate? It was a choice between guaranteed nothing and a chance to have everything. She had to take that chance.

She raised her head and smiled faintly, struggling to control her trembling lips. "All right. I accept your proposal."

HOLLY TURNED the narrow gold band on her finger and leaned against the wall next to the window. Married less than an hour and Mac had already disappeared to make a phone call. She supposed she was going to have to get used to that kind of thing. After all, her husband wasn't in an ordinary nine-to-five job.

"Husband." She repeated the word in her mind and then said it out loud once or twice, trying to make it seem real. Her lips tilted faintly. It wasn't going to seem real until Mac was there to hold her in his arms and make it feel real. He had swept her onto a plane, not even giving her time to pack her things, and she had thought ruefully that it was the second time in recent months that she had left a place and left everything behind.

The ceremony at the chapel had been brief and formal. Not really the stuff dreams were made of, but Holly didn't care. Mac was standing next to her and, for a few minutes, she indulged herself in a fantasy, pretending that they were marrying for all the right reasons. Reciting her vows in a trembling voice and hearing Mac's husky tones echoing them, she was suddenly confident that she had made the right decision.

A brief knock on the hotel room door drew her away from the window and she crossed the room. "Who is it?" Surely it was too late for maid service.

"It's Mac."

Her brows arched in surprise and then came together in a frown. He had a key to the room; why would he be knocking? Unless he was just being extra considerate? Her fingers worked the latch and opened the door to him.

He stepped into the room and leaned back against the door, watching her as she crossed to the mirror and picked up a brush. She began pulling it through her hair, more out of nervousness than anything else.

"I just thought I'd stop by and make sure you had everything you needed."

He didn't offer an explanation of the phone call, she noticed, and she knew better than to ask. His words registered as she realized that he was reaching for the doorknob. She hadn't had time to think about their sleeping arrangements, but she had assumed that they would be sharing a room, like any other couple. Despite the problems between them, she wanted their marriage to be a real one. How could they ever hope to work things out if they couldn't communicate on even that most fundamental level?

Holly turned to look at him, her hair falling in tousled curls around her face. "Where are you going?"

He cleared his throat, trying not to notice how incredibly desirable she was, trying to forget that she was now his wife. "I have a room on the floor above this one."

"But I thought...I mean, aren't we..." she stammered to a halt. There was no subtle way to tell him what she had thought. Obviously he didn't plan on sleeping with her. She could hardly beg him to stay, not even if her pride would permit it. She managed a smile but she half turned away so that he could not read the hurt in her eyes. "Never mind. Good night, Mac."

He hesitated, his hand on the doorknob. He should just leave it there, he told himself. Why look for trouble? He didn't want to stay, did he? But she looked so hurt.

"Holly, I..." He released the knob and ran his fingers through his hair, disarranging it into dark waves. "It's enough that you agreed to marry me. I bullied you into this but I'm not going to assume that gives me the right to your bed." One corner of his mustache twisted in a rueful smile. "I'm not quite that much of a monster."

Now it was her turn to hesitate. Pride told her to let him go. She moved to the small dresser and fiddled nervously with the few bottles she had set out there. The gleam of her wedding band caught the light. "I wouldn't think you were a monster."

The words were so low that he had to strain to hear them. For a moment his heart stopped beating, and when it started again, it was with a slow, heavy thud that almost suffocated him. He didn't want her—she had destroyed that by using him. He couldn't possibly want her.

Like hell he couldn't.

He crossed the room to stand behind her, his hands coming up to settle hesitantly on her shoulders. For a moment Holly was very still beneath his touch and then, with a sigh, she leaned back against his chest, letting the hard muscles support her. She felt his breath stir her hair and then his lips touched her temple in the lightest of kisses.

"Holly, you don't have to do this."

She opened her eyes as his lips continued their gentle, undemanding massage of her temple and her gaze was caught and held by her reflection in the mirror. In her silky dress, with her hair falling in soft disarray and her dark eyes wide with uncertainty, she looked fragile and wholly feminine.

In contrast, Mac's broad shoulders were surely the essence of solid masculinity. The darkness of his tanned hands stood out on the delicate fabric of her dress, the almost black of his hair mingling with the lighter brown of her curls as his mouth brushed her forehead. It was going to work out, she told herself. It had to.

His hands loosened on her shoulders, allowing her to turn into his arms. Her hands slid around his neck, her face tilting up to his. The look of need he read there was his undoing. All his rage and hurt ebbed away, leaving him nothing to hold between them. With a muffled groan of surrender, he bent to slip an arm beneath her knees and carried her to the bed. He set her down long enough to throw back the covers and then laid her gently on the sheets.

His eyes never left her face as he hastily discarded his jacket and yanked impatiently at his tie. Holly felt a sharp pang of anticipation in her stomach as he pulled off his shirt and she could see the naked breadth of his chest. Suddenly it seemed like years since he had touched her.

Her lashes fluttered down as he sank, naked, onto the bed beside her, his weight tilting the mattress. He undressed her slowly, his fingers just brushing her body, his touch almost impersonal. But the trembling in his hands and the ragged catch to his breathing told her that he was anything but impersonal.

She flushed, suddenly self-conscious as he lifted her dress over her head and then deftly peeled off her hose, dropping them at the foot of the bed. His fingers were shaking and it took him a moment to master the front catch of her lacy bra, but then she was lying almost naked beneath him, a pair of silk and lace panties her only covering.

He stared at her for a long, silent moment, the expression in his cerulean eyes hidden by the thickness of his lashes. Uncertain in the face of his silence, she moved her hands to cover the gentle swell of her stomach. Was he repulsed by the sight of her? His fingers caught hers and drew them away.

"No, don't hide from me. So beautiful." His huge palm pressed lightly on her belly and she was stunned to see the glitter of tears in his eyes before his gaze dropped away. He bent to place a heartbreakingly tender kiss against the mound that held his child and then laid his face against her silken skin.

Holly's hands came to rest in his thick, dark hair and she cradled him to her, blinking rapidly to control the sudden surge of moisture to her eyes. She felt a stab of guilt. How could she have planned to keep his child from him?

Gradually, tenderness eased into desire and the gentle pressure of his mouth on her stomach yielded to the more demanding touch of his mouth at her breasts. Whatever the problems that remained unresolved between them, physically they were still in tune.

There was an extra element of tenderness in his lovemaking but no less desire. Holly was swept up in a whirlwind until every last ounce of response was wrung from her. They came together at last in an explosion of passion that left them both panting and spent.

Holly snuggled against his side and was deep in sleep moments later. Mac lay next to her and stared at the darkened ceiling, wrestling with the confusing mixture of emotions that churned within him. How was it possible to both love and hate someone at the same time? Or was it himself he hated?

He still hadn't found the answers to his question, even when dawn found its way slowly into the room.

Chapter Eleven

A silver Ferrari was parked in the driveway and Ken was leaning casually against its side. Mac muttered a curse under his breath, almost the first words he had spoken since they had left Las Vegas, and pulled the sedan in next to the sports car.

"Is something wrong?"

He threw her a quick glance and she wondered if he'd forgotten her presence. It would certainly account for the hours of silence since they woke that morning.

"I don't know. Wait here a minute, would you?" He didn't wait to hear her murmur of agreement. He already had the door open and was swinging his long legs out.

Holly gave a soft sigh and reminded herself that Rome wasn't built in a day. She couldn't expect to establish a wonderful rapport with Mac without giving it some time. But wouldn't it be nice if he didn't pretend she wasn't there, she thought acidly.

Last night had been beautiful, far more than she had expected of her wedding night, considering the odd circumstances of their marriage. Mac had been tender and loving, and for a little while she had been able to pretend that everything was fine, that there were no lies, no secrets to come between them. She had imagined the last several weeks had never existed.

She hadn't expected that euphoria to last, but she hadn't expected to wake up next to a total stranger, either. Mac was polite but cold. No, "cold" was too active a word. He was distant, as if he didn't know her very well and didn't care to pursue the acquaintance.

Give it time, she cautioned herself. *Don't expect everything to sort itself out magically. There's a lot of hurt on both sides.* She was still working out her own pain, and she had to allow him that same privilege.

MAC APPROACHED KEN WARILY, a hint of stiffness in his lazy strides. "Problem?"

Ken nodded. "Reggie has been invited on a short boat trip and he's taking his financial consultant along. We're leaving in about two hours. It's a good thing you called last night to let me know when you were coming back. I managed to get the cruise set back a couple of hours." He glanced at Mac's car. "Daniels is not happy about your unscheduled trip."

"Daniels will just have to learn to live with it. Holly's pregnant."

"I know."

Mac stiffened, his eyes flaring brilliant sparks. "You knew about it?"

Ken held up one hand. "Before you tear my head off, I just found out yesterday. When you did your disappearing act, I checked the files. It wasn't hard to figure things out." He waited until Mac relaxed, and then smiled. "You're a little quick on the draw, aren't you, partner?"

Mac's fingers combed his hair. "I guess I'm a little uptight right now." He glanced at the car where Holly waited and felt his gut twist. "Listen, I'll go pack my financial adviser bag. Why don't you get Holly?" He was gone before Ken could reply.

It was cowardly. He knew it was cowardly but he welcomed the chance to get away for a while. He needed some time to gather himself together. As Ken had pointed out, he was a little quick on the draw these days, not quite in control. And being that little bit on edge was not a good thing. An agent had to be in control of himself. It was the only thing he could count on.

Holly smiled at Ken as he opened the car door and offered his hand to help her out.

"Hello, Holly. How are you?"

His eyes were a chill gray and his words were equally cool. Despite herself, Holly felt tears rise. She was beginning to feel as if the whole world was against her. She blinked and managed a tremulous smile.

"I think that's the first time you've ever used my name. I got kind of used to being called Lady."

He leaned into the back to get her two small bags on the back seat and then slammed the car door shut before turning to look at her.

"Things change. People change."

He would have gone around her but she reached out and caught his arm. He stiffened and she was afraid he would pull away and walk off, but after a long, tense moment, he turned to look at her, his youthful features unfamiliarly hard.

"I haven't changed, Ken."

"No? Well, maybe I have."

"Why are you so angry? What happened was between Mac and me. It had nothing to do with you."

She didn't know why she was bothering. It was obvious that he was carrying some kind of grudge. Naturally he would be on Mac's side. As Mac's partner, he must be investigating her brother, too. A familiar rush of anger stiffened her backbone when she thought of their spying on James.

"Never mind. I should have known you wouldn't be interested in both sides. You've tried and hanged my brother already. I don't see why I should expect any different treatment."

Ken dropped one of the bags, and it was his turn to catch her by the arm. "This has nothing to do with your brother, Lady." Neither of them noticed his slipping into the old form of address.

"It has everything to do with James! That's what started this whole mess! The two of you were sneaking around and trying to get me to give you information to use against him."

"What started this whole mess was your not having the sense of a peahen, Lady! If you had half the brains you lay claim to, you would never have stayed in that bar in Tijuana waiting for your snotty roommate's sleazy boyfriend to show up and deliver some souvenir!"

"It was not a souvenir! It was an heirloom and it meant a great deal to Maryann."

Ken went on as if Holly hadn't spoken. "And then Mac

wouldn't have been using the agency computers—illegally—to track you down and we wouldn't have been assigned to this stupid case.''

"And Maryann is not snotty!" She stopped as his last sentence registered. "Was Mac really using the computers to find me?"

"Yes, and he's lucky he didn't get docked five years' pay. They frown rather heavily on using the company computers for personal reasons. Didn't he tell you that?"

Holly frowned, trying to remember what had been said during that horrible scene after she found the folders. Yes, Mac had said something about trying to find her, but she had just dismissed it at the time.

"I think so, but I didn't believe him."

"*I* don't believe *you*," he muttered disgustedly, thrusting his fingers through his hair and ruining Reginald C. Naveroff's neatly combed waves. "What do you want from him? Are you *trying* to destroy him?"

"Of course not!" she snapped.

"Well, you damned near succeeded when you left before. And I'll tell you what makes it my business. I'm the one who scraped him off the floor and tried to put the pieces back together again. I don't think it would work a second time, Lady. You keep that in mind next time you get in a snit."

"I wasn't in a snit. He was investigating my brother. Do you hear what I'm saying?" It would have been difficult not to hear when her voice had risen to just under a shout. She took a deep breath, glancing at the peaceful neighborhood around her, and lowered her tone.

"He was using me to try to get evidence against my brother. He lied to me."

"He was doing his job. He didn't want this lousy case, but if he hadn't taken it, another agent would have. Would you have preferred someone else 'spying' on you?"

It was the same question Mac had asked her, and she still didn't have an answer. "Yes. No. I don't know."

"Well, while you're trying to make up your mind, think about the fact that Mac is the best in the business."

"All the better to hang my brother," she muttered bitterly.

"We're not trying to hang your brother. He was suspected long before we ever heard of him. All we're trying to do is find out the truth. And if you think he's so all-fired wonderful, then you shouldn't have any doubts that we'll find he's innocent. But one way or another, we've got to find out."

Holly blinked back tears. He had struck right at the root of her bitterness. "I'm not sure he is innocent," she whispered painfully. "I don't even know what he's accused of."

Ken hesitated, and she thought he was going to tell her what James was suspected of. With a sigh he released her arm and shook his head. "Sorry, Lady. I can't tell you anything."

"Your job." Her tone was laced with distaste, and his face hardened again.

"My job. And you might try looking at my job and Mac's as trying to prove your brother innocent, instead of acting as if we've already got the noose made up. We're not out to get anybody. We just want the truth."

"You can't expect me to like what you're doing."

He sighed. "No, but you can respect it. Don't torture Mac with it. He isn't even working on the case anymore, except to back me up when it's necessary."

She swallowed hard and looked up at him, her eyes bright with unshed tears. "I do love him, Ken, really I do, but it hurts sometimes."

His face softened. He never had been very good at staying angry. She was back. That was what really mattered. "He loves you, too, Lady. Don't ever doubt that. It almost killed him when you left him. I don't think he'd pull out of it again."

The front door slammed and both of them jumped slightly. Mac's long strides carried him across the lawn to where they stood, giving Ken time only to pick up the bags again. Mac had changed into a beautifully tailored suit more in keeping with his role. Horn-rimmed glasses dimmed the brilliance of his eyes, making him seem like a stranger. He took the glasses off, tucking them in an inside pocket, his gaze skimming alertly from Ken to Holly.

"I didn't realize the bags were so heavy you couldn't get them into the house."

Ken shrugged. "I was just asking Holly how her former roommate was doing."

Mac's brows shot up. "*You* were asking about Maryann?"

"Well, you know how it is, Mac. I like to keep track of the only woman who's ever resisted my fatal charm. We'd better hurry."

Mac reached out to take the bags from Ken, setting his own suitcase on the ground. "I'll take these in."

"I knew if I just delayed long enough, I could get out of carrying them in." Ken gave Holly an easy smile. "Nice to have you back, Lady. I'll take care of Mac for you."

"Thanks." Her smile was slightly shaky. She turned to follow Mac, feeling as if she had made a small start on putting things in order. Ken had forgiven her. Now if she and Mac could only learn to forgive each other.

Mac set her bags down just inside the door and turned to look at her, his eyes shadowed by thick lashes. "I don't know how you're situated financially, so I left some cash and a couple of credit cards on the breakfast bar, along with the keys to the sedan."

"Thanks. I left Baby with Maryann. I suspect she'll be glad to get rid of it."

He shifted restlessly. "I'd rather you drove the sedan. It's a lot safer." The tentative glow his concern brought was quenched by his next words. "I'd feel better about you and the baby."

"The baby. Yes, of course. How could I forget?" Her tone was flat, concealing hurt.

Mac arched one dark brow. "I don't know. It was the reason for this marriage." He regretted the cold words the moment they were said, but he didn't take them back. He was wrestling with the jealousy that had risen when he saw her on such apparently easy terms with Ken.

A chill silence settled between them. Holly didn't speak, afraid that her voice would betray how close to tears she was. Mac, too, was torn between conflicting urges. One was just to walk away and the other was to pull her close and promise her the moon if she'd only smile at him.

He shifted at last. "Well, I'd better get going. I shouldn't be gone more than a few days, ten at most. There's a card with a phone number along with the cash. If an emergency comes up, you can call and somebody will try to get a message to me."

"I'm sure I won't need it," she told him coolly. "I can always call on Maryann."

"Of course." His voice beat hers for sheer indifference. He took a step away, his eyes never leaving her downbent head. She said nothing. His hands clenched into fists. Damn her! Why did she tie him up in knots like this? With a muffled curse he closed the distance between them.

Holly's head jerked up in startled surprise as his fingers closed around the delicate bones of her shoulders. She caught only a glimpse of tormented blue eyes before his mouth met hers. It was a kiss that demanded everything she had to give and at the same time returned it a thousandfold. It was an all-too-brief glimpse of heaven.

He drew back, his eyes dark and disturbed. One palm came to rest possessively against the swell of her stomach but she knew his words were for her and not just the child she carried.

"Take care of yourself."

He was gone before she could do more than lift shaky fingers to her tingling mouth.

THE NEXT WEEK AND A HALF was made bearable by the fact that there were so many things to be done. She didn't have time to sit and brood. Her first move was to call Maryann to let her know that she was back in town. She also had to let Maryann's friend know that her parents' house was empty. That turned out not to be a problem. Nancy had just broken up with her fiancé and she was grateful for the excuse to spend some time somewhere other than on her previously arranged trip to Hawaii with her ex-fiancé. She'd just take that time and go stay at her parents' home. She could also pack up Holly's things and ship them back.

Maryann, however, was not quite so easily dealt with. She arrived at Mac's house within an hour of getting Holly's message.

"So explain to me how you ended up marrying Mac. When you left him a couple of months ago, you said he was a lowlife and I think that was about the best thing you said about him."

She fixed her friend with bright, inquiring eyes and Holly shifted restlessly. "I was upset."

Maryann's eyes widened. "Now there's a masterpiece of understatement. What happened to un-upset you?"

"I had some time to think about it and I realized that perhaps what Mac had done had not been entirely his fault, that maybe I'd been a little too hard on him."

Maryann stirred her tea thoughtfully. "Mac's not a cop, is he?"

Holly's tea sloshed into the saucer. She shook her head silently. "Not exactly."

"I didn't think so. You were so cagey about why you'd gone from being madly in love to hating the man that I did a lot of thinking about it. Did it have something to do with his job?"

"Yes. But I can't talk about it, not even with you."

"I wouldn't dream of asking. But I would like to know why you got married in such a rush. Last I'd heard, you were going to raise your baby in solitary splendor and you weren't even going to tell Mac about it."

Holly smiled. "I never used the words 'solitary splendor,' not even at my most maudlin." She took a swallow of tea and sighed. "To tell you the truth, I don't feel particularly married yet. Mac swooped in out of the blue and informed me that I was going to marry him or he'd kidnap me until I gave in."

"What?" Maryann spluttered on a swallow of tea. "You're joking, of course."

Holly laughed. There was something about telling her friend the story that made it seem ridiculous. "Cross my heart," she said solemnly. "He really did."

"And you let him get away with it?"

She shrugged, and her smile became rueful. "I think I was glad to have an excuse. Gloria Steinem would probably drum me out of the corps for saying that. But it was almost a relief to have him tell me what to do. I was so confused. I love him, and yet my pride didn't want to forgive him. Actually, I'm not sure I've completely forgiven him yet."

"Don't you think you're asking for trouble? Marriage isn't easy at the best of times, but you're starting out on all the wrong feet."

"I had to give it a try. Maybe it won't work, but I have to try."

Maryann shook her head and then lifted her cup in salute. "Well, here's looking at you, kid. I hope it works."

Holly's cup clinked against her friend's. "I hope so, too."

They were silent for a long moment and then Maryann spoke again. "I suppose that creep is his partner or something."

"Ken isn't a creep." Holly was relieved to have the subject shifted from her relationship with Mac. She had too many doubts about it herself to be comfortable defending it. "I don't know why you're so hostile to Ken. He's really a nice guy."

"You could have said the same thing about Jason, and look what a creep he turned out to be."

Holly stared at her friend in surprise. "You're not comparing Ken to Jason, are you? He isn't anything like Jason."

"You wouldn't have said that Jason was anything like Jason, either, until you got to know him."

Holly had no trouble sorting out this garbled sentence, and she shook her head. "Jason was a weak, womanizing fish and he showed his true colors from the start. You just didn't want to see it because he was a hotshot in bed."

"How do you know what he was like in bed?" Maryann's cheeks flushed, the color clashing with her fiery hair.

"You told me."

The flush deepened until her whole face was on fire. "I must have been drunk if I said anything like that. I never talk about my sex life."

"Well, as a matter of fact, you were drunk. It was New Year's Eve and Jason had stood you up, and we sat around the apartment drinking. I asked you why you kept seeing him and that's when you told me that he was—"

"I know, I know." Maryann rubbed her hand over her face as if trying to rub away the heat that flushed it. "I can't believe I said that."

"Was it a lie?"

"Yes. No. Well, sort of." She met Holly's curious eyes and heaved a sigh. "Did anyone ever tell you that you're awfully pushy?"

"Not since the last time you said it." Her interested expression didn't fade, and Maryann sighed again.

"Jason was very good, and I suppose, at first, I did tend to let myself be blinded to some of his faults." Holly rolled her eyes. "All right, I was blind to a lot of his faults. Great sex can be very distracting."

"So what happened?"

"Nothing cataclysmic. I just gradually realized that great sex couldn't make up for a mind like a turnip. All the man ever thought of was food and money and sex. Even the sex was getting old. Without any real emotion behind it, it got to be a sort of competition.

"Jason was so vain and shallow. I just couldn't take it anymore. I just wish I'd gotten my grandfather's watch back before I told him to drop dead."

"I don't see how you can compare Ken to him. Ken is warm and caring and definitely not shallow."

Maryann shrugged and got to her feet. "If you say so." She was unconvinced, but Holly didn't know what more she could say, so she let the subject drop.

BETWEEN SETTLING INTO a new home and getting ready for the start of the new school year, Holly found she had very little time to worry about the future. It was always there in the back of her mind, but it was pushed aside by the day-to-day business of living.

Mac's time away stretched into a full ten days and Holly began to doubt that she'd really married him. It could have been a figment of her imagination. The whole rushed trip to Las Vegas could have been a dream.

She clung to the memory of that last kiss. No matter how cool he seemed, there had been real passion in that kiss, passion and need. Whenever she began to wonder if the whole thing had been a mistake, she remembered that kiss and the emotions it revealed.

The least he could have done was called her, she thought irritably as she climbed into bed. Tomorrow would be the eleventh day since he'd left. What if something had happened to him and nobody had notified her? She pushed the idea away. Nothing was going to happen to Mac. She had to keep telling herself that or she'd go completely crazy.

Holly plumped up the pillows and thumped her head down into the center of them. To be fair, she supposed that he couldn't just walk to the nearest phone booth and give her a call. She had to remember that he wasn't doing a nine-to-five job. He couldn't just wrap things up and come home for dinner. But who said she had to be fair? She was lonely and worried and she wanted Mac home and safe. What a way to start a marriage, she thought morosely.

The room was dark when she awakened. Pale moonlight provided a dim illumination. Her eyes searched the darkness, trying to decide what it was that had disturbed her. The quiet jingle of change in a pants pocket and the soft thud as the garment hit the floor answered her. She rolled over.

"Mac?" She could just make out his outline on the other side of the bed. He froze for a moment, then put his watch on the night table and turned toward her.

"I didn't mean to wake you. It's late. Go back to sleep."

She stifled a yawn as she rose on one elbow. Her eyes were adjusting to the darkness and she could see that he was naked. The paler strip of skin that circled his thighs contrasted with his tan.

"I know it's late," she told him grumpily. "Tomorrow is eleven days. I was beginning to worry."

He paused in the act of sliding under the covers and she caught the gleam of his eyes as he looked at her. "Sorry. If it had taken any longer, I would have tried to get word to you, but I can't ever guarantee things like that, Holly."

He slid into bed and lay on his back. If she had been more alert, she would have noticed the rigid way he held himself. But she was still half asleep and all she was conscious of was that he was home and safe, at least for the present. She scooted across the few inches that separated them and cuddled up against his side.

"I know, but I can't help but worry. I missed you," she muttered plaintively, her eyelids already drooping.

For a moment Mac remained still and then, with an almost

convulsive movement, his arm slid under her neck and he pulled her close so that her head rested on his shoulder. He turned his face to inhale the clean fragrance of her hair.

"I found someone to send my stuff from Michigan." Her fingers threaded idly through the mat of hair on his chest, enjoying the strong beat of his heart against her palm.

"Did you?" His hand pressed against her back, bringing her closer still. He had spent the last ten days living on the edge of danger. One wrong move from either himself or Ken could have gotten them both killed. He had burrowed deep beneath the skin of Mason Dobson, financial adviser, hiding anything of Mackenzie Donahue that didn't fit the other persona. Stepping off the yacht with Ken had been like stepping into clean air after a week in a sewer.

Holly's warm presence in his bed was both a soothing balm and a niggling torture. He rebelled at the desire he felt building for her. He didn't want to want her, didn't want to love her.

Holly was sleepy but would have had to be dead not to feel the stirring of his masculinity beneath the pressure of her thigh.

"Mac?"

His hand moved from her arm to her chin, drawing her face up to his. Her eyes searched his shadowed features, trying to define his expression, but she could see little beyond the glitter of his eyes.

"I want you, Holly."

She had little doubt of that. If his words didn't convince her, the hard length of his arousal would have. She moistened her dry lips.

"Are you asking me or telling me? Because if you're telling me, I'm glad to hear it in words, and if you're asking me, then the answer is yes."

His lips found hers before the last word was complete. Her mouth parted eagerly beneath his, and Mac felt a surge of desire and relief.

He was home.

Chapter Twelve

It was difficult to build a marriage when you never saw your husband, Holly thought angrily a month after she and Mac were married. No, that wasn't fair. She couldn't say that she never saw Mac. He spent plenty of time around the house. He was there physically but he wasn't there mentally. It was like living with a stranger.

The only place he dropped the polite facade was in the bedroom. There, in the dark privacy of their bed, he became the lover she remembered from the days before she found out who he really was. But even those precious moments of sharing were not flawless. It was as if he resented himself for wanting her, seeing his wanting as a sign of weakness.

She told herself over and over again that she had to give it time. What they really needed was to sit down and talk, bring some of the hurts out into the open, where they could be healed. She had to tell him that she had been lying about using him to conceive a child. And she had to tell him that she had at last come to terms with the lies he had told her.

She had been delaying that talk, telling herself that she was too busy getting started on a new school year to worry about it then. But six weeks into the new year, she still hadn't done anything about talking to Mac, and she had to admit that she was afraid to disturb the fragile balance of their relationship. Once she admitted that, she no longer had an excuse to put it off.

When Mac arrived home a little before six o'clock, Holly was in the kitchen. He hesitated in the doorway, his peripheral vision taking in the beautifully set table. His nose twitched at the appetizing aromas that filled the room, but the main focus of his attention was his wife.

She had her back to him, unaware of his arrival as she stirred something on the stove. The *1812* Overture was on the stereo and she had the sound up so that she could hear it in the kitchen. Her free hand was waving time to the blasting cannons.

She was wearing a pair of dark slacks and a silky blue blouse that he had once said he liked. He felt his muscles tighten in a familiar surge of desire, followed by an equally familiar anger. Did she know how hard it was for him to stay away from her?

He should move into the guest room. At least then he wouldn't have to endure the torture of sleeping next to her. A thousand times he cursed his weakness. He had sworn again and again that he was not going to make love to her. But he had only to feel the softness of her body and smell the warm womanly scent of her and he could no more stop himself from being with her than an alcoholic could resist a drink.

But afterward he would lie there listening to her peaceful breathing as she slept, and he hated himself. He hated the part of him that was so weak that he could let himself be used. His hand would move to the bulge of her stomach and his heart would swell with a confusing tangle of pain and pleasure.

His child. She sheltered his baby inside her. How could he not love her? And then he would hear her telling him that she had used him to conceive that child and he wanted to rage at her. Part of him kept insisting that she must have lied, that she couldn't have used him like that, but he was always confronted by the undeniable fact of her pregnancy. He lost count of the nights he had lain beside her, eyes wide open and staring, until he saw the light of a new day fill the room.

Now he looked at her, consideringly. It was obvious that she had gone to quite a bit of trouble in her preparation for tonight. The question was, why?

Before he could speculate further, Holly turned and saw him. For a moment they looked at each other in silence. Mac noticed the carefully applied makeup that failed to conceal the faint tension in her eyes. Holly saw the lines of tiredness that bracketed his mouth, the wary look in his blue eyes and the tense line of his lower lip. Her heart sank. It definitely did not look like a good night to start a discussion about the future of their relationship.

But she had not spent all day gathering up her courage and determination to scrap her plans because he was not in a receptive mood. All through dinner she made every effort to coax him into conversation. Tonight he was more taciturn than usual, and she finally gave up and took comfort from the fact that he appeared to be enjoying his food. Maybe that old wives' tale was right after all and the way to a man's heart *was* through his stomach.

After the meal he helped her clear the table and load the dishwasher, still with a minimum of conversation. But when it looked as if he was going to try to escape to his study, she stopped him.

"Mac?" He hesitated in the doorway, his shoulders taut, and she was afraid that he was going to ignore her. But he turned slowly, his face completely expressionless, his eyes hooded. He didn't say anything, only looked at her. She was daunted for a moment but then a tingle of anger brushed aside her uncertainty. He had no reason to treat her like a pariah.

"I think we need to talk about some things," she told him firmly.

"Can't it wait?"

She shook her head, stifling the cowardly urge to say yes. "No, it can't wait. We've been putting it off for too long as it is."

He studied her in silence for a moment, gauging her determination, and then he shrugged and gestured toward the living room with one large hand. "After you."

Holly ignored the mild sarcasm in his tone and walked by him to settle herself into a soft chair. Mac sat down on the sofa opposite. Now that the moment was actually here, she felt surprisingly calm and she was proud of her even tone.

"I think you know as well as I do that we can't go on like this forever."

"What's wrong with the way we've been going?" he drawled.

She subdued the flash of irritation that his deliberate obtuseness brought. "I don't like living in an atmosphere that stops just short of outright hostility. You said that you were willing to work at making our marriage work. My idea of a working marriage doesn't include one partner who pretends there is no marriage.''

He sat silently, only the white knuckles of his clenched fist showing that he had even heard her.

''Why did you marry me, Mac, if you couldn't stand the sight of me?''

''It's not as simple as I thought it would be.''

She had to strain to hear his muttered words.

''Things that are worthwhile are often difficult.''

He said nothing and she could read nothing in his face. Frustrated, she took the bull by the horns.

''You haven't forgiven me for saying that I used you just to get pregnant, have you?'' That got more reaction than she was prepared for.

His lashes swept up and she shrank back in her chair at the rage that burned in his eyes. ''Did you expect me to forgive you for using me? Should I be flattered?'' His calm facade disappeared, and Holly realized that she'd struck a nerve. He came to his feet in a surge of power that expressed all the pent-up anger that burned inside.

Holly suppressed a shiver. Lord, he was big! He moved with such easy grace that it was only at a moment like this that she realized how intimidating his bulk could be. He bent down and put his hands on the arms of her chair, trapping her in its depths.

''Do you have any idea how it made me feel when you told me that?'' He spit the words out in a voice so low, it rasped out of his throat. ''I felt dirty. I hated you at that moment. I stood there listening to you and I felt as if something precious between us had been extinguished forever.'' He stared at her for a moment, and Holly bit her lip, her eyes wide and locked on his.

She flinched as he jerked away, standing with his back to her, one hand clasped at the back of his neck. ''I've never been so angry in my life.''

Holly had to clear her throat before she could get out any words in the supercharged silence that followed his rasped confession. She waited until he turned to face her before she replied.

''I lied to you about using you to get pregnant.'' His brows shot up in cynical disbelief, and she continued hurriedly. ''I was so angry when I found those files that I wanted to hurt you, and I grabbed at the first weapon I thought of.''

''An amazing coincidence that you should turn up pregnant,'' he murmured sarcastically. Holly felt her cheeks warm.

''I already knew I was pregnant but I didn't plan it, Mac. I swear I didn't.''

''Then why don't you tell me just how it happened, Holly? Explain to me how you came to be carrying my child when you told me that you were taking precautions against it.'' His voice was all the harsher because he wanted to believe her. No matter what ridiculous story she concocted, he wanted to believe it.

''It was a misunderstanding.''

''A misunderstanding?'' He gave a short bark of laughter. ''That's an interesting excuse. Did you misunderstand the principles of reproduction? Did you think it wasn't possible to get pregnant during that phase of the moon?''

''Stop it!'' Her voice shook, but the short command cut into his bitter words and he broke off. She didn't say anything more. She wasn't sure she could without bursting into tears. She'd had no idea how deep his bitterness went.

Mac ran his hand over his face, shaking his head dazedly as if waking from a bad dream. He looked at Holly, seeing the whiteness of her face and the blank pain in her dark eyes, and he sat down abruptly, resting his elbows on his knees and burying his face in his hands. A quivering silence fell over the room, a silence Holly was afraid to try to break.

''I'm sorry.'' He raised a ravaged face and repeated the words. ''I'm sorry. Attacking you isn't going to change anything. And you're right; we do need to talk. How was it a misunderstanding?''

Holly searched his face, seeing the weariness of defeat there but seeing also an openness that hadn't been there before. She began hesitantly, praying that he would listen.

''That first night we made love, when you asked me if it was safe, I didn't really hear you. I was...thinking of other things.'' A delicate flush rose in her cheeks as she remembered just what she had been thinking of, but she plowed on. ''I didn't realize until the next morning what you meant. I know that sounds ridiculous, but it's the truth.''

Mac shook his head, his eyes skimming her earnest features. ''It's almost ridiculous enough to believe,'' he admitted tiredly. ''But if I accept that, it still doesn't explain why you didn't come to me right away to tell me what had happened. I had a right to know, Holly.''

Her flush deepened and her eyes dropped to where her fingers plucked restlessly at the arm of her chair. ''I didn't tell you because I felt like an idiot. It seemed like such a stupid thing to have done. And it wasn't just that. I've always wanted children, Mac. I can't remember a time when I didn't want them, and I was afraid that maybe it hadn't been a misunderstanding,'' she admitted in a whisper. ''I was afraid I'd done it deliberately. And I have to be honest and tell you that I can't regret that I am pregnant. I regret the way it happened, but I love having your child inside me.''

Her eyes swept up to meet his, shimmering with tears but open and honest, almost black with the intensity of her need to make him understand. ''I never meant for you to be hurt and I wish I'd never said the things I did, but I can't be sorry I'm carrying your baby.''

''I want to believe you, Holly.'' She was silent, hardly daring to breathe. ''You know what I can't quite deal with? You weren't going to tell me that you were pregnant. Whether you deliberately got pregnant or not, if I hadn't found out about it myself, I'd never have known.''

She blinked beneath the intensity of his eyes and groped frantically for something to say, something to take the hurt out of his face. She came up empty. She could not lie and say that she had planned to tell him. It was lies that had gotten them into this mess.

She shrugged unhappily. ''I should have told you. I know that. But I was so hurt and angry, and then when the anger left, I just couldn't get up the courage to contact you.''

Mac shook his head, his expression resigned. He had wanted to hear her say that she had planned to tell him all along. But she wouldn't lie about it.

"Maybe another man wouldn't have reacted so violently to that particular lie." Her eyes swept to his face, surprised to see weary resignation there. She knew that whatever he was about to tell her was something he didn't like to remember. "You touched a raw place that I guess has never really healed." His eyes focused on the carpet between his boots.

"I went to college at UCLA on a football scholarship and I joined the marines right after I graduated. I would have been caught in the draft anyway, so I preferred to enlist and at least retain the illusion of making a free choice. That was right at the height of the war and enlisting was pretty well tantamount to abdicating from your generation, but it seemed the smartest thing to do at the time.

"While I was in college I fell in love with Diane. She came from a very wealthy family and she was very beautiful. I didn't really fit in with her crowd. Both my parents were dead and they'd never been upper-class when they were alive.

"We had absolutely nothing in common, so we fell madly in love. I thought she was utterly perfect. I knew her parents wouldn't approve, but she said that I meant more to her than anything else."

He leaned back in his chair, his eyes focused on distant memories. Holly wasn't sure if he was even aware of her anymore. "Diane didn't want me to join the marines but when I insisted, she seemed to accept it. We vowed undying love for each other and she promised to marry me when I came home on leave. Unfortunately, I had hardly completed basic training when they were shipping my unit off to 'Nam. I barely had time to write and tell Diane what was happening.

"A few weeks after I went over, I got a letter from her. She was pregnant and I had to come home immediately to marry her. Her family was old money, very conservative, and Diane couldn't take the humiliation of being an unwed mother.

"I couldn't get home, so I wrote to her and sent her money. I had an aunt living in Oregon and I told Diane to go there and Aunt Maggie would take care of her until I could get home."

He paused, lost in thought, his mouth twisted in a bitter smile.

Holly said nothing, afraid to break his unusually revealing mood by reminding him that she was there.

"It was almost ten months before I made it home. I never got another letter from Diane. Aunt Maggie wrote and said that Diane had gotten in touch and told her that she was going to stay with her family in California but she never answered any of the letters I sent there.

"I flew to L.A. as soon as I hit the States and I went to her parents' home. At first they refused to tell me anything, but finally her mother told me that Diane no longer lived with them and gave me her address. I knew they had never approved of me. Nobody mentioned a baby and I thought maybe they had set her up in an apartment somewhere so that none of their friends would know about the baby.

"I went to the address. It was a beautiful home in Palos Verdes. I can still remember the smell of the roses that lined the walk. I was almost frantic to see Diane and the baby. It seemed incredible to think that I had a child and I didn't even know whether it was a boy or a girl.

"I hadn't expected Diane to fall into my arms. I knew she would be upset that she'd gone through so much alone, but I thought we could work everything out. After all, we loved each other. What I wasn't expecting was the absolute horror on her face when she saw me. It wasn't the home of a relative or friend. It was her home, hers and her husband's. She had been married for almost two months."

He didn't hear Holly's gasp of horror. "He was out of town on business, which is probably why her parents felt it was safe to let me know where she was. It was apparently their idea of an amusing way to let me find out that she was married. Of course, they didn't know about the baby or they might have been more concerned about my reaction.

"She explained it all to me very carefully. Apparently she had decided that she didn't want to marry someone who didn't share her background, but the baby was a real complication. Her parents would never have forgiven her, so she took the money I sent her and went to stay with a cousin in New York. Abortions were still difficult to get, so she had the baby without telling anyone and then came home to L.A. and married the son of one of her father's partners.''

He stopped talking and after a while Holly dared to prod him softly. ''What about the baby?''

His hands tightened into fists but his voice remained flat and unemotional. ''It was a healthy baby boy. She never saw him before she gave him up for adoption. I have a son who's almost thirteen years old and I wouldn't even know him if I saw him on the street.''

''Did you...did you try to find him, maybe fight the adoption?'' She hesitated to ask the question, frightened of intruding on his private grief.

''And offer him what?'' he asked bitterly. ''I was on my way back to Asia and had no idea if I'd come back in a box next time. No family. It was one thing to ask Aunt Maggie to let Diane stay with her, but I couldn't ask an old lady to take care of an infant. I didn't have any money or any prospects of earning any. It seemed best for the boy just to leave things as they were. But then I sometimes wonder if I didn't con myself into thinking that was best for him because I didn't want the responsibility.

''Oh, hell, what a bloody mess!''

Tears flooded her eyes at the raw agony in that final sentence. What had she done? She could not have found a more potent weapon with which to hurt him.

There was really nothing left to be said, she realized dully. She got to her feet and looked down at his bowed head. She ached to comfort him, to hold him and make the pain go away, but she was the last person who could do that.

''I...I think I'll go to bed,'' she said vaguely, more to define her next step for herself than to inform him.

There was no reaction from Mac. With a small, helpless gesture of one hand, she turned and left the room, leaving him alone with his bitter memories.

HOLLY WAS NOT SURPRISED to wake alone the next morning. After the trauma of the night before, the real surprise would have been if he *had* slept with her.

She felt lethargic as she went about her morning routine and avoided looking in the mirror until she was dressed. The reflection there made her wish she had avoided it then. She looked every one of her twenty-eight years. In fact, she looked—and felt—a few years older. There were violet shadows under her eyes and her mouth had a pinched look that depressed her. She experimented with a few smiles and then decided that the grimaces she was producing looked even worse than the original expression.

As she walked down the hall that led from the bedrooms to the main living area, she became aware of the aroma of brewing coffee. She glanced at her watch. It was almost ten o'clock, and even on Sundays, Mac was usually gone by then. On Sundays, he played racquetball.

She stopped in the entrance to the dining room. Mac's huge frame was sprawled carelessly in the big oak rocker that stood in one corner of the room. That rocker had been a present from Ken, who said that all pregnant women liked to rock and all babies should have a rocker. The fact that the rocker was miles too big for Holly's small frame and that the motion made her seasick was irrelevant beside the meaning of the gesture. She treasured it for the friendship it represented.

Mac's eyes were closed, the lines of exhaustion etched in his face a mute testament to his lack of sleep. He was wearing the same clothes he had worn the night before, the jeans rumpled and the light cotton shirt open down the front, the fabric wrinkled and creased. He had removed his boots and one stockinged foot was draped carelessly over the arm of the rocker. A mug of coffee was clutched in one hand, held against the bare skin of his stomach as if he were cradling it to him for warmth. He looked so alone and vulnerable that she had to blink back tears as she looked at him.

Holly crossed the room quietly and peeked into the cup. It was half full of tepid liquid, and if he twitched in his sleep, it was going to spill all over him. She grasped the cup and eased it gently out of his hand, trying not to jar him. But even that slight movement was enough to penetrate his uneasy sleep, and his eyes opened as she pulled the cup away.

He blinked at her sleepily for a moment as if trying to place where he was, and then he sat up straight, groaning as his twisted muscles fell back into place. She stepped back, uncertain of the next move. Should she just act as if last night had never happened?

While she was trying to make up her mind, he got to his feet and arched his back in a bone-popping stretch. "Hell of a stupid place to fall asleep," he muttered. "I think I've done permanent damage to my back."

His eyes moved to where she stood, their expression unreadable beneath the fringe of his lashes. "We didn't really finish talking last night. I need to go take a shower. Why don't you have a cup of tea or something and we'll talk as soon as I get cleaned up." He reached out to touch her lightly on the cheek. "We'll work it out."

She watched him leave the room before turning to the sink to dump the cold coffee out of his cup, rinsing and drying it with automatic movements. That last sentence sounded positive.

When Mac came back into the room twenty minutes later, Holly was sitting at the table, a cup of tea in front of her and fresh coffee made for him. She flicked quick glances at him while he poured himself a cup of the rich dark liquid. He still looked tired but fresh jeans, a clean shirt and a shave had made a vast improvement. He hadn't bothered with shoes or socks, and he looked endearingly boyish with his feet bare and his dark hair still damp from the shower.

She dropped her gaze back to her cup as he pulled out the chair across from her and sat down. It was left to Mac to break the uneasy silence.

"I did a lot of thinking last night after you went to bed." He took a quick swallow of coffee, giving himself a moment to organize his thoughts. "You were right. I did say that I was willing to do my best to make this marriage work, and I haven't done that." He shrugged. "Whatever happened between us before is in the past, and we've got to put it behind us and think about the future."

His eyes swept up with a suddenness that surprised her. She had no time to drop her gaze, and once his eyes caught hers, she could not look away.

"I do want us to have a future together. Maybe I've been

punishing you for what happened with Diane without even realizing it. But that's over and done with and long past changing. I'd like to try starting over, if you're willing. This time without bitterness. I may not be the best husband material but I'm trainable.''

He gave her a lopsided grin that tugged at her emotions, but she pushed aside the impulse to agree to anything he asked. This wasn't just her future they were discussing. It was her baby's future.

Her eyes dropped to her teacup again and she swirled the amber liquid around, noticing with absent attention the patterns formed by the bits of tea in the bottom of the cup. It was a pity she didn't read tea leaves, she thought. It would be nice to be able to put her faith in the pattern of the leaves and let them make her decision. But she didn't read tea leaves and there was no one who could make this choice for her.

The choice was a very simple one. She could stay with Mac and hope that he really could put aside the past and learn to love and trust her, or she could leave him and make a life for herself and her child apart from him.

Her mouth twisted in a rueful smile. So much for weighing all her options. There really was no choice. How could she leave him as long as there was a chance they could make it work? She looked across the table into his eyes and her decision was reinforced by his obvious anxiety. He really wanted her to stay. She smiled at him, her expression making it clear that she was more than willing to meet him halfway.

"I'd like for us to have a future together, too." She held her hand across the table and it was engulfed by his much larger palm. Her heart swelled on an upsurge of hope.

Chapter Thirteen

The phone rang just as she was throwing the last of the clothes in the dryer. Holly muttered irritably as she started the machine. Why was it that phones never rang when you were standing right next to them? They always waited until you were halfway across the house before going off.

She hurried out of the utility porch and across the living room. Why was she hurrying? It was probably going to be someone calling to sell her newspapers or tickets to a charity ball, or someone who wanted donations left on the front porch. Of course, if she didn't hurry, it would probably be a call to tell her that she'd won a million dollars in the *Reader's Digest* sweepstakes. And one way or another, she always hated to miss a call because then she had to wonder who it had been.

She snatched the receiver up at the end of the fifth ring. "Hello?" She half expected to get a dial tone, but there was still someone on the line.

"Holly? This is your long-lost and forgotten brother."

"James!" Unconsciously she lowered her voice and glanced around as if expecting agents to pop out of the fireplace. But there was no one there. Mac wasn't even home, since Ken had needed his support.

"James, where are you?"

"I'm in Europe. Where did you think I was, Outer Mongolia? That would explain why I found out from Mom and Dad that you were married. You didn't know how to get a letter to me."

Holly flushed guiltily. "I'm sorry. Things have been sort of confused lately. I would have written soon."

"Like maybe when I became an uncle. Mom tells me you're about to produce a grandchild—any minute now, from the way she talks."

"Not until January, actually. Did they seem upset or anything?"

"You mean because you're producing a husband and an heir almost simultaneously? Not really. You know how easygoing Dad is, and Mom is too thrilled about the baby to care. What I'd like to know is why I wasn't among those who received notice of your nuptials."

"I did call about a week after we got married, but you weren't there." Holly sat down at the breakfast bar and twisted the phone cord nervously.

"Have you ever heard of leaving a message?" She twisted the cord harder, hearing the hurt underlying his light tone.

"It didn't seem like the kind of news one left in a message."

"How about calling back? Or has your new husband forbidden you to use the phone more than once a month?"

How could she explain that she hadn't called again because she didn't know what to say. "I've just been so busy, James. I didn't realize how much time had gone by. I'm sorry I didn't call sooner."

"I suppose absentmindedness is something to be expected from newlyweds. Mom and Dad didn't seem to know much about the new member of the family. I take it I haven't met him?"

"No. Mac hasn't met anyone in the family yet. Mom and Dad are coming out for Thanksgiving. I don't suppose there's any chance that you could make it home then?" Even as she said the words, she was praying he would say no. What if he returned to the States to meet her new husband and was arrested?

"Sorry. There's no way." Holly released her breath in a silent rush of relief.

"That's too bad." She managed to inject sincere regret into the words. "When do you think you'll be able to get home?"

"I'm not really sure. Probably not until spring."

"Not till after the baby's born, then."

"By the time I get to see him, he'll be past the red and wrinkled stage. I'm counting on it. That way I don't have to pretend to think that he looks terrific."

"I can see you're going to be a devoted uncle."

"You bet. Tell me all about Mac."

She swallowed hard. "What do you want to know?"

"What does he do for a living?"

She could feel the color draining from her face as she searched for a way to answer him. "He works for the government." Was that her voice? She sounded so normal.

James laughed. "Doesn't everyone? What does he do?"

Her fingers tightened around the receiver until her knuckles ached. This was James, her brother. She had to tell him the truth. But then, what could she say to Mac? "Oh, I don't know. Paperwork of some kind," she said vaguely.

"No matter what you do for the government, you end up doing paperwork," James said with disgust. He paused, and she could hear the change in his tone when he continued. "Listen, you remember what we talked about when you called from Michigan?"

"I remember." Holly was surprised to hear her own voice. Her throat felt as if it had closed tight.

"Some things have happened that I don't like. My phone was tapped, for one thing. Don't worry; it isn't anymore. But I don't think it was tapped as part of a general precautionary measure."

"James, are you...are you in trouble?"

"Aren't I always in trouble?"

Her hand knotted around the receiver until the plastic creaked in protest. "I'm serious. Are you doing something you shouldn't?"

She had hoped—prayed—for a quick denial, and her heart seemed to stop as the pause between them lengthened.

"I think that would depend on how you looked at things," he finally answered. "I wanted to let you know that I may be dropping out of sight for a while."

"James! What are you involved in?"

"Don't get upset, Holly. I just wanted to let you know so you wouldn't worry if you didn't hear from me for a while. I told the parents that I might be out of touch and let them think it was something to do with my job—which, in a way, I suppose it is.'' He gave an odd laugh.

''Jamey.'' In her distress she fell back on the old childhood name. ''Please don't do anything stupid.''

''Hey, when have I ever done stupid things? Listen, this call is going to cost me a fortune. Don't worry about me. I know what I'm doing. Tell your new husband 'welcome to the family' for me, and I'll be in touch as soon as I can. I love you, Half-pint.''

''I love you, too.'' But the line was already dead.

She set the receiver back on the base very slowly, staring at it as if seeking answers to all her questions from it. She should have told James about Mac. But what about her loyalty to Mac? Who had first call on her loyalties, her brother or her husband?

Tears burned at the back of her eyes. Why did everything have to get so complicated? Her head fell onto her crossed arms and she let the tears fall. She was so tired of making choices and decisions. She didn't want to have to worry about what or who was right or wrong.

''Holly!'' She was so lost in emotion that she hadn't heard the front door open. She didn't realize that she was no longer alone until Mac spoke her name. His hands came down on her shoulders and she stumbled off the stool and into his arms.

''What's the matter?'' His arms closed around her automatically, holding her against his chest, letting her tears soak his shirt. ''Are you hurt?'' He bent his head over her, seeking some sign of injury. Finding none, he allowed some of the tension to ease out of his muscles.

He cradled her closer. ''Holly? What's wrong?'' She shook her head, mumbling incoherently into his shirt. He gave up trying to get an answer out of her and lifted her into his arms, carrying her to the sofa and sitting down with her across his lap. He let her cry herself out and then handed her a fistful of tissues to mop up with.

Holly wiped her swollen eyes and blew her nose. ''I'm sorry.'' Her eyes shifted around the room, looking anywhere but at the questioning blue of his gaze. ''I don't know what got into me.''

"Did something happen to upset you?" His long fingers brushed a tangled curl off her forehead.

"I...I..." Her eyes fell on the television. "I just watched a sad movie."

His brows rose slightly as he looked from her to the silent television set. "Must have been a doozy." If he wondered why she'd been crying in the dining room over a sad movie that she had watched in the living room, he didn't ask, allowing her that privacy. His thumb brushed across her cheek, wiping away the dampness left by her tears.

Holly closed her eyes, feeling miserably guilty. She hadn't told James about Mac and now she hadn't told Mac about the call. She was caught between them, unable to make a final decision, not being honest with either of them.

"I must look awful," she mumbled, trying to turn her face away.

"You look beautiful." His fingers caught her chin and turned her face back to his.

"What? With my eyes all swollen and a belly to match I'm sure I look devastating."

"You're gorgeous." And looking into his eyes, she could almost believe it. Her fingers closed around his wrist, holding his hand pressed to her face.

"Am I?" she asked wistfully. "You don't think I look like a watermelon?"

A slow smile lifted his dark mustache. "I think you're the prettiest watermelon I've ever seen." His lips closed over hers, swallowing her laughing protest.

THE NEXT AFTERNOON Holly sank back onto the sofa with a sigh of relief. Barely two more months and she'd be able to turn her class over to another teacher and relax. She was going to miss her students and her job, but the Christmas break was the perfect time to turn things over to someone else.

She sipped a cup of tea and looked out the patio doors to where the first rain of the season was coming down in depressingly heavy sheets. But she didn't feel depressed. She was at home and dry. Mac had put a stew in the Crockpot that morning and an appetizing smell was wafting through the house.

The baby moved strongly and Holly laid her hand lightly over the bulge of her belly, a contented smile curving her mouth. What more could she ask for? A home, a job she loved, a baby on the way and a husband. She closed her eyes and leaned her head against the back of the sofa. Mac hadn't said he loved her yet, but it was only a matter of time.

Life hadn't been perfect in the weeks since he'd told her about the son he had lost. There were still adjustments to be made and some rough spots to smooth over but perhaps no more than could be expected in any new marriage. Mac had been true to his word. He was really working at their marriage. The old hurts hadn't disappeared overnight but they were on their way out.

The front door slammed and she opened her eyes slowly, contentment making her drowsy. The contentment vanished as Mac came into the room on a wave of dark emotion. She sat up straight, bracing herself as she took in the hooked line of his brows and the tightness of his lower lip. He shrugged out of his wet jacket and ran his fingers through his damp hair.

"What's wrong? Has something happened that I should know about?" Her worries ran from some tragedy befalling Ken to her brother's having been convicted of attempted assassination.

"No. Something happened that *I* should know about. Why didn't you tell me that your brother had called?"

She gasped, her fingers tightening around her teacup as she stared at him. "How did you find out?"

"The phone is tapped."

Her eyes widened, and indignation began to edge aside guilt. "Do you mean you've been listening to every call I've made?"

He gestured impatiently with one hand. "Of course not. I'm not on this case anymore."

"You mean some total stranger is listening in on my private conversations? That's even worse!"

Mac thrust his hands deep in his pockets and scowled down at her. "Nobody is listening in on your conversations. The only thing we're interested in is what your brother has to say to you."

"So you only eavesdrop when I talk to James? Is that supposed to make me feel better?"

"Holly—" he ground her name out with hard-won patience "—we're investigating your brother. Naturally we're interested in what he has to say."

"Why didn't you tell me that the phone was bugged? This is my home. I have a right to know when I'm being spied on in my own home."

"To tell the truth, I assumed you must have guessed."

"Well, I hadn't guessed and I don't like it."

"*I* don't like the fact that you didn't tell me that he'd called," Mac snapped angrily. "Is that why you were crying yesterday when I got home? I knew it didn't have anything to do with an old movie."

"As a matter of fact, yes. Not that it's any of your business." She set her teacup down with a thump and started to struggle up off the sofa. Mac crossed the short distance between them and reached out a hand to help her, but Holly jerked her arm away with a glare and got up by herself. He raised his hand defensively and backed a step away.

"Even though I'm not on the case officially, I think it's my business when you lie to me." He looked at her angry expression and sighed, the anger draining out of him. "Why didn't you tell me why you were crying?"

"Would you have run straight to your superiors with what I told you, even if it was something that I told you in the privacy of our home?"

He ran his fingers through his hair, ruffling the still-damp curls. "I don't know. It's my job and yet... Oh, hell, what a mess!"

"You feel torn in two directions, between me and your job. Imagine how I feel, Mac. You're investigating *my brother*. I've managed to come to terms with your job but I'll be damned if I'm going to help you hang James!"

"I've already told you we're not trying to hang him! We're trying to find out the truth."

"Well, you can find it without my help. I didn't tell James about you, but I won't discuss him with you, either. I owe him that much."

"You're right. I have no right to expect you to help actively with the investigation. But, Holly, please, next time you hear from him, tell me about it. I won't go to the agency with it," he added quickly. "But I'd rather find out about it from you. Please."

Holly studied his face and then slowly nodded. "All right. If I hear from him again, I'll tell you."

"Thank you." His hand came out, and she allowed him to grasp her fingers and pull her close. She let her forehead come to rest on his chest as his arms encircled her. Life was so miserably complicated and she was so tired of worrying.

"Everything will work out okay." He whispered the promise into the silky darkness of her hair and, for a little while, Holly allowed herself to believe it.

THAT CONFRONTATION MARKED a new change in their relationship. It was as if they'd established a new level of trust. Mac was more open with her and willing to discuss his work a little more. He hated being tied to a desk all day, but Holly hoped that he wouldn't get another assignment. As long as he was tied to a desk, she didn't have to sweat out every moment that he was away from her, wondering if he was in danger.

November flew by. Before she had a chance to worry about the holiday, Thanksgiving was upon them and her parents came to visit for the long weekend. If Holly worried about how her parents might react to Mac, she needn't have. Her father, diplomat that he was, would probably have pretended to like Ivan the Terrible if that was who his daughter wanted. But he didn't have to pretend with Mac. The two men slipped into an easy relationship that showed signs of developing into true friendship, given time.

Holly's mother was instantly smitten by her son-in-law's slow smile and quiet courtesy. She made no secret of the fact that in her opinion Holly had made a wonderful choice. The coming grandchild simply made everything perfect as far as she was concerned.

Holly wondered how they would feel about Mac if they knew that he could be instrumental in destroying James's career, but she kept the question to herself. She hadn't heard from her brother since he called to tell her that he might be dropping out of sight, which hadn't been that long ago. She could only pray that whatever he was involved in was not going to get him killed.

She enjoyed the Thanksgiving holiday. The only blot on the general good cheer was the continued hostility between Maryann and Ken. The two combatants joined in the spirit of thankfulness, just as long as they didn't have to speak to each other. When they did speak, it was with acid-tongued politeness on Maryann's part and exaggerated patience on Ken's. Holly washed her hands of the whole problem, refusing to worry about it. If they were bound and determined to dislike each other, it wasn't her problem.

Her parents left on Sunday morning, and that afternoon Holly and Mac went to the opening of a new art gallery. The owner was an old friend of Holly's family and she had promised her father that she would make an appearance at the opening since he and her mother couldn't stay long enough to be there.

Holly had purchased a new maternity gown especially for the occasion and the admiration in Mac's eyes told her that the money hadn't been wasted. The amber silk cast a warm glow over her complexion and contrasted richly with her dark hair. Standing in one corner of the gallery with Mac's large presence beside her, she watched the other guests swirl through the open spaces of the gallery.

Mac kept one hand against the small of her back, a warm, comforting weight that made her feel cared for and protected. She had already said hello to her father's old friend, so they really could have left at any time. But it was pleasant to linger and watch the crowd.

Mac glanced around the room uneasily. The back of his neck itched and it was a sign he had learned to trust, a sign that something was not right. Yet there was nothing wrong that he could see. This was not one of the galleries suspected of dealing in stolen art treasures. The reputation of the man who owned it was as clean as the proverbial whistle. But the back of Mac's neck still itched.

He sipped his champagne, letting his eyes scan the room, seeking the source of the niggling feeling. He froze, his gaze flickering slightly, his fingers tightening on the fragile stem of the champagne flute. Of all the lousy luck! Across the room, standing in front of a free-form sculpture that bore a vague resemblance to an anteater, was Ken...or more appropriately, Reginald C. Naveroff.

The crowd thinned between them, and Ken saw Mac at almost the same instant. His eyes widened slightly and then skimmed over Mac without pausing. Mac set down his champagne glass and turned to Holly. Just by being here they were compromising Ken's cover. If someone should recognize Mac as Ken's financial consultant, things could only get more dangerous.

"Let's get out of here." But it was already too late. Holly's eyes skimmed past his shoulder and widened in surprise.

"Oh, look. There's Ken." She caught her breath on a little gasp of surprise when Mac's fingers captured her hand before she could wave at the other man.

"No, it's not."

"Yes, it is." Her bewildered laugh cut off when she met the intensity of his look.

"That is not Ken." Her dark eyes flickered from him to the other man and then back to her husband. "Let's go home now."

Holly nodded, finally grasping what he was telling her. She allowed him to find her coat and shepherd her through saying farewell to her friend. Not once did her eyes stray in Ken's direction, though she felt as if she were telegraphing her awareness of him for the whole room to see.

They were halfway home before she spoke. "Does this have something to do with my brother?"

Mac swore mildly as he braked to avoid a car cutting into the lane ahead of them. "Yes."

"I want to know what James is suspected of doing, Mac. I think I have a right to know that much. I've been patient and not asked too many questions, just like a good little girl, but now I want to know."

He was silent for so long that she had time to wonder what she would do if he refused to tell her anything. Since she couldn't come up with a firm plan, she was grateful when he spoke.

"During World War II, a lot of the great art treasures in Europe disappeared. Some of them were hidden away and surfaced again after the war. Some of them were taken to Germany and were returned after the war. But there were quite a few masterpieces that never showed up again. Undoubtedly, some of these treasures were destroyed in the bombings, but every once in a while, somebody stumbles upon a cache of them in a forgotten attic or an abandoned cellar or a long-ignored secret passageway in one of the great old houses.

"Lately several things that had been missing for over forty years have been turning up in private collections, starting about the time your brother was sent to Europe."

"Is that all you have against him? The fact that he happened to go to Europe at the wrong time?"

"There's also his admitted interest in art. He has the knowledge to identify and evaluate great art works. And," he overrode her protest, "James has been acting a little odd. He disappears for several days at a time without explanation. Some of those disappearances coincide with known shipments into this country."

To his amazement, Holly began to laugh, not hysterical cackles but a deep chuckle of genuine amusement and relief. It was as if she knew something he didn't. He pulled the car into the driveway and shut the engine off, leaning his arm on the back of the seat as he turned to look at her.

"Want to share the joke?"

"Oh, Mac, if only you'd told me months ago what you were after him for, I could have saved you so much time and myself so much worry."

He raised his brows, studying her expression in the dim light of late afternoon as if trying to decipher her senseless words.

"I must be a little dense today. I don't get it."

"Of course you don't. That's because you don't know James. Yes, James loves art and he probably *could* identify the great masters. But James absolutely despises private collections." As his face remained blank, she continued. "He thinks that all art belongs to the people and that nobody has a right to keep it hidden for his own enjoyment. Don't you see, Mac? He would never, ever, be involved in anything that would put art treasures in the hands of private collectors. He's innocent!"

Despite his trained skepticism, Mac was impressed by Holly's words. It was obvious that she firmly believed what she was saying. If she had any doubts about her brother, they were gone now. Mac didn't feel quite as positive but he couldn't deny the words carried weight.

"Don't expect my employers to be quite as sure as you are, but I'll pass your opinions along."

But Holly found that it was no longer quite so important what Mac's superiors thought. In her own heart she knew that James was innocent, and the knowledge lifted a huge burden from her. Everything was going to be all right.

WHY IS IT that late night phone calls always herald disaster? Two days later, at three o'clock in the morning, their phone rang. Mac woke with the quickness provided by years of training and snatched up the phone. Holly rolled over in bed, feeling her heart start to thump with fright as she took in the grim expression on his face.

"All right. I'll be there in half an hour. Thanks for calling."

The terse words were less than enlightening, and Holly grabbed his forearm, her nails digging in. "What's wrong?"

"That was Maryann. They just brought Ken into the emergency room."

"Oh, my God!" She swung her feet off the bed, tossing off her nightgown as she moved. Mac was already stepping into a pair of jeans and grabbing a shirt as Holly struggled to unfold the maternity pants she had pulled out of a drawer.

"You don't have to go, Holly. Why don't you stay here and try to get some sleep? You've got school tomorrow." He was stuffing his wallet and keys into his pockets as he spoke.

"They'll just have to get a substitute." She grabbed for a loose sweater and pulled it over her head, tugging it impatiently over the bulge of her stomach before slipping into a pair of soft loafers.

"Holly." Mac caught her by the arms when she reached for her purse. "It's not going to be pretty."

The quietness of his tone made her go still. Wide brown eyes searched solemn blue. "What happened?" she whispered through a dry throat.

"He's been beaten—badly, from what Maryann said."

"Is he going to die?"

"I don't know. They were still working on him when she called, and she didn't know all the details yet. It might be better if you stayed here."

She swallowed hard. "I'm going with you. Ken is my friend and he doesn't have any family. He's going to need all the cheering on he can get. I can handle it."

Chapter Fourteen

But handling it was easier said than done. First came all the hours of waiting, endless hours when no one seemed to know what was happening. When Maryann's shift ended at four in the morning, she joined Mac and Holly in the waiting room but she couldn't tell them much more than they already knew. Ken had been beaten, but the extent of his injuries was not yet known.

The shaken tone of Maryann's voice caught Holly's ear, drawing her out of her concern for Ken. Looking at her friend, Holly was surprised to see that her face had paled until the dusting of freckles stood out like blotches across her cheeks.

"Are you all right?" She kept her voice low.

"Of course I'm all right. I'm a nurse, remember? I see lots of cases come through that are worse than this." But her hand was shaking so badly that she almost spilled her coffee when she tried to lift it to her mouth.

Holly reached out to steady the plastic cup while the other woman took a drink. She glanced across the room at Mac, who sat slumped on a hard chair; only the restless clenching and relaxing of his fist betrayed his inner disturbance.

Maryann rubbed her fingers tiredly across her forehead. "I wish I smoked. I'd kill for a cigarette right about now."

"Is there something you're not telling us? Is Ken in worse shape than we thought?" Holly kept her voice low.

"I don't see how he could be much worse. When they brought him in, I thought he was dead. There was so much blood, and he wasn't moving." Her voice began to shake and she ran her hands up and down her arms as if to ward off a chill, her eyes blank with remembered fright. "I couldn't even find a pulse at first. There was blood everywhere, so much blood."

"Maryann?" Holly reached out and put her hands tentatively on the other woman's shoulders. "Are you all right?"

Maryann blinked and her shadowed eyes focused on Holly. Tears welled up and began to trickle down her pallid cheeks. "It was horrible, Holly. I could almost feel him dying under my hands. I've seen people die but never someone I knew. And there was all that blood. I had it on my uniform. It was so awful." The words ended in a choked whisper as Holly pulled her close. With a sob Maryann put her head on her friend's shoulder and began to cry quietly.

Holly blinked back her own tears and held Maryann, patting her awkwardly on the back and whispering vague reassurances. Her eyes met Mac's and she shook her head in answer to his questioning gaze. There was nothing he could do right now, nothing that any of them could do except wait.

Fortunately, they didn't have to wait much longer. When the doctor came into the waiting room, Mac stood up immediately, balancing lightly on the balls of his feet as if ready to take a blow. Holly and Maryann were frozen, hardly daring to breathe.

"Are you people waiting for news of Mr. Richardson?"

"How is he?" Mac's voice was even huskier than usual, his eyes brilliant blue points of life in his face, his skin pale under the layer of tan.

"Are you a relative?" The doctor was a short, stocky man in his fifties, and he wasn't intimidated in the least by Mac's looming presence.

"He doesn't have any relatives. I'm his partner."

"Well, then, I suppose I can tell you how he's doing. He had some internal bleeding, several cracked or broken ribs, a couple of nasty head wounds, three broken fingers and a broken leg. We've repaired the internal damage, stitched his head back together, splinted the fingers and we're putting a cast on the leg. All in all, he looks like hell, but he should survive."

"When can I see him?"

"Not until tomorrow I'm afraid. I'd like to keep him quiet for the next twenty-four hours or so."

"Doctor, I need to see him as soon as possible. I'm an agent of the federal government and Ken was working on a case. This beating was probably connected to what we were working on. For his own protection, as well as that of other agents, we need to find out what he remembers."

The doctor tugged thoughtfully on one bushy eyebrow, his eyes shrewd as they looked at Mac. "I'll tell you what, you show me some proof that you are who you say you are and I'll let you see Mr. Richardson as soon as he regains consciousness." He studied the badge Mac held out and then nodded. "All right, I'll see that you're informed as soon as he's conscious."

"Thank you, doctor. I'm afraid I'm going to have to call in some security. We'll want to station someone outside his room."

The gray brows lowered. "Just see that no one interferes with hospital routine." He turned on one worn heel and left.

Though Mac got in to see Ken that afternoon, Holly was not allowed to visit until the next day. And then she wasn't sure she was grateful for the privilege. Nothing had prepared her for his battered appearance. She stopped beside the bed, grateful for the strong support of Mac's hand at her waist.

Ken opened his eyes—or, rather, he opened one eye. The other one was swollen completely shut. And the one that did open was surrounded by deep blue bruises. There was hardly an inch of visible flesh that wasn't bruised.

His mouth twisted in a painful smile. "Hello, Lady. Sorry I can't offer you my seat."

She swallowed hard and forced back the stinging tears that threatened. If her smile was shaky, she hoped he was too doped up to notice. "Hi, yourself. How are you feeling, or shouldn't I ask?"

"You shouldn't ask. I feel as if I had an argument with a steamroller and lost. They tell me I'll survive, though."

"Mac went over to your apartment and packed up some of your stuff and cleaned out the food. We're fixing up the spare room for you. The doctor says you should be able to come home by the end of the week." She tried to keep her doubts out of her voice. Looking at Ken's battered figure, it was hard to believe that he'd be able to be moved in anything less than six months.

"Thanks, Lady." His good eye dropped to the bulge of her stomach. "How's the little creature doing?"

"Fine. The doctor says I'm healthy as a horse."

"I'll be up and around by the time it's due to arrive. Mac will probably panic and somebody's going to have to stay calm enough to rush you to the hospital."

"I'm counting on it. Listen, I'm not supposed to stay too long, but I'll be back tomorrow. Maryann is going to keep an eye on you and make sure they treat you well."

Ken tried to grimace and then groaned as he tugged at the stitches along his cheek. "If it's left up to her to see that I'm okay, I'm doomed for sure."

She managed a tremulous smile and turned away. Mac said softly, "I need to talk to Ken for a minute. Are you okay?" She nodded blindly in answer to his question and left before he could pursue it further. His worried eyes followed her until the door shut. When he turned back to Ken, he found the other man had also watched her leave.

"She's pretty shook up."

Mac nodded. "I know. She's been really worried about you."

"Nice to have friends." His eye closed for a moment, revealing his weariness. "What did you need to talk to me about?"

"I just wanted to go over some of the things you told me yesterday. Daniels asked me to confirm everything. You were pretty groggy."

"I wasn't that far out. They brought in another shipment right under our noses, Mac. It came in sometime last week."

"I know. We just got word of it from the other end. What brought this on?" He gestured silently at Ken's bandaged condition.

Ken started to shake his head and then stopped at the warning twinge of pain. "I don't know for sure. I do know that the goons who jumped me didn't know who I was. From what I could piece together, they were from a rival group that also feels they have a claim to the art. I was seen snooping around one of their warehouses and they were teaching me a lesson. But they didn't know I was a fed.''

"Just as well."

"Damn right. If they'd known, you'd be talking to my corpse right now. This was meant as a warning. Too bad they didn't just write a letter."

Mac saw the exhaustion in his partner's face and brought the conversation to a close. "The chief is sending someone to take down your report." Ken groaned, and Mac gave him a sympathetic grin. "Paperwork must be done, come hell or high water, you know. I'll be back tomorrow. Don't drive the nurses too crazy."

Mac walked down the hall to the waiting room, his brows drawn together. Ken was lucky to be alive. Next time he might not be so lucky. Next time it might not be Ken. He shook the thought away. It didn't do any good to anticipate trouble.

Holly was sitting on the edge of a chair in the waiting room, her eyes straight ahead, their expression blank. "Holly?" She didn't acknowledge him, and he repeated her name more urgently, crossing the room and dropping to one knee in front of her. "Holly? What's wrong?"

Her eyes refocused slowly until she was looking at him. "I want to go home."

"Of course, I'll take you home." He spoke soothingly, as if talking to someone who was mentally disturbed. She didn't say another word on the drive home. She sat silently staring out at the passing streets, her skin pale, her face expressionless.

Mac came around to her side of the car and helped her out, keeping his arm around her as they entered the house. Her skin felt cold and clammy, and he wondered if he'd done the wrong thing by bringing her home. If she was ill, she needed a doctor.

She began to shake as he led her into the bedroom. "I'm going to be sick," she muttered tightly.

And sick she was, violently and thoroughly. Mac held her head until her stomach had emptied itself. He murmured soft reassurances as he stroked her hair back from her hot forehead. Holly leaned against him weakly as she rinsed her mouth and he dabbed at her flushed face with a damp cloth. When it was clear that she wasn't going to be sick again, he lifted her in his arms and carried her into the bedroom.

"I'm going to call the doctor." Holly grabbed his arm as he reached for the phone.

"I don't need a doctor. I just need you to hold me."

"Honey, you've been sick. And your hands feel like ice. There's something wrong." In her dazed condition she didn't even notice the endearment that would have meant so much to her at another time.

"I don't want a doctor. I just want you to hold me."

"All right. It's all right." He sat on the edge of the bed and drew her into his arms, cradling her while she shivered convulsively.

"It could have been you. I kept thinking that it could have been you."

Mac laid his cheek against the top of her head. "Hush. It's all right. Ken is going to be fine and I'm fine. Everything is going to work out. Don't cry, baby."

He rocked her gently, holding her until the shivering and the soft sobbing ebbed to an occasional shaken breath. He eased her back down onto the pillows. If Holly could have seen his face at that moment, all her doubts would have been put to rest.

But her lashes formed dark crescents against her cheeks and she didn't stir while he loosened her clothing and covered her with a light blanket. He stood beside the bed for a long time, deep lines of tension bracketing his mouth.

IT WAS A SOURCE of constant amazement to Holly how quickly things return to normal after a crisis. A week after Ken's beating, she saw the last of her small students off for the weekend and stood looking around the empty classroom. One hand rubbed absently at the slight ache in her lower back.

Only one more week, she thought as she straightened up the room. One more week and then Christmas break and then the baby. She patted her stomach. She was going to miss teaching, but having the baby was going to more than make up for any pangs of regret. Besides, nobody had said that she was giving up teaching forever. Mac had made it clear that it was her choice and he'd support whatever she decided to do.

Mac. Her mouth curved in a tender smile. There had been something different about him this past week—an extra touch of caring, a warmth that hadn't been there before. He was finally putting the past behind him. He might not be ready to say the words yet, but he loved her.

Ken was recovering nicely. He had settled into the spare room, and soon it felt as if he'd always been there. He still looked as if he'd been hit by a train, but Maryann assured her that the bruises and scars would fade in time. Holly's smile deepened. Maryann was spending quite a bit of time visiting Ken. She said it was just professional concern, but Holly knew for a fact that Ken had been released when he was because Maryann had told the doctor that she would keep an eye on him. Holly had a suspicion that her interest was more than professional.

As she stepped out of the building, she squinted to see through the pouring rain. They might not have a white Christmas but it sure looked as if it might be a wet one. Of course, there were still a few weeks left until the holiday, and in Southern California a few weeks could mean the difference between a downpour and a heat wave.

Mac's sedan pulled up to the low steps and Mac was beside her before she had gone more than three steps. His arm captured her waist, supporting her protectively as he saw her into the car. She shook her head in loving exasperation as she watched him circle around the hood.

"You know, I'm pregnant, not dying. You don't have to help me down stairs. You don't even have to pick me up at work. My stomach still fits behind the wheel."

"I worry about your driving in this kind of weather," he told her calmly, "and it doesn't do any harm to help you down stairs, does it?"

"I suppose not, but you're spoiling the image of the modern woman who can take on anything during pregnancy."

"I know you can take on anything. I just don't see any reason why you should have to when I'm there to help." He came to a halt at a red light and dazzled her with a smile, his teeth flashing white beneath the dark mustache. "Actually, I feel guilty. You have to do all the work, and I get to enjoy the rewards."

"I'll tell you what, just so it won't make you feel bad, I'll let you change all the diapers after he's here."

Mac winced, edging the car through a flooded intersection. "I was afraid you'd say something like that."

"Always trying to be fair."

"Have you heard from James?" The question was so far away from what they had been discussing that it took Holly a minute to sort the words out.

"I told you that I'd let you know if I heard from him." Her voice was tight, revealing her hurt.

Mac grimaced. "I didn't mean it to sound like that. James has disappeared. I don't mean disappeared in an ominous way," he reassured her quickly. "He's just dropped out of sight. We've had people watching him, and two days ago he ditched his tail and hasn't been seen since. And it was pretty clear that he knew exactly what he was doing," he finished grimly.

"Do you think he's in trouble? He's not helping anybody steal art treasures, Mac. I know he isn't."

"You've almost managed to convince me. Whatever he was up to, he obviously didn't want to be tailed. It could be something as simple as a rendezvous with a woman. Maybe he wanted some privacy. I figured you would want to know what was happening."

"Thank you." She twisted her fingers restlessly. *Oh, Jamey, what are you up to? What have you gotten involved with?* she thought, shaking her head. James knew how to take care of himself. She'd have to trust in that. There was nothing else she could do.

THE FEW WEEKS LEFT before Christmas seemed to whirl by so quickly that Holly had the feeling she should grab hold of them and try to slow them down. That wasn't possible, so she threw herself into the festive spirit with enthusiasm. Her parents weren't going to be able to make it for the holidays. They were saving their next visit until after the baby was born. That left just Mac and Holly and Maryann and Ken, which suited Holly just fine. The four of them were beginning to seem like a family.

She was baking cookies one afternoon when Ken appeared in the kitchen. He clumped in on his crutches and leaned against the breakfast bar, watching her as she lifted a tray of buttery pressed cookies from the oven and slid another tray in.

"You realize, of course, that there's no way you're ever going to find enough people to eat all these cookies you've been baking." Holly was putting the oven-fresh cookies out on racks and he reached over to snitch one, juggling it back and forth between his palms until it cooled enough to pop in his mouth.

"At the rate you've been eating them, I don't have any worries at all."

"I do my best to help out in any way I can," he acknowledged humbly.

"Ha! You've got an appetite like an underfed anaconda. I don't know where you put it all. All I have to do is look at cookies and I gain weight."

"So I noticed." He eyed her bulging belly and Holly lifted the spatula threateningly. "You've got to remember that I'm an invalid. I need lots of nourishing food."

"Butter cookies are not nourishing food. If you're an invalid, you should be eating spinach and chicken broth."

He snitched another cookie. "The doctor says I should eat lots to keep up my strength."

"Funny, I don't remember Maryann mentioning that you were supposed to be eating like a pig."

He threw her a hurt look and withdrew to the other side of the breakfast bar, but not before he'd picked up two more cookies to sustain himself. Holly shook her head and went back to carefully pressing wreaths and Christmas trees onto a clean cookie sheet.

"Speaking of Maryann..." Ken's voice was casual, and Holly bit her lip to hide a smile. She wondered if they really thought they were keeping their feelings a secret.

"What about her?" She pressed out a row of plump angels.

"When we met you in Tijuana, you had gone down there after something of hers, hadn't you?"

"Her grandfather's watch. She had been dating a guy named Jason Nevin and he told her he knew someone who was a pro when it came to repairing old watches. She gave him the watch just a couple of days before they broke up. He went back East and she couldn't get the watch back. Then he called and said he'd meet her in Tijuana. He was pretty upset that she'd been the dump*er* instead of the dump*ee*, and I guess he figured he'd teach her a lesson by sending her into that bar." She sprinkled colored sugar crystals over the cookies.

"Did she ever get the watch back?"

"Nope. I heard through a mutual acquaintance that Jason moved back to L.A. He's living somewhere in West Hollywood. I told Maryann that she ought to go beat the watch out of him but she didn't want to see him again, even to get the watch back. I figure he either sold it or he kept it out of spite. That's the kind of weasel he was."

She opened the oven door and pulled out a sheet of delicately browned cookies and slid in the one she had just readied before looking at Ken. "Why do you ask?"

He shrugged and then winced as the movement pulled at his healing ribs. "No reason in particular. I just got to thinking about that first meeting with you, and I wasn't sure I remembered the details exactly right."

CHRISTMAS EVE DAWNED bright and clear, but the weather forecast promised rain by nightfall. Holly hoped the weather bureau was right. Snow wasn't possible, but rain would make a worthy substitute. Even without rain, the temperature was wonderfully chill. Mac was out of bed before she was awake, and when she came into the living room, she was greeted by the warm crackle of a small fire.

She inhaled deeply, taking in the rich scent of burning oak and the tangy smell of evergreen. She wandered over to the Christmas tree, lifting one delicate crocheted snowflake on her fingertip. The snowflakes had been Maryann's contribution to their first tree. Ken had provided some charming hand-carved reindeer. Mac and Holly had shopped for the rest of the traditional trimmings and she was very pleased with the results.

She rested her hands on her belly and smiled mistily. Their first Christmas together. Next year there would be a baby. Just a few more weeks and she would be able to hold her child in her arms. Would it be a boy or a girl?

"No fair shaking the packages." Mac's teasing words made her turn, her face still soft with anticipation. She had grown accustomed to his silent approach and she wasn't surprised to find him right behind her.

"I was just thinking about the baby. You know, it's funny but I've never even asked you whether you want a boy or a girl."

"I think it's a little late to change the order. I'll take whatever comes. Just as long as you and the baby are healthy."

"Just a few more weeks and we'll know, one way or the other." Her voice shook slightly, and Mac slipped his arms around her, drawing her close and resting his chin on the top of her head.

"Are you worried?"

"I don't know. It's kind of scary sometimes. What if I scream and make a fool of myself?"

"You could never make a fool of yourself. You're going to be too busy having the baby to think about it. I'm the one you should worry about. What if I faint on the delivery room floor? Think of how humiliating that would be."

Her soft giggle told him that she wasn't worried about that, and he smiled. "You're going to do just fine. I'll be right beside you all the time, and between the two of us and the doctor, we're going to deliver our baby."

She laid her palm against his chest and leaned back until she could look up into his eyes. Her teasing words died. His strong features were gentled by tenderness, the blue of his eyes a soft promise. "Mac, are you really, truly happy about the baby?" They weren't the words she had intended to say at all, and they tumbled out in a rush.

He bent to brush his lips gently over hers. "I'm really, truly happy about the baby."

"I never meant to hurt you." Her eyes were dark with sincerity.

"I know. That's over and done with, Holly. It's past."

"Is it? Sometimes I'm afraid it won't ever go away," she admitted wistfully.

"Holly, I—" But whatever he had been going to say was lost.

"Aha! I might have known I'd catch you two by the Christmas tree. You've probably been shaking the packages and trying to guess what's in them."

Mac's eyes seemed to express some of Holly's own frustration at the interruption, but the expression was gone so quickly, she thought she might have imagined it. When he turned to Ken, his smile was easy.

"Actually, I caught this wench in the act and I was just trying to decide on a proper punishment."

Ken limped heavily across the room, the sound of his new walking cast accenting every step. He raised one sandy brow. "I can see that you're holding on to her in case she tries to escape."

"Oh, please, officers, have mercy on me. It's my first offense and I'll never do it again." Holly fluttered her eyelashes innocently and Mac frowned heavily.

"That's what they all say. Today it's shaking packages but tomorrow it could be armed robbery. There's just no stopping the criminal mind."

She walked her fingers up the sleeve of his pale-blue shirt. "I was planning to make waffles for breakfast and I can't do that if you throw me in jail."

"Bribing an officer is a criminal offense, young lady," Mac reminded her sternly.

"Waffles? Don't you think we could let her off with a warning this time, Mac?" Ken pleaded, rubbing his stomach to indicate imminent starvation.

"With vanilla ice cream and ripe peaches," Holly added invitingly.

Mac wavered. "Well, I suppose if you truly promise not to do it again, we could go easy on you this time."

AS IT TURNED OUT, Mac ended up making the waffles, while Holly sliced out-of-season peaches and stirred the ice cream to soften it. Ken sat at the breakfast bar and kibitzed, offering worthless bits of advice until Mac threatened to put his head in the waffle iron or drown him in the ice cream.

The day was wonderfully lazy. Holly spent her time embroi-

dering tiny flowers on a smock that her mother had made for the
baby. In the late afternoon, Holly carefully stuffed a fat capon
with a sage-and-pecan dressing, following an old family recipe,
and slipped the bird into the oven to roast.

Maryann arrived about the same time as the rain, and Mac built
the fire higher. Dinner was perfect. The food was exactly right
and the conversation was warm and lively, bouncing easily back
and forth across the table. While Mac and Ken loaded the dishwasher, the two women went into the living room, relaxing with
cups of subtly spiced cocoa.

"You've been looking very happy the last month or two,"
Maryann observed. "Do I take it that the gamble of marrying
Mac has paid off?"

Holly smiled, snuggling deeper into her chair. "Definitely.
We've still got some things to work out, but I made the right
choice."

"You're so sure of that. Doesn't it worry you that things might
change, that it might not last forever?"

Holly studied her friend in the flickering light cast by the fire
and the winking bulbs of the Christmas tree. "Nobody can guarantee forever, Maryann. I love Mac so much that I couldn't just
let him go without taking a chance."

"But what if it doesn't work out? What if ten years from now,
you decide it isn't working anymore?"

"Then we'll have had ten good years together. How could I
regret having that? Maybe in some ways the fact that we started
off on such bad footing will work to our advantage. We've proved
that things don't have to be perfect from the start."

"I don't know. It seems so risky." Maryann stirred restlessly,
her auburn hair taking on fiery lights from the dancing flames.

"It is risky. But it's worth it. Ken's worth it."

Maryann's head jerked toward her and then away, as if she was
afraid of what her expression would reveal. "Who said this had
anything to do with Ken?"

"Just a guess. Am I wrong?"

The other woman lifted her shoulders in an elaborate shrug that
put Holly in mind of Ken whenever Maryann's name came up.
"He's not so bad when you get to know him." Holly said nothing

and Maryann's casual pose changed. "I'm scared to death, Holly. What do I do if he wants some kind of commitment from me?"

"You mean like marriage?"

Maryann gestured wildly with one hand. "I'm not even ready for going steady. I'm frightened. What if we're not really suited?"

"How will you know if you don't give it a chance?"

Before Maryann could answer that, the two men came into the room and the conversation was dropped.

"I don't know about anybody else but I'm ready to open some of these boxes." Ken rubbed his hands together, and Holly laughed at the avid expression on his face.

An hour later the room was strewn with wrapping paper and discarded boxes. The area under the tree, so full at the start of the evening, was beginning to look empty and rather forlorn. Holly's present to Mac lay beside him and she noticed that he had a tendency to touch the beautiful pair of antique dueling pistols as if he couldn't quite believe in their presence.

She smiled, satisfied that the effort of finding them had been worthwhile. She had searched every antique shop in the city, looking for just the right addition to his small collection of historic pistols. When she finally found them, she had almost emptied her bank account to buy them, but seeing the expression on his face made it worth being broke.

Ken reached beneath the tree and lifted the last box, handing it to Maryann with an uncertain smile that seemed odd on his usually confident face. "This isn't exactly something I picked out for you, but I think it's something you'll enjoy."

Maryann took the box hesitantly, her eyes searching his. Holly felt Mac stiffen beside her and she looked at him, arching a brow in inquiry. Whatever was in that box, Mac knew about it. He shook his head and nodded toward the couple who sat across from them.

"Oh, Ken." The soft exclamation broke from Maryann as the wrappings fell away to reveal a worn velvet case. Her fingers were shaking as she opened the lid and looked down at the etched gold case of the watch.

"Actually, you should probably thank Mac more than me." Maryann was silent so long that Ken broke into nervous speech.

"He's the one who did the intimidating. I'm afraid that I'm not very frightening-looking right now. Oh, hey, don't cry."

Holly's eyes were wet as Mac nudged her to her feet. Ken was dabbing futilely at Maryann's cheeks with the edge of his shirt sleeve as they left the room; Holly didn't think that the other couple even noticed their leaving.

Mac switched on a soft lamp in their bedroom and silently handed her a tissue. "That was the most beautiful gift." Her voice shook with emotion as she wiped her watery eyes. "How did he get it back?"

"It wasn't hard once we found Nevin. I'm afraid I'm once again guilty of using the agency computers for something personal. You seem to have corrupted me totally in that respect. I took Ken over to see the guy last week and we...persuaded him that it was in his best interests to return the watch. Luckily, he hadn't sold it. You were right; he was just hanging on to it for spite. I think he's seen the error of his ways, though."

"Maryann's face was so beautiful. I can't imagine a more wonderful gift."

Mac cleared his throat. "Well, actually, I hope you'll change your mind about that." He reached into his pocket and pulled out a small jeweler's case of royal-blue velvet. "We got married in kind of a hurry and we didn't have time for an engagement ring."

Holly's heart began to thud as he opened the case and lifted out a ring. He took her left hand and slipped off her wedding band, sliding it onto the end of his little finger. His eyes met hers and her chest began to swell as she saw all her dreams coming true in those brilliant blue depths.

"We started off on the wrong foot, but maybe that's made our marriage stronger." She smiled shakily at hearing him echo her words. "I'm not always good at letting go of the past, and it's taken me a lot longer than it should have to see how much more important the future is."

He slid the wedding ring onto her finger. "With this ring I thee wed." He slipped the engagement ring into place and Holly saw it through a haze of tears, a simple cluster of diamonds on a plain gold band.

"I love you, Holly."

"I love you, too." The words came out on a sob of happiness as she threw her arms around his neck.

Chapter Fifteen

The only person who was taken by surprise when Ken moved in with Maryann was Maryann herself. She didn't seem quite sure of how it had happened, but she didn't seem unhappy with the arrangement, either. Holly was thrilled. Now that she and Mac had worked out the last of their problems, she wanted her friend to be as happy as she was.

The only dark spot on her rainbow was the fact that no one seemed to know where her brother was. Mac pointed out frequently that no news was good news. If something had happened to him, chances are they would know about it. James had ditched the agent following him and disappeared quite deliberately, which meant that he had known what he was doing. He hadn't accidentally stumbled into something.

After Ken's beating, Reginald C. Naveroff went home to the South to recuperate from a terrible car wreck, which meant that Ken and Mac were both officially retired from the case.

"You know, if you get any more contented-looking, you're going to begin to worry me," Ken remarked to his partner.

Mac glanced up from his menu and arched his brow at Ken. "You aren't looking any too miserable yourself. How's the leg doing without the cast?"

"Not too bad. Of course, Maryann was a lot more sympathetic while I was tied down with it."

They gave their orders to the waiter and then Ken turned an inquiring look to his friend. "You said you had something to discuss. Have you heard anything more about Reynolds?"

Mac shook his head. "No. As far as we're concerned, he's dropped off the face of the world."

"Well, I for one am glad to be off the case. I had a hard time looking Holly in the eye while we were on it."

"Yeah."

"You don't sound sincere. Would you rather not be off it?"

"No, it's not that. I've just had this funny feeling lately, as if everything is coming to a head and I'm going to get caught in the eruption." He took a swallow of his drink and shook his head. "I can't put my finger on it. There's just something that tells me that we're not as far out of it as we'd like to be."

"Is that what you wanted to talk to me about?" Ken had worked with Mac long enough not to discount one of his "feelings." It was something a good agent developed, a sort of sixth sense that helped to keep him alive.

Mac shrugged off the niggling itch at the back of his neck. "No, it isn't." He toyed idly with the silverware. "Have you ever thought of quitting?"

"Sure. Lots of times."

"Why didn't you?"

Ken's shoulders lifted. "I don't know exactly. I'd look around and see that there wasn't anything else I was trained to do. Besides, I like the excitement."

"Try riding herd on an endless stack of papers as I've done for the past few months. That's real excitement," Mac told him sourly. He glanced around the restaurant, taking in the lunchtime crowd. At the table just across from them was a young couple with two children and an infant. Mac had a sudden image of Holly sitting all alone at that table, a small child beside her, but without him, because he'd been killed by some drugged-out junkie. A cold chill worked its way up his spine.

"I'm getting out, Ken." His eyes swept to his partner. "I'm tired of the whole game. I've spent fifteen years living on the edge, ever since 'Nam, and I want something more now. I don't want Holly to be a widow before she's thirty-five. I want to see my child grow up, maybe have other children."

Ken didn't seem surprised. He nodded slowly, leaning back to let the waiter put his plate in front of him. He spoke as soon as the waiter was gone again. "I could see it coming. You've got a lot more to lose now."

"It's not just that. Holly hasn't said anything, but I can see it in her eyes each time I leave for work. She's wondering if today I'm going to be sent out on assignment again. But I can't blame it on Holly. I'm getting too old for this, Ken. I'm beginning to lose my ideals. You know, motherhood and apple pie and keeping the country safe for your kids. Sometimes I look around and feel as if we haven't accomplished a damn thing. Fifteen years of my life and there's still the same old stuff going down on the streets."

"You can't look at it that way. You've got to look at the ones you've managed to put away, not the ones who are still out there."

Mac stabbed restlessly at his baked potato. "I know that, but I'm getting out while I still believe it."

Ken chewed thoughtfully on his hamburger. "You're not the only one who's been thinking along those lines. Maryann and I haven't worked out all the bumps yet, but I think we will, and I'd like a chance to build some kind of a life with her. I've even thought once or twice that maybe having a kid might not be quite so bad." He grimaced as Mac threw back his head and laughed. "I hate to admit that after all my comments about the little animals, but the thought has slipped in once or twice.

"But I keep coming back to the same problem over and over again. What else am I trained to do?"

Mac shoved aside his uneaten food and leaned over the table. "Security consultants. We've got the knowledge and we've got the perfect background to inspire confidence in the hearts of clients."

Ken stopped chewing and stared past Mac's shoulder for a moment, his eyes distant. "Security consultants. Not bad. We wouldn't be stuck at a desk all day. We could probably hire a secretary to do the paperwork once we get things off the ground. Not bad."

"Think about it. I'm not giving my notice tomorrow, but I will be soon. There's nothing I'd like better than for you to continue as my partner."

"I'll give it some thought."

"Excuse me. A gentleman asked me to give you this note." Mac's contented mood vanished as he heard the waiter's words. He took the folded sheet of paper, murmuring his thanks. The hair on the back of his neck stood up as he unfolded it, vaguely aware of Ken's sudden alertness.

The printing was simple block capitals, simple but effective: "DO YOU KNOW WHERE YOUR WIFE IS?"

China rattled and slid to the floor as he shoved the table aside and surged to his feet. Ken was hastily throwing money on the table as Mac ran from the restaurant like a man possessed, pushing his way past anyone who got in his way and hurtling over a low planter when a woman in a wheelchair blocked the aisle around it.

He was pulling out of the parking lot when Ken caught up with him. Mac tapped the brakes just long enough for the other man to swing in, stepping on the gas before the door had shut behind him. Ken fastened his seat belt and picked up the crumpled sheet of paper, reading the one line.

"Oh, my God!" The words were a prayer and they were the only words said during the mad drive to Mac's home. Mac kept the gas pedal to the floor, using the horn to clear intersections ahead of them. Ken glanced over his shoulder when he heard the wail of a siren but he said nothing, knowing that Mac must have heard it, too.

By the time they fishtailed their way into the driveway, they had picked up a two-car escort. Knowing that Mac wasn't going to take time to explain, Ken got out his wallet and opened his door, holding his identification in a prominent position as the police cars skidded to a halt and the officers leaped out, guns drawn.

Mac was oblivious to them; his long legs had already carried him across the lawn. His palm hit the front door, noting the already broken lock as the panel thudded back against the wall. Some remnant of training had him flattening against the door, reaching beneath his arm to pull out his automatic.

"Holly?" But the house was empty. He could almost smell the emptiness. He went through it room by room, coming to the bedroom last. Each room had been thoroughly searched. But until the bedroom, there was no sign of unnecessary destruction. Even there the destruction was minor. Drawers gaped open, their contents strewn around them. He noticed vaguely that the false bottom on the lowest drawer was still intact, which meant that they hadn't taken time to really search the place. But what drove the color from his face was the shattered lamp that lay in pieces next to the bed and, on the pale bedspread, the bright, unmistakable tint of blood.

THE FIRST REALIZATION Holly had that something was wrong was when she looked up from making the bed and found two strange men entering the bedroom. There wasn't time for more than a startled, convulsive movement toward the bathroom to lock herself in before one of them was across the room, his fingers closing around her upper arm.

"Do not scream and we won't hurt you. Understand?"

She nodded. Her throat felt as if it had permanently closed. She didn't think she could have forced a scream out if she'd tried. In fact, she couldn't even find the voice to ask who they were and what they wanted.

The one who stood beside her was short and stocky. The other one, who proceeded to search the room, was taller and slimmer. Both had dark hair and eyes and both wore neat gray suits, white shirts and conservative ties. She stifled a hysterical giggle. They looked as if they'd stepped out of an ad for the perfect IBM man.

"Nothing." The slim one had finished his search.

"Are you sure?"

"What did you expect to find? Even if he did have records at his home, they'd be only copies."

They'd missed the false bottom, Holly realized. Looking at the clothes strewn about the room, the drawers hanging drunkenly open, the closet door gaping wide, she felt a tingle of healthy anger. How dare these men search her home and intrude on her privacy like this? The anger burned away some of her fear-born paralysis. The short one had taken a step toward his companion and they were now arguing in a language that sounded vaguely German, their attention shifting away from her for the moment.

She reached behind her with one hand, fingers groping for the table lamp. If she could just make it to the bathroom, she might have a chance of escaping. The two men continued to argue as her fingers closed around the lamp. It was nice and solid. She'd have to jerk it from behind her and bring it down on his head in one smooth move and then sprint for the bathroom.

One of the intruders was leaning over the bed, gesturing with one hand to emphasize his point. Holly took a deep breath, jerked the lamp away from the table and smashed it down on his head. The other man was too near the bedroom door, but the bathroom was within reach. She was on her way before he hit the bed. She slammed the door behind her, leaning back against it for a breathless moment. She would have only seconds. Bathroom locks had never been intended to keep a determined man out. To give herself an extra edge, she wedged the back of a wicker chair beneath the knob. She threw open the medicine chest, searching for some kind of weapon. Why couldn't Mac shave with a nice, vicious straight razor? She discarded his electric shaver and finally settled on a can of hair spray. It wouldn't be fatal, but it might blind someone for an instant.

The wicker chair creaked ominously and she cast one glance over her shoulder before opening the door on the other side of the bathroom and slipping into the baby's room. Mac had put that door in less than a month earlier, when they'd decided that it would provide convenient access to the nursery.

Holly hurried through the nursery and cracked open the hall door. With any luck, they would spend a few minutes trying to get the bathroom door open and give her enough time to get to the front door. Being almost nine months pregnant was not conducive to speed but she didn't need much time. Her purse was on the hall table and the car keys were in it. All she needed was a few precious minutes.

She didn't get them. She was only a few feet away from the door when hard fingers caught her from behind, spinning her around and pushing her back against the wall. Her wrist tingled from the force of the blow that knocked the pathetic hair spray can from her fingers. She stared wide-eyed into hard, dark features, the almost-black eyes as cold as sin.

"We do not want to hurt you, Mrs. Donahue. If you cooperate

with us, it will be much easier for everyone. And if you do not cooperate, it will not only be more difficult for you, it will go much harder on your brother.''

Holly went limp. "James? You have James?"

"You will be more cooperative. Yes?"

"Yes. Is he all right?"

"You may judge that for yourself."

His partner staggered out of the bedroom then, one side of his head covered in blood and murder in his eyes. Holly shrank back against the wall, grateful that Icy Eyes stood between her and the bleeding man. The conversation was short and harsh. It was obvious that Icy Eyes was in charge and equally obvious that Tubby wanted to extract revenge but the other man wasn't going to let him. After a moment, Tubby shrugged and stalked out of the house, giving Holly a baleful glare as he went by.

She was led out and seated in the back of a dark van. They didn't tie her up, but Icy Eyes did point out the damage that trying to leap from a moving vehicle would do to the human body. Tubby got into the driver's seat, using a rather grubby rag to clean up his face.

She cleared her throat nervously as the van moved away from the curb. "Who are you?"

"He is David Brown and my name is John Smith."

Brown and Smith? Holly muttered a mental *Ha!* but didn't say anything. Smith sat in the back across from Holly and closed his eyes, but she was sure that he was aware of her every move.

The drive was not long, but it gave her plenty of time to reflect on the situation. Her hands rested lightly on the swollen mound of her stomach. Her first consideration had to be protecting her child. Mac would find them.

From her position in the back of the van, she was unable to see much of their direction, but they hadn't driven far enough to be out of the city, so they were staying in L.A. They parked the van in an underground garage and led Holly into the apartment building above. The elevator was old and rickety and smelled musty. It creaked its way upward, threatening to grind to a halt at any moment. When the doors slid sluggishly open, the three of them stepped out into a long narrow hallway with a tattered

carpet. Smith kept one hand around her upper arm, his hold relaxed but tight enough to let her know that he wasn't going to let
her escape, not that there was any place to escape to.

The larger man knocked twice on a door that had long ago
been white. It was now a grubby tan, the paint peeling in places.
He paused and then knocked three times, and the door was opened
by a man who could have been his twin brother, down to the dark
hair on the back of his hands.

Reluctantly Holly entered the apartment, her nose wrinkling at
the smell of stale onions. It was a good thing she was past the
queasy stage of her pregnancy. There was a babble of conversation between David Brown and his clone, and from the gestures
Brown was making, she assumed that he was explaining how he'd
come by the gash in his head.

Smith led her farther into the room and gestured to her to be
seated. Holly suspiciously eyed the sofa he indicated and then
decided that it was probably just as well that the dark brown fabric
hid most stains and flaws. She sat down gingerly and looked up
at her captors.

"Where's my brother?"

Smith shrugged. "I have no idea. We were rather hoping that
you could tell us that."

"You said you had James!"

"You are mistaken, Mrs. Donahue. I said that it would be
harder for your brother if you did not cooperate. It was your
assumption that we 'had' him."

Holly didn't bother with recriminations. "Well, I don't know
where he is. If I did know, I would hardly have come along
without an argument, would I?"

He sat down in a sagging chair, scowling as a broken spring
snagged his pants. "The accommodations are most distressing,"
he muttered before turning his attention to her question. "A
woman in your delicate condition cannot afford to fight too many
battles, Mrs. Donahue. If I implied that we had your brother under
control, it was as much for your sake as for my own. Despite the
circumstances under which we have met, I assure you that I am
not in the habit of harming pregnant ladies."

He smiled, and a chill worked its way up Holly's spine. The

polite gesture might have been intended to reassure her, but his eyes remained cold and frightening. She quelled her fright, lifting her chin unconsciously.

"You've made a mistake, because I can't help you, even if I wanted to. I don't know where James is."

"Yes, I had guessed that when you so easily believed that we might have him. This will do just as well, though. He will come when he knows that we have his sister."

"If you don't know where he is, how are you going to let him know that you have me? You may not have realized this, but my baby is due within the next week. With James in Europe, it could take days to track him down. No offense, but I really don't want to have my child in this seedy apartment."

"Seedy?" He raised a dark brow. "This is slang for poor accommodations, no?" He lifted his shoulders. "I cannot argue with your opinion. To answer your question, we know that your brother is in this country. As to how we will get a message to him, we will deliver a note to your husband and I'm sure that he will contact your brother."

"But Mac doesn't know where James is, either."

Again he parted his lips to display a row of shiny teeth that put her strongly in mind of a piranha. "Your husband works for your FBI. The power of this agency is well known. I'm quite sure he will find a way to contact James Reynolds."

"But..." Holly bit off her protest. What difference did it make what he thought? He was going to contact Mac and that was all that mattered. He probably got his ideas from old reruns of *The Untouchables*. If he wanted to equate Mac with Robert Stack, then he was welcome to the comparison, just as long as he told Mac where she was.

"What do you want with my brother?"

He had pulled a nail file out of his wallet and was carefully filing his nails. His hands were long and slim, and Holly had no trouble at all imagining them around her throat. He glanced up and appeared to consider her question.

"Your brother has caused my friends and me considerable trouble. We would like to talk to him, to see if we can't come to a better understanding of each other." He fingered the pointed tip of the file as he spoke, and she felt another chill slide up her spine.

"What if Mac can't find him?"

"I'm sure he will." He tucked the file back into his wallet and leaned back in the lumpy chair. She was vaguely aware that Brown and friend had disappeared into one of the other rooms but she wasn't all that interested in them. Smith was the man to watch.

"You see, we did not make the connection until we realized just who your husband was. We thought your brother was working alone, trying to cut himself in for a piece of the action, as they say on TV. But when we found out about your husband, it became clear that he must have been working for your government all along. A very good cover. It would have been perfect if we had not found out that his sister was married to a fed."

He was obviously rather pleased by this last bit of slang, and Holly had to swallow the urge to laugh hysterically. The whole situation was like something out of a bad movie. Mac thought James was working for these people, and they thought he was working for Mac. Both sides were unknowingly united in the common goal of finding James, each for its own reasons and each mistaken in what it thought he was doing.

And while they were all stumbling around looking for him, he had managed to slip between them and disappear. There was a certain sisterly pride in the thought, but it was dampened by a strong urge to shake him until his teeth rattled. James must have suspected something about the art thefts and decided to play Lone Ranger.

Holly leaned back against the sagging sofa and closed her eyes. She was tired and scared, and all she wanted was to be home, safe in Mac's arms. He would hold her and tell her he loved her and make everything right again.

Chapter Sixteen

The twenty-four hours that followed Holly's kidnapping were a nightmare for Mac. The agency responded rapidly, mobilizing agents to canvass the neighborhood to see if any of the neighbors had seen anything. A description of the van allowed them to identify the men as members of the ring of smugglers that Holly's brother had been suspected of being involved with.

Since Mac and Ken pulled out, the case had been progressing and was nearing a resolution. Now that Holly had been kidnapped, the case itself had become of minor importance to Mac. All he wanted was his wife back, safe and sound.

"Mac, you've got to slow down, or you're going to burn yourself out before we ever get to Holly."

Mac knew the truth in Ken's words, and he forced himself to stop pacing and sit down. His hands flexed into fists and then relaxed as he sought to work the tension out of his body.

Ken handed him a glass of Scotch. "Drink it. You didn't get any sleep last night. Maybe this will help you get some tonight."

"I can't sleep in that bed. All I can think about is that Holly should be there. And I wonder where she is and if she's scared or cold or hungry or—"

Ken pushed the glass into his hand. "Drink it. The note said they were taking care of her, and they have no reason not to. In fact, they've got good reason *to* take good care of her. Lady's a lot stronger than she looks. She'll be all right."

Mac took a swallow of Scotch, letting it burn its way down his throat and settle in a knot in his stomach. "I know she's strong, but she's nine months pregnant. She shouldn't be trying to deal with kidnappers at a time like this.''

"You mean there's a good time to deal with kidnapping?"

"You know what I mean." Mac took another swig, draining the glass.

"Yeah, I know." Ken poured himself a drink and sank onto the sofa. "You've just got to believe that she's okay. You don't have any choice. We've got people tracking them down, and as soon as we get the call telling us where to meet them, we'll get your lady out."

Mac's fingers tightened around the glass. "I'd give a lot to know where James Reynolds is right now. Whatever damn stupid game he's been playing has gotten Holly kidnapped. If anything happens to her, I'll track him down myself and tear him into bite-size pieces. I may do it anyway, just for the satisfaction it would give me."

"I have a feeling Lady wouldn't like it if you killed her brother. She seems to be rather fond of him."

"Then she can be fond of him in pieces," Mac growled.

As if the words had conjured up the man, the conversation was interrupted by a commotion of raised voices at the front door. One of the agents watching the house was protesting angrily, and there was another voice, softer but determined.

"I've got to get in. I'm James Reynolds, I tell you. My sister lives here."

Mac was on his feet before the words stopped fadded. He was vaguely aware of Ken moving with him, but his attention was centered on the man who stood in the hallway, arguing vehemently with the agent.

"What the hell is going on? This is my sister's house and I want to see her. Has something happened to her? I'm her— What the hell?" The exclamation was startled out of him as Mac's left hand closed on his shoulder, spinning him around to meet the hard knuckles of his right fist.

The force of the blow knocked him into the wall. Mac reached for him again but Ken was there first, standing between his partner and the other man. "Cool off, Mac. Punching her brother isn't going to do Holly any good."

Mac glared at him for a long moment, his blue eyes brilliant with rage and fear. Ken met his gaze calmly, aware of James Reynolds getting to his feet behind him. With a visible effort Mac bridled his anger, banking the fires in his eyes and forcing his strained control into place.

"Where's my sister?" James's words were muffled by the hand at his injured lower lip. Mac's eyes flickered over Ken's shoulder, still holding a smoldering hostility.

"It's okay, Dick. This really is my brother-in-law." The agent nodded and stepped outside, shutting the door behind him.

Mac strode back into the living room and went straight to the bar, pouring himself a short Scotch, a very short Scotch. He wasn't looking to get drunk, just to give his hands something to do other than beat James Reynolds to a pulp.

"Where's Holly?" The words were a bit clearer this time, and Mac turned as James and Ken entered the living room. He leaned back against the bar, his hand tightening around the squat glass and his eyes skimming over the other man.

There was a definite resemblance between Holly and her brother. They shared the same dark eyes and hair. Holly's soft features appeared in a more masculine version in her brother, but the resemblance was marked.

Those eyes were now dark with hostility and concern as he stared at Mac's lounging figure. "Where's my sister?"

"Funny, that's just the question we've been asking about you for the last two months. You did a good job of dropping out of sight, Reynolds. If you hadn't been so damn good at it, Holly might be here to greet you right now."

"We? Who's we? And what's happened to Holly?"

Ken's eyes skipped between the two men. Mac's reclining position didn't fool him. His partner was about as relaxed as a cobra ready to strike. And Reynolds looked as if he was just about angry enough to start throwing punches himself. All Mac's iron control had disappeared when his wife was kidnapped. It was like being around a stick of dynamite with a faulty fuse; you couldn't tell just when he was going to blow up, but the explosion was inevitable.

"Sit down, Reynolds. I'm Ken Richardson and this is Mac Donahue. We're the FBI."

James ignored the invitation and remained standing, his angry gaze locked on his brother-in-law. "FBI? Why didn't Holly tell me?"

"Out of loyalty to me," Mac told him shortly, his voice rough as he remembered how she had agonized over that decision.

"Loyalty or sheer terror?" James rubbed his swelling jaw.

"Loyalty. And for what it's worth, she never gave me any information about you, either. It was her misguided attempt to protect you."

"Protect me from what? You? Why would you be after me?"

"Spare me the protestations of innocence, Reynolds. We've been watching you for months now and we know all about the art thefts. Holly swore you'd never be involved in them, but your recent disappearance makes that a little hard to buy."

"I wasn't involved in the thefts. I was trying to get information on them. My boss is in on it and I stumbled onto the whole thing."

"If that's true, why didn't you go to the authorities with what you suspected?"

"He's my boss. He's got a lot of years in with the diplomatic corps. Nobody was going to take my word for it. I had to get some proof. And I've got it. That's why I'm back in the States— to turn the evidence over to the authorities. Now, is somebody going to tell me where Holly is?"

"While you were out playing at cops and robbers, the men you were spying on kidnapped her."

James paled. "Kidnapped? Holly? Why?"

"Because her brother was causing them problems and this seemed like a good way to draw him out of the woodwork."

Stung by the accusation implicit in the words, James struck back. "I suppose it had nothing to do with the fact that her husband is a fed?"

"Cool down, both of you." Ken's tone was wearily disgusted. "None of this is helping any. What we need to do is put our heads together and pool information."

Mac shook his head tiredly, the aggression draining out of him.

"You're right. I'm not thinking too clearly right now. Tell us what you know, Reynolds."

HOLLY PACED RESTLESSLY across the room. Ten paces to the wall with the faded wallpaper and then ten paces back to the wall with the bathroom door. Her hands rested protectively on the swollen mound of her baby, and her lips moved in silent prayer.

It was almost dawn. Less than forty-eight hours ago she had been contemplating nothing more frightening than the birth of her child. Now she was wondering if she was going to live to see that birth.

I must stop it! They haven't hurt me yet. I've got to think positively. Mac will find me. He'd never let them hurt me. The mental pep talk broke off on a stifled gasp as pain rippled through her abdomen. It faded briefly but it left her with renewed fear. It was probably just false labor, she told herself. She'd certainly been through enough to bring it on. But something told her that this was the real thing, and she had to struggle with the hysterics that threatened to break free.

Mac. She had to concentrate on Mac. Smith had told her that he was going to meet with Mac today. She could be free by nightfall. She patted her stomach soothingly. "Hang on, little one. Just hang on. Daddy's going to get us out."

Outside, the sun struggled to come up, hampered by thick gray clouds that promised rain. Holly barely glanced out the window as early-morning blackness gave way to dim illumination. She had already explored all the possibilities offered by the window. As Smith had promised her when he showed her this room, there was no way out unless she grew wings. They were four stories up over an alley. Holly was thankful that they had given her a room and even a bathroom of her own. At least she'd had some privacy.

With the pain gone, she resumed her pacing, her mind skipping wildly from thought to thought. James, Mac, her family. They all flitted through her mind. Where *was* James? What was Mac doing to find him? What if he couldn't find him? What if—

Her frantic thoughts were interrupted by a light tapping. She turned to the door, feeling her pulse accelerate. So far, Smith had

offered her no harm, but what if he changed his mind now? She
waited for the door to open, but the tapping sound was repeated.
She took a step toward the door, cocking her head. There it was
again, but it wasn't at the door.

She turned as quickly as her ungainly figure would allow. Her
breath caught, and for a moment she was afraid her heart would
stop. A dark shape hung outside the window, a black silhouette
against the still-dim morning light. Wild thoughts of vampires,
burglars and crazed killers flitted through her mind. Before fear
could drive out rational thought, the tapping was repeated, and
this time she could make out a human hand against the window.

Hesitantly she approached the window, squinting to try to make
out something of the dark figure. His hand came up and tugged
a dark cap off his head. The gray light caught in sandy hair and
Holly gave a sob of relief, her footsteps hurrying across the short
distance to the window. Ken! Oh Lord, it was Ken!

She released the catch on the window and tugged at the edge
of the aluminum frame. It refused to budge, and tears filled her
eyes. To be so close and have a damn window keep her trapped.
Ken held up his hand, motioning her to stay calm. He waved one
arm in a wide circle and a moment later the grinding sound of a
garbage truck began in the alley below.

Holly caught the white gleam of his smile as he pulled a hammer out of the belt at his waist. She shook her head in a frantic
no, but he held up his hand in a gesture of reassurance. Instead
of shattering the glass, he began to tap lightly at the edges of the
frame, breaking loose the accumulated grime of several years.

The truck continued to grind away in the alley, masking any
noise Ken might have made. Holly held her breath, letting it out
on a gasp as another pain rippled across her abdomen. *Please
don't let Smith decide to check on me.* She muttered the prayer
over and over again. Suspended outside the window as he was,
Ken would be a totally vulnerable target.

Ken tucked the hammer back into his belt and gestured to her
to try the window again. Holly straightened as the contraction
faded, and she reached for the window, barely breathing as she
tugged at the frame. For a moment it stubbornly refused to budge
and then it let loose with a speed that almost knocked her over.

"Step back."

She hurriedly moved away from the window and Ken swung his feet through the opening, slipping out of the harness that had supported him, and landed lightly on the floor.

"Ken!" The name was a breathless gasp. He put his arms around her, hugging her briefly.

"It's okay, Lady. Are you all right?"

She nodded against his shoulder, clinging to him. He put his hands on her arms, holding her away. "We're going to get you out of here. Mac is on the roof, and as soon as we get you into a sling, he's going to pull you up. Trust us?"

"Of course," she answered without hesitation. If he had told her that they were going to put a rocket on her back and shoot her out of her prison, she would have uttered not a word of protest. If Mac thought it was okay, she would go along with it.

"I'm going to lift the window out of the frame so there's room to accommodate you and then we'll get you settled in one of the slings. It's going to be just like sitting on a swing, Lady. You'll be perfectly safe. Mac is waiting for you on the roof." He was working as he spoke, using the hammer, which she could now see was rubber-tipped, to break the frame loose. He then lifted it out and put it on the floor just inside the window.

He leaned out the window to snag a sling and pulled it in before turning to look at her. "Ready?"

Holly swallowed hard and nodded. She'd walk across hot coals without a qualm if it meant getting to Mac.

MAC LAY FLAT on the roof, his head sticking out over the edge as he looked down the side of the building. Ken swung suspended at the end of the rope, looking amazingly fragile. Below him, the garbage truck was grinding endless mounds of trash into a pulp, the noise successfully obliterating all other sounds. The captors hadn't had the apartment long; chances were they had no way of knowing when regular trash pickup was.

Mac's throat tightened as Ken disappeared inside the window and the rope went slack. He found himself murmuring childhood prayers he had thought forgotten long ago. It seemed like forever before Ken leaned out the window again and signaled for Mac to take up the slack in the rope. Mac got to his feet and picked the rope up in his gloved hands. Behind him, three other men followed his lead, lifting the rope and bracing themselves to pull.

Once they had located Smith's hiding place, there hadn't been time to set up anything more elaborate. No fancy high-tech rescues, just plain old muscle power. Mac pulled gently until he felt weight on the end of the rope. His shoulders bunched beneath the black turtleneck he wore as he took the weight of Holly and Ken. Behind him, the other agents added their strength.

Sweat beaded on Mac's forehead. In his mind's eye, he could picture what was happening over the side of the building. Ken was in one sling and Holly in another, Ken supporting her against his side as he used his feet and arms to keep them both away from the building. Mac cursed his inability to be the one at the end of the rope. His smaller size had made Ken the only practical choice. Mac's strength could be put to better use just where he was, but that didn't stop him from wanting to be the one sheltering his wife now.

He kept up the steady pull, with first one hand and then the other. With every foot of rope that coiled behind him, Holly was that much closer, that much nearer to safety. *Please, God, let her be all right.*

Ken's gloved hand clamped on to the edge of the roof, and Mac walked hand over hand along the rope until he knelt at the edge of the roof. Behind him, the other men took up the slack on the rope as he released it, one of them coming forward to brace Mac as he reached over to grasp Holly beneath the arms, lifting her to safety.

Holly felt Mac's strong arms close around her, pulling her back from the edge of the roof. Her hands clutched at him, her fingers digging into the thick knit of his sweater as she pulled him still closer, burying her face in his shoulder.

"Holly. Holly. Holly." He kept repeating her name, his head bent over her as he held her. After a long moment his hands came up to cup her head, tilting her face up until he could see her eyes. "Are you all right?"

She nodded, sniffing back tears of relief. "I'm all right."

"There was blood all over the bed." He ran his hands lightly over her body, seeking some sign of injury.

"It wasn't mine. I hit one of them over the head with a lamp. Oh, Mac, I'm so glad to see you."

He gave a shaky laugh. "The feeling is mutual, believe me. I've never been so frightened in my life. If anything had happened to you..."

"Nothing happened. They didn't hurt me at all. They're looking for James."

"I know. James is okay. He showed up at the house yesterday. You were right. He wasn't involved in the thefts."

"Thank goodness. How did you know where I was?"

"It's a long story. Let's get off this roof and then we can talk. What's wrong?" Her fingers suddenly dug into his arm, her face paling.

"I...think...you're...about...to...become...a...father," she got out between shallow breaths.

"Holly! Ken, tell them we need the ambulance. Holly's in labor."

He scooped her up in his arms, ignoring her murmured protest. "Mac, I'm too heavy for you to carry. I can walk. Besides, the contractions are still quite a ways apart. There's no need to panic."

She might as well have saved her breath. Ken ran ahead of them as Mac carried her carefully down the stairs, then climbed into the waiting ambulance with her. After taking one look at his determined face, the attendants decided not to argue with him.

Michael Kenneth Donahue came into the world some three hours later, squalling a loud protest that brought a satisfied smile to the doctor's face. Holly held up bravely throughout the labor, bolstered by Mac's huge presence. Mac's fears of disgracing himself by fainting proved to be unfounded. The only sign of nerves was the faint tremor in his hands when the doctor handed the baby to him and he laid his son on Holly's suddenly flatter stomach.

Holly touched her fingers lightly to the thick mop of dark hair that covered the baby's head and then looked up at Mac, her eyes brimming with tears. His fingers closed around her free hand, while the other touched the baby's tiny back, uniting them in a complete circle of love.

Chapter Seventeen

"You're such a good little boy. I just don't know what I ever did to deserve a baby as sweet as you."

"You married me."

Holly straightened up and turned away from the crib, frowning at Mac. "You scared me out of six years' growth," she scolded lightly. "What if I'd been holding the baby? I might have dropped him on his head. When did you get home?"

Mac grinned and crossed the room to drop a kiss on her nose before leaning over the crib to admire his son. "A few minutes ago. Anyway, I waited until you'd put him down. Is it going to create some hideous trauma if I pick him up again?"

Holly pretended to consider the matter before giving in with a laugh. "I suppose not. Just don't get him too excited or I'll never get him to sleep."

As always, she found herself entranced by the contrast of Mac's broad hands against Michael's tiny frame. He picked the baby up gently, supporting his head with one palm before cradling him in his arms.

"He looks as if he's grown another inch since this morning."

"Not quite, but my mother swears he's going to be at least as big as his father. She claims she can tell by his feet."

Mac looked up from the baby, his eyes bright with amusement. "His feet? You mean like a puppy?"

Holly nodded solemnly. "She says you can always tell that way."

Michael blinked up at his father. At six weeks his eyes were beginning to darken and show signs of matching the brilliant blue of Mac's. With his dark hair and those eyes, there was no doubt about whose child he was. Watching the two of them now, Holly had to blink back tears. Mac was such a good father.

He ran his finger gently over the baby's soft cheek, murmuring nonsense words to him for a few minutes before replacing him carefully in the crib and arranging the blanket just so. He ignored the fact that in a matter of minutes, Michael would kick it off.

Did he ever think about the son he'd never know? Holly wondered. Did he look at Michael and wonder what the other boy had looked like as a baby, what he was like now, where he was and what he was doing?

Mac looked up, his brows coming together when he saw the tears in her eyes. "Hey, what's the matter?" He hooked his hand behind her neck to pull her close, his thumb brushing a lone tear from her cheek. "What's this?"

She shook her head. "I was just being silly."

"You're always silly," he teased softly. "But you don't always cry. What's wrong?"

She hesitated, her eyes searching his. He had told her about the other child, but he had never again mentioned him. Was she treading on thin ice by bringing him up?

"I was just thinking about the other boy." His fingers tensed against the back of her neck and his lashes fell, shielding his eyes, but she had come too far to back out. She drew a deep breath and went on. "Do you think about him when you look at Michael?"

There was a tense moment of silence, and then he shook his head. "No, not really. Once in a while I wonder what he looked like at Michael's age, but I've come to terms with the fact that things can't be changed."

He shook his head, dispelling the faintly melancholy atmosphere. "Come on, I've got champagne in the fridge and I brought dinner home." His arm slid around her back and urged her out of the room.

Holly fell into his mood easily. "What are we celebrating?"

"Today I have joined the ranks of the unemployed."

She came to a halt in the living room, turning to look at him, her eyes dark with concern. "Oh, Mac, are you sure?"

"Of course I'm sure. Hey, don't look so serious. I didn't get fired. I quit. Remember?"

She let him lead her toward the kitchen, but her brow stayed wrinkled. "Are you absolutely sure this is what you want? I don't want you to quit just for my sake."

"Holly, we've been over this before. This is what I want. I'm getting old and tired and I don't want to become another statistic on burned-out agents, or dead ones. And after what happened to you, I'd never be able to concentrate as wholeheartedly as I'd need to."

She ran her fingers restlessly over the smooth wood of the breakfast bar while he got the champagne out of the refrigerator. "I should argue some more, but I'm selfish enough to admit that your job scares me to death."

"It had begun to scare me to death, and that's a sign that it's time to get out. I want to be here for you and Michael and any other children we might have. Besides, I've always wanted to run my own business. I've already made a bunch of contacts, and in less than a month I'll have all the licenses we need to start consulting like crazy." The sentence was punctuated by a bang as the cork popped out of the champagne. "Ken is going to work at it part-time until things stabilize enough to support both of us, and then he's going to quit and the firm of Donahue and Richardson will soon join the ranks of the *Fortune* five hundred."

Holly laughed, taking the glass he handed her and lifting it in a toast.

"To us," Mac offered. "We've come a long way together. May we go much farther."

"What's for dinner?"

"Pizza."

"With champagne?"

"A gourmet delight," he assured her as he lifted the pie out of the oven. She watched him cut it, admiring the play of muscles beneath his shirt and remembering the first night they had eaten pizza and then made love.

"James called today."

"Wonderful. Did you tell him he had a wrong number?"

"Mac, he really did think he was doing the right thing," she coaxed.

"Napoleon probably thought he was doing the right thing, too."

"Don't you think you could forgive him?" She accepted a plate from him and set it on the bar, pushing a stray mushroom around the plate. "Everything worked out."

"But not until you almost got killed," he snapped, feeling his skin tighten with anger at the memory of the fraught hours after she had been kidnapped. "If your brother hadn't been so anxious to play Superspy, you wouldn't have been put in that kind of danger." He drew in his breath and let it out in a sigh, seeing the distress in her eyes. He reached across the bar and caught her hand in his, running his thumb lightly over her wrist in an unconscious caress.

"I'm sorry. I know it wasn't all his fault. I take a large share of the blame myself. But it would have saved so much trouble if he'd gone to the authorities when he first suspected something was wrong." He forced a rueful smile. "I'll get over it. It may take a while, but I'll get over it. Who knows, give me a while and I may even decide that James is a great guy. He made up for a lot by being so impressed by Michael. He can't be all bad, I suppose. Now, are we going to eat this celebratory feast before or after it gets cold?"

Holly drew her hand away from his and let her fingers drift casually to the neck of her soft blouse. "I suppose we could celebrate with a pizza, but I had something a little more adult in mind," she murmured, slipping the buttons loose.

"Holly?" Mac's voice was husky, his eyes never leaving her tantalizing movements.

"I saw the doctor today and she gave me a clean bill of health. I thought I might slip into something more comfortable and then we could..."

A muscle worked in Mac's jaw as she slid the last button free and began to ease the blouse off her shoulders. "We could..."

"We could go for a swim. The pool should be nice and cold this time of year." Her eyes sparkled with mischief as he swung around the counter and caught her up in his arms, startling a muffled squeal from her.

"Brat. It would serve you right if I threw you into the pool." His arms tightened, pulling her closer to his chest. "Is it really safe?"

She nodded, feeling suddenly shy beneath the warm hunger in his eyes. Her arms came up to circle his neck as he carried her down the hall to their bedroom.

"I love you, Mac."

He placed her gently on the bed, leaning over her, his figure outlined against the light from the doorway.

"I love you."

She caught a glimpse of the tender expression in his eyes just before his mouth claimed hers. Those brilliant eyes had haunted her dreams for over a year. From a tacky bar in Tijuana, they had followed her everywhere she went, promising heaven if only she could find the key. She had found that key, and it wasn't the baby who lay sleeping in the next room. It was simply love, a love that would grow for a long time to come. It had been a long, sometimes rocky road, but it had been worth every step.

She was his lady and she couldn't ask for anything more.

LOOK FOR OUR FOUR FABULOUS MEN!

Each month some of today's bestselling authors bring
four new fabulous men to Harlequin American Romance.
Whether they're rebel ranchers, millionaire power brokers
or sexy single dads, they're all gallant princes—and
they're all ready to sweep you into lighthearted fantasies
and contemporary fairy tales where anything is possible
and where all your dreams come true!

You don't even have to make a wish...
Harlequin American Romance will grant your every desire!

Look for Harlequin American Romance
wherever Harlequin books are sold!

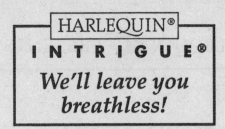

HARLEQUIN PRESENTS®

HARLEQUIN PRESENTS
men you won't be able to resist
falling in love with...

HARLEQUIN PRESENTS
women who have feelings
just like your own...

HARLEQUIN PRESENTS
powerful passion in
exotic international settings...

HARLEQUIN PRESENTS
intense, dramatic stories that will keep you
turning to the very last page...

HARLEQUIN PRESENTS
The world's bestselling romance series!

Harlequin® Historical

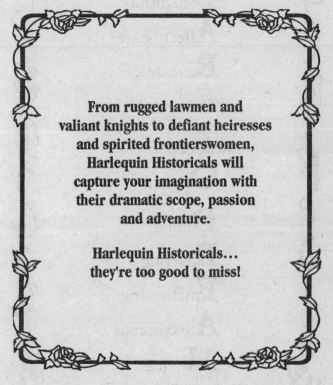

From rugged lawmen and
valiant knights to defiant heiresses
and spirited frontierswomen,
Harlequin Historicals will
capture your imagination with
their dramatic scope, passion
and adventure.

Harlequin Historicals…
they're too good to miss!

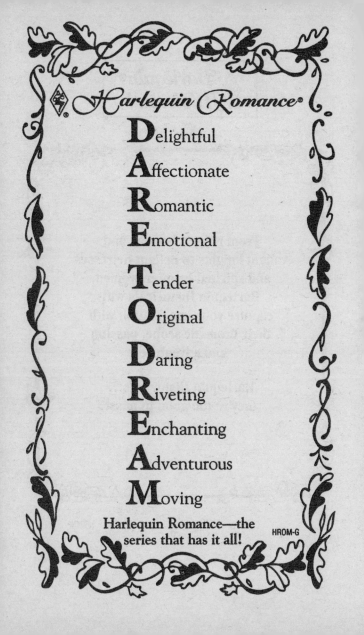

Harlequin Romance®

Delightful

Affectionate

Romantic

Emotional

Tender

Original

Daring

Riveting

Enchanting

Adventurous

Moving

Harlequin Romance—the
series that has it all!

HROM-G

HARLEQUIN SUPERROMANCE®

...there's more to the story!

Superromance. A *big* satisfying read about unforget-
table characters. Each month we offer
four very different stories that range from family
drama to adventure and mystery, from highly emotional stories to romantic comedies—and
much more! Stories about people you'll
believe in and care about. Stories too
compelling to put down....

Our authors are among today's *best* romance writ-
ers. You'll find familiar names and
talented newcomers. Many of them are
award winners—and you'll see why!

If you want the biggest and best
in romance fiction, you'll get it
from Superromance!

Available wherever Harlequin books are sold.

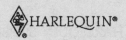 **HARLEQUIN®**

Not The Same Old Story!

 **PRESENTS®**
Exciting, glamorous romance stories that take readers around the world.

Sparkling, fresh and tender love stories that bring you pure romance.

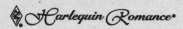
Bold and adventurous—Temptation is strong women, bad boys, great sex!

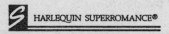 **HARLEQUIN SUPERROMANCE®**
Provocative and realistic stories that celebrate life and love.

Contemporary fairy tales—where anything is possible and where dreams come true.

 **INTRIGUE®**
Heart-stopping, suspenseful adventures that combine the best of romance and mystery.

Humorous and romantic stories that capture the lighter side of love.